# The Call of the Wild
## by
## Jack London

A Casebook with Text,
Background Sources,
Reviews, Critical Essays,
and Bibliography

# The Call of the Wild by Jack London

## A Casebook with Text, Background Sources, Reviews, Critical Essays, and Bibliography

Compiled with an Introduction by
Earl J. Wilcox

Nelson-Hall nh Chicago

**Library of Congress Cataloging in Publication Data**
London, Jack, 1876-1916.
  The call of the wild.
  Includes index.
  Bibliography: p.
  1. London, Jack, 1876-1916. The Call of the Wild.
I. Wilcox, Earl J., 1933-  II. Title.
PZ3.L846Cal 1980  [PS3523.046]  813'.5'2  79-21647
ISBN  0-88229-381-8 (Cloth)
ISBN  0-88229-756-2 (Paper)

Manufactured in the United States of America

10  9  8  7  6  5  4  3  2  1

# Contents

1. Introduction                                                          1
2. *The Call of the Wild*, by Jack London                                7
3. "Bâtard," by Jack London                                             89
4. Letters from Jack London                                            105
5. Gold Creek and Gold Town, by Franklin Walker                        123
6. Selected Early Reviews of *The Call of the Wild*                    147
7. Critical Essays                                                     161
   Bibliography                                                        243
   Index                                                               251

# Chapter 1

## Introduction

When Jack London died on November 22, 1916, he left behind not only a considerable variety and quantity of literature but also a reputation as varied and uneven as the quality of his work. A glance at *Jack London: A Bibliography* (Hensley C. Woodbridge, et al.) attests to a continuing and expanding interest in the writer and his work. Born an illegitimate son in rankest poverty but with an obsession to rise above his low station, London worked and wrote and lived in his forty years a short life that only the literary specialist has been aware of. Indeed, his struggle to rise above his meager beginning appropriately epitomizes the very age in which he was born: an age of unusual ferment in sociological, political, and ideological patterns. Prominent names which flash across the mind and which one associates with that almost distant era are Charles Darwin's *Origin of Species*, Herbert Spencer's *First Principles*, and Marx and Engles' *The Communist Manifesto*. Like a twentieth century Rabelais, London read—sometimes carefully, often sporadically—with an eager appetite. And he wrote with an equal fervor in an attempt to assimilate into his literary credo the dramatic ideas and changes taking place during his lifetime.

More than thirty years ago Irving Stone wrote *Sailor on Horseback*, a popular version of Jack London's life and works. Stone's account for many years channeled many of the attitudes taken by the general reading public and some scholars toward London's fiction. Stone's "biography" meant that truly serious study of London the artist was delayed to a considerable extent until university students and professors began to discover him. This discovery is reflected in the past two decades of scholarly theses and dissertations written on London. Perhaps the reason for this enthusiasm is not too difficult to justify. Even though London's era does seem remote, his perplexing attempt to find a destiny for himself via his literary creations has been the pursuit of many other writers. But particularly is this quest obvious in the twentieth century. Is the "struggle for survival" merely a biological phenomenon that one ponders on formal study; is the "class struggle" of sociological concern only in Russia and China? A related concern is the question of individual will versus the will of the majority. These rhetorical questions have obvious answers, and their relevance should be equally apparent. Jack London wrestled with these concepts all of his life, and his writings are burdened with his endeavor to come to some answers.

Excellent studies that pursue the ways in which London came to grips with his dilemmas have been done by Earle Labor, Sam Baskett, Maxwell Geismar, Gordon Mills, and others. Together these scholars have shown that though London was not consistently a consummate artist he was nevertheless a gifted and talented writer. That London was not an original thinker can be easily shown. But he did have the courage and the skill to inculcate provocative and unorthodox ideas into his stories, an asset that raises him significantly higher than many of his literary contemporaries. Clearly, one of the most stimulating and controversial ideas that intrigued London throughout his life were those spinning out from Darwin's writing, especially *Origin of Species*.

Franklin Walker's study (see Bibliography) examines London's apprenticeship in the Klondike, the place where London first met Darwin's ideas seriously. The three volumes of stories that London published from 1900-1902 gave him his reputation, but they did not give him a form of sufficient length to explore in depth the ideas that had been fermenting in his mind. *The Son of Wolf* (1900), *The God of His Fathers* (1901), and *Children of the Frost* (1902) were the first collections of tales. The first novel came in the form of *A Daughter of the Snows* (1902). Unfortunately, London was not equipped from his reading or through his writing to handle the sets of ideas he introduced in the novel. The result was a work marred with Victorian platitudes and improbable plot action. Nevertheless, he was on the verge of his finest piece when he decided to write a "dog story" that would balance his earlier short story about a vicious husky, "Bâtard." Little more than a month after he started writing, London had finished his prose masterpiece, *The Call of the Wild*. Superficially, the novel is London's most famous dog tale. On a more complex level, among other views, it is his rendering of the Darwinian world in all its mystery, its awesomeness. Buck, it is apparent, has all the longings and urges of primitive and sophisticated man. London could hardly have stated his case more openly.

The literary reputation of Jack London in academic disciplines is currently at its peak. Available to students and scholars alike now are an impressive bibliography, a published collection of his letters, a journal devoted to London studies, and several excellent university theses. The zenith of London's academic reputation was perhaps achieved in the finest critical study yet done in Earle Labor's *Jack London* (Twayne Publishers, 1974) from which an excerpt is printed in this volume. A special issue of *Modern Fiction Studies* (Spring, 1976) printed several important essays dealing with a wide range of London studies. And so the list grows.

The format of this casebook is simple: the presentation of a collection of materials setting forth historical and critical perspectives on London's most widely acclaimed novel, *The Call of the Wild.* The text of the beautiful prose poem is also here. One aspect of the background of the novel is pictured in Franklin Walker's chapter from his book, *Jack London and the Klondike,* and another part of the background to study with the novel is the reprinting of London's own story, "Bâtard." Some early reviews, letters from London reflecting some of his pervasive thoughts, and the best of criticism on the novel make up the collection. The items listed in the bibliography are taken from a large and impressive accumulation of criticism in the western world.

Perhaps it is of special importance to note that in our tension-filled world—characterized by the United States/Soviet Union ambivalence—the one writer who has broad appeal for both countries is Jack London. Recent surveys in the Soviet Union indicate that of all twentieth century American writers whom Russians most admire, Jack London is their first choice. Somewhere in the struggle, the mystery, and yet the enthusiasm for life, East and West may yet meet on friendly terms. A Jack London novel seems an appropriate starting ground.

# Chapter 2

---

# The Call
## of
# the Wild

---

## by Jack London

# I
# Into the Primitive

"Old longings nomadic leap,
  Chafing at custom's chain;
Again from its brumal sleep
  Wakens the ferine strain."

Buck did not read the newspapers, or he would have known that trouble was brewing, not alone for himself, but for every tidewater dog, strong of muscle and with warm, long hair, from Puget Sound to San Diego. Because men, groping in the Arctic darkness, had found a yellow metal, and because steamship and transportation companies were booming the find, thousands of men were rushing into the Northland. These men wanted dogs, and the dogs they wanted were heavy dogs, with strong muscles by which to toil, and furry coats to protect them from the frost.

Buck lived at a big house in the sun-kissed Santa Clara Valley. Judge Miller's place, it was called. It stood back from the road, half hidden among the trees, through which glimpses could be caught of the wide cool veranda that ran around its four sides. The house was approached by gravelled driveways which wound about through wide-spreading lawns and under the interlacing boughs of tall poplars. At the rear things were on even a more spacious scale than at the front. There were great stables, where a dozen grooms and boys held forth, rows of vine-clad servants' cottages, an endless and orderly array of outhouses, long grape arbors, green pastures, orchards, and berry patches. Then there was the pumping plant for the artesian well, and the big cement tank where Judge Miller's boys took their morning plunge and kept cool in the hot afternoon.

And over this great demesne Buck ruled. Here he was born, and here he had lived the four years of his life. It was true, there were other dogs. There could not but be other dogs on so vast a place, but they did not count. They came and went, resided in the populous kennels, or lived obscurely in the recesses of the house after the fashion of Toots, the Japanese pug, or Ysabel, the Mexican hairless—strange creatures that rarely put nose out of doors or set foot to ground. On the other hand, there were the fox terriers, a score of them at least, who yelped fearful promises at Toots and Ysabel looking out of the windows at them and protected by a legion of housemaids armed with brooms and mops.

But Buck was neither house-dog nor kennel dog. The whole realm was his. He plunged into the swimming tank or went hunting with the Judge's sons; he escorted Mollie and Alice, the Judge's daughters, on long twilight or early morning rambles; on wintry nights he lay at the Judge's feet before the roaring library fire; he carried the Judge's grandsons on his back, or rolled them in the grass, and guarded their footsteps through wild adventures down to the fountain in the stable yard, and even beyond, where the paddocks were, and the berry patches. Among the terriers he stalked imperiously, and Toots and Ysabel he utterly ignored, for he was king—king over all creeping, crawling, flying things of Judge Miller's place, humans included.

His father, Elmo, a huge St. Bernard, had been the Judge's inseparable companion, and Buck bid fair to follow in the way of his father. He was not so large—he weighed only one hundred and forty pounds—for his mother, Shep, had been a Scotch shepherd dog. Nevertheless, one hundred and forty pounds, to which was added the dignity that comes of good living and universal respect, enabled him to carry himself in right royal fashion. During the four years since his puppyhood he had lived the life of a sated aristocrat; he had a fine pride in himself, was ever a trifle egotistical, as country gentlemen sometimes become because of their insular situation. But he had saved himself by not becoming a mere pampered house-dog. Hunting and kindred outdoor delights had kept down the fat and hardened his muscles, and to him, as to the cold-tubbing races, the love of water had been a tonic and a health preserver.

And this was the manner of dog Buck was in the fall of 1897, when the Klondike strike dragged men from all the world into the frozen North. But Buck did not read the newspapers, and he did not know that Manuel, one of the gardener's helpers, was an undesirable acquaintance. Manuel had one besetting sin. He loved to play Chinese lottery. Also, in his gambling, he had one besetting weakness—faith in a system; and this made his damnation certain. For to play a system requires money, while the wages of a gardener's helper do not lap over the needs of a wife and numerous progeny.

The Judge was at a meeting of the Raisin Growers' Association, and the boys were busy organizing an athletic club, on the memorable night of Manuel's treachery. No one saw him and Buck go off through the orchard on what Buck imagined was merely a stroll. And with the exception of a solitary man, no one saw them arrive at the little flag station known as College Park. This man talked with Manuel, and money chinked between them.

"You might wrap up the goods before you deliver 'm," the stranger said gruffly, and Manuel doubled a piece of stout rope around Buck's neck under the collar.

"Twist it, an' you'll choke 'm plentee," said Manuel, and the stranger grunted a ready affirmative.

Buck had accepted the rope with quiet dignity. To be sure, it was an unwonted performance: but he had learned to trust in men he knew, and to give them credit for a wisdom that outreached his own. But when the ends of the rope were placed in the stranger's hands, he growled menacingly. He had merely intimated his displeasure, in his pride believing that to intimate was to command. But to his surprise the rope tightened around his neck, shutting off his breath. In quick rage he sprang at the man, who met him halfway, grappled him close by the throat, and with a deft twist threw him over on his back. Then the rope tightened mercilessly, while Buck struggled in a fury, his tongue lolling out of his mouth and his great chest panting futilely. Never in all his life had he been so vilely treated, and never in all his life had he been so angry. But his strength ebbed, his eyes glazed, and he knew nothing when the train was flagged and the two men threw him into the baggage car.

The next he knew, he was dimly aware that his tongue was hurting and that he was being jolted along in some kind of a conveyance. The hoarse shriek of a locomotive whistling a crossing told him where he was. He had travelled too often with the Judge not to know the sensation of riding in a baggage car. He opened his eyes, and into them came the unbridled anger of a kidnapped king. The man sprang for his throat, but Buck was too quick for him. His jaws closed on the hand, nor did they relax till his senses were choked out of him once more.

"Yep, has fits," the man said, hiding his mangled hand from the baggageman, who had been attracted by the sounds of struggle. "I'm takin' 'm up for the boss to 'Frisco. A crack dog-doctor there thinks that he can cure 'm."

Concerning that night's ride, the man spoke most eloquently for himself, in a little shed back of a saloon on the San Francisco water front.

"All I get is fifty for it," he grumbled; "an' I wouldn't do it over for a thousand, cold cash."

His hand was wrapped in a bloody handkerchief, and the right trouser leg was ripped from knee to ankle.

"How much did the other mug get?" the saloon-keeper demanded.

"A hundred," was the reply. "Wouldn't take a sou less, so help me."

"That makes a hundred and fifty," the saloon-keeper calculated; "and he's worth it, or I'm a squarehead."

The kidnapper undid the bloody wrappings and looked at his lacerated hand. "If I don't get the hydrophoby—"

"It'll be because you were born to hang," laughed the saloon-keeper. "Here lend me a hand before you pull your freight," he added.

Dazed, suffering intolerable pain from throat and tongue, with the life half throttled out of him, Buck attempted to face his tormentors. But he was thrown down and choked repeatedly, till they succeeded in filing the heavy brass collar from off his neck. Then the rope was removed, and he was flung into a cagelike crate.

There he lay for the remainder of the weary night, nursing his wrath and wounded pride. He could not understand what it all meant. What did they want with him, these strange men? Why were they keeping him pent up in this narrow crate? He did not know why, but he felt oppressed by the vague sense of impending calamity. Several times during the night he sprang to his feet when the shed door rattled open, expecting to see the Judge, or the boys at least. But each time it was the bulging face of the saloon-keeper that peered in at him by the sickly light of a tallow candle. And each time the joyful bark that trembled in Buck's throat was twisted into a savage growl.

But the saloon-keeper let him alone, and in the morning four men entered and picked up the crate. More tormentors, Buck decided, for they were evil-looking creatures, ragged and unkempt; and he stormed and raged at them through the bars. They only laughed and poked sticks at him, which he promptly assailed with his teeth till he realized that that was what they wanted. Whereupon he lay down sullenly and allowed the crate to be lifted into a wagon. Then he, and the crate in which he was imprisoned, began a passage through many hands. Clerks in the express office took charge of him; he was carted about in another wagon; a truck carried him, with an assortment of boxes and parcels, upon a ferry steamer; he was trucked off the steamer into a great railway depot, and finally he was deposited in an express car.

For two days and nights this express car was dragged along at the tail of shrieking locomotives; and for two days and nights Buck neither ate nor drank. In his anger he had met the first advances of the express messengers with growls, and they had retaliated by teasing him. When he flung himself against the bars, quivering and frothing, they laughed at him and taunted him. They growled and barked like detestable dogs, mewed, and flapped their arms and crowed. It was all very silly, he knew; but therefore the more outrage to his dignity, and his anger waxed and waxed. He did not mind the hunger so much, but the lack of water caused him severe suffering and fanned his wrath to fever-pitch. For that matter, high-strung and finely sensitive, the ill treatment had flung him into a fever, which was fed by the inflammation of his parched and swollen throat and tongue.

He was glad for one thing: the rope was off his neck. That had given them an unfair advantage; but now that it was off, he would show them. They would never get another rope around his neck. Upon that he was resolved. For two days and nights he neither ate nor drank, and during those two days and nights of torment, he accumulated a fund of wrath that boded ill for whoever first fell foul of him. His eyes turned blood-shot, and he was metamorphosed into a raging fiend. So changed was he that the Judge himself would not have recognized him; and the express messengers breathed with relief when they bundled him off the train at Seattle.

Four men gingerly carried the crate from the wagon into a small, high-walled back yard. A stout man, with a red sweater that sagged generously at the neck, came out and signed the book for the driver. That was the man, Buck divined, the next tormentor, and he hurled himself savagely against the bars. The man smiled grimly, and brought a hatchet and a club.

"You ain't going to take him out now?" the driver asked.

"Sure," the man replied, driving the hatchet into the crate for a pry.

There was an instantaneous scattering of the four men who had carried it in, and from safe perches on top the wall they prepared to watch the performance.

Buck rushed at the splintering wood, sinking his teeth into it, surging and wrestling with it. Wherever the hatchet fell on the outside, he was there on the inside, snarling and growling, as furiously anxious to get out as the man in the red sweater was calmly intent on getting him out.

"Now, you red-eyed devil," he said, when he had made an opening sufficient for the passage of Buck's body. At the same time he dropped the hatchet and shifted the club to his right hand.

And Buck was truly a red-eyed devil, as he drew himself together for the spring, hair bristling, mouth foaming, a mad glitter in his blood-shot eyes. Straight at the man he launched his one hundred and forty pounds of fury, surcharged with the pent passion of two days and nights. In mid air, just as his jaws were about to close on the man, he received a shock that checked his body and brought his teeth together with an agonizing clip. He whirled over, fetching the ground on his back and side. He had never been struck by a club in his life, and did not understand. With a snarl that was part bark and more scream he was again on his feet and launched into the air. And again the shock came and he was brought crushingly to the ground. This time he was aware that it was the club, but his madness knew no caution. A dozen times he charged, and as often the club broke the charge and smashed him down.

After a particularly fierce blow he crawled to his feet, too dazed to rush. He staggered limply about, the blood flowing from nose and mouth and ears, his beautiful coat sprayed and flecked with bloody slaver. Then the man advanced and deliberately dealt him a frightful blow on the nose. All the pain he had endured was as nothing compared with the exquisite agony of this. With a roar that was almost lionlike in its ferocity, he again hurled himself at the man. But the man, shifting the club from right to left, coolly caught him by the under jaw, at the same time wrenching downward and backward. Buck described a complete circle in the air, and half of another, then crashed to the ground on his head and chest.

For the last time he rushed. The man struck the shrewd blow he had purposely withheld for so long, and Buck crumpled up and went down, knocked utterly senseless.

"He's no slouch at dog-breakin', that's wot I say," one of the men on the wall cried enthusiastically.

"Druther break cayuses any day, and twice on Sundays," was the reply of the driver, as he climbed on the wagon and started the horses.

Buck's senses came back to him, but not his strength. He lay where he had fallen, and from there he watched the man in the red sweater.

" 'Answers to the name of Buck,' " the man soliloquized, quoting from the saloon-keeper's letter which had announced the consignment of the crate and contents. "Well, Buck, my boy," he went on in a genial voice, "we've had our little ruction, and the best thing we can do is to let it go at that. You've learned your place, and I know mine. Be a good dog and all'll go well and the goose hang high. Be a bad dog, and I'll whale the stuffin' outa you. Understand?"

As he spoke he fearlessly patted the head he had so mercilessly pounded, and though Buck's hair involuntarily bristled at touch of the hand, he endured it without protest. When the man brought him water he drank eagerly, and later bolted a generous meal of raw meat, chunk by chunk, from the man's hand.

He was beaten (he knew that); but he was not broken. He saw, once for all, that he stood no chance against a man with a club. He had learned the lesson, and in all his after life he never forgot it. That club was a revelation. It was his introduction to the reign of primitive law, and he met the introduction halfway. The facts of life took on a fiercer aspect; and while he faced that aspect uncowed, he faced it with all the latent cunning of his nature aroused. As the days went by, other dogs came, in crates and at the ends of ropes, some docilely, and some raging and roaring as he had come; and one and all, he watched them pass under the dominion of the man in the red sweater. Again and again, as he looked at each brutal performance, the lesson was driven home to Buck; a man with a club was a law-giver, a master to be obeyed, though not necessarily conciliated. Of this last Buck was never guilty, though he did see beaten dogs that fawned upon the man, and wagged their tails, and licked his hand. Also he saw one dog, that would neither conciliate nor obey, finally killed in the struggle for mastery.

Now and again men came, strangers, who talked excitedly, wheedling, and in all kinds of fashions to the man in the red sweater. And at such times that money passed between them the strangers took one or more of the dogs away with them. Buck wondered where they went, for they never came back; but the fear of the future was strong upon him, and he was glad each time when he was not selected.

Yet his time came, in the end, in the form of a little weazened man who spat broken English and many strange and uncouth exclamations which Buck could not understand.

"Sacredam!" he cried, when his eyes lit upon Buck. "Dat one dam bully dog! Eh? How moch?"

"Three hundred, and a present at that," was the prompt reply of the man in the red sweater. "And seein' it's government money, you ain't got no kick coming, eh, Perrault?"

Perrault grinned. Considering that the price of dogs had been boomed skyward by the unwonted demand, it was not an unfair sum for so fine an animal. The Canadian Government would be no loser, nor would its despatches travel the slower. Perrault knew dogs, and when he looked at Buck he knew that he was one in a thousand—"One in ten t'ousand," he commented mentally.

Buck saw money pass between them, and was not surprised when Curly, a good-natured Newfoundland, and he were led away by the little weazened man. That was the last he saw of the man in the red sweater, and as Curly and he looked at receding Seattle from the deck of the *Narwhal,* it was the last he saw of the warm Southland. Curly and he were taken below by Perrault and turned over to a black-faced giant called François. Perrault was a French-Canadian, and swarthy; but François was a French-Canadian half-breed, and twice as swarthy. They were a new kind of men to Buck (of which he was destined to see many more), and while he developed no affection for them, he none the less grew honestly to respect them. He speedily learned that Perrault and François were fair men, calm and impartial in administering justice, and too wise in the way of dogs to be fooled by dogs.

In the 'tween-decks of the *Narwhal,* Buck and Curly joined two other dogs. One of them was a big, snow-white fellow from Spitzbergen who had been brought away by a whaling captain, and who had later accompanied a Geological Survey into the Barrens.

He was friendly, in a treacherous sort of way, smiling into one's face the while he meditated some underhand trick, as, for instance, when he stole from Buck's food at the first meal. As Buck sprang to punish him, the lash of François's whip sang through the air, reaching the culprit first; and nothing remained to Buck but to recover the bone. That was fair of François, he decided, and the half-breed began his rise in Buck's estimation.

The other dog made no advances, nor received any; also, he did not attempt to steal from the newcomers. He was a gloomy, morose fellow, and he showed Curly plainly that all he desired was to be left alone, and further, that there would be trouble if he were not left alone. "Dave" he was called, and he ate and slept, or yawned between times, and took interest in nothing, not even when the *Narwhal* crossed Queen Charlotte Sound and rolled and pitched and bucked like a thing possessed. When Buck and Curly grew excited, half wild with fear, he raised his head as though annoyed, favored them with an incurious glance, yawned, and went to sleep again.

Day and night the ship throbbed to the tireless pulse of the propeller, and though one day was very like another, it was apparent to Buck that the weather was steadily growing colder. At last, one morning, the propeller was quiet, and the *Narwhal* was pervaded with an atmosphere of excitement. He felt it, as did the other dogs, and knew that a change was at hand. François leashed them and brought them on deck. At the first step upon the cold surface, Buck's feet sank into white mushy something very like mud. He sprang back with a snort. More of this white stuff was falling through the air. He shook himself, but more of it fell upon him. He sniffed it curiously, then licked some up on his tongue. It bit like fire, and the next instant was gone. This puzzled him. He tried it again, with the same result. The onlookers laughed uproariously, and he felt ashamed, he knew not why, for it was his first snow.

# II
# The Law of Club and Fang

Buck's first day on the Dyea beach was like a nightmare. Every hour was filled with shock and surprise. He had been suddenly jerked from the heart of civilization and flung into the heart of things primordial. No lazy, sun-kissed life was this, with nothing to do but loaf and be bored. Here was neither peace, nor rest, nor a moment's safety. All was confusion and action, and every moment life and limb were in peril. There was imperative need to be constantly alert; for these dogs and men were not town dogs and men. They were savages, all of them, who knew no law but the law of club and fang.

He had never seen dogs fight as these wolfish creatures fought, and his first experience taught him an unforgettable lesson. It is true, it was a vicarious experience, else he would not have lived to profit by it. Curly was the victim. They were camped near the log store, where she, in her friendly way, made advances to a husky dog the size of a full-grown wolf, though not half so large as she. There was no warning, only a leap in like a flash, a metallic clip of teeth, a leap out equally swift, and Curly's face was ripped open from eye to jaw.

It was the wolf manner of fighting, to strike and leap away; but there was more to it than this. Thirty or forty huskies ran to the spot and surrounded the combatants in an intent and silent circle. Buck did not comprehend that silent intentness, nor the eager way with which they were licking their chops. Curly rushed her antagonist, who struck again and leaped aside. He met her next rush with his chest, in a peculiar fashion that tumbled her off her feet. She never regained them. This was what the onlooking huskies had waited for. They closed in upon her, snarling and yelping, and she was buried, screaming with agony, beneath the bristling mass of bodies.

19

So sudden was it, and so unexpected, that Buck was taken aback. He saw Spitz run out his scarlet tongue in a way he had of laughing; and he saw François, swinging an axe, spring into the mess of dogs. Three men with clubs were helping him to scatter them. It did not take long. Two minutes from the time Curly went down, the last of her assailants were clubbed off. But she lay there limp and lifeless in the bloody, trampled snow, almost literally torn to pieces, the swart half-breed standing over her and cursing horribly. The scene often came back to Buck to trouble him in his sleep. So that was the way. No fair play. Once down, that was the end of you. Well, he would see to it that he never went down. Spitz ran out his tongue and laughed again, and from that moment Buck hated him with a bitter and deathless hatred.

Before he had recovered from the shock caused by the tragic passing of Curly, he received another shock. François fastened upon him an arrangement of straps and buckles. It was a harness, such as he had seen the grooms put on the horses at home. And as he had seen horses work, so he was set to work, hauling François on a sled to the forest that fringed the valley, and returning with a load of firewood. Though his dignity was sorely hurt by thus being made a draught animal, he was too wise to rebel. He buckled down with a will and did his best, though it was all new and strange. François was stern, demanding instant obedience, and by virtue of his whip receiving instant obedience; while Dave, who was an experienced wheeler, nipped Buck's hind quarters whenever he was in error. Spitz was the leader, likewise experienced, and while he could not always get at Buck, he growled sharp reproof now and again, or cunningly threw his weight in the traces to jerk Buck into the way he should go. Buck learned easily, and under the combined tuition of his two mates and François made remarkable progress. Ere they returned to camp he knew enough to stop at "ho," to go ahead at "mush," to swing wide on the bends, and to keep clear of the wheeler when the loaded sled shot downhill at their heels.

"T'ree vair' good dogs," François told Perrault. "Dat Buck, heem pool lak hell. I tich heem queek as anyt'ing."

By afternoon, Perrault, who was in a hurry to be on the trail with his despatches, returned with two more dogs. "Billee" and "Joe," he called them, two brothers, and true huskies both. Sons of the one mother though they were, they were as different as day and night.

Billee's one fault was his excessive good nature, while Joe was the very opposite, sour and introspective, with a perpetual snarl and a malignant eye. Buck received them in comradely fashion, Dave ignored them, while Spitz proceeded to thrash first one and then the other. Billee wagged his tail appeasingly, turned to run when he saw that appeasement was of no avail, and cried (still appeasingly) when Spitz's sharp teeth scored his flank. But no matter how Spitz circled, Joe whirled around on his heels to face him, mane bristling, ears laid back, lips writhing and snarling, jaws clipping together as fast as he could snap, and eyes diabolically gleaming—the incarnation of belligerent fear. So terrible was his appearance that Spitz was forced to forego disciplining him; but to cover his own discomfiture he turned upon the inoffensive and wailing Billee and drove him to the confines of the camp.

By evening Perrault secured another dog, an old husky, long and lean and gaunt, with a battle-scarred face and a single eye which flashed a warning of prowess that commanded respect. He was called Sol-leks, which means the Angry One. Like Dave, he asked nothing, gave nothing, expected nothing: and when he marched slowly and deliberately into their midst, even Spitz left him alone. He had one peculiarity which Buck was unlucky enough to discover. He did not like to be approached on his blind side. Of this offence Buck was unwittingly guilty, and the first knowledge he had of his indiscretion was when Sol-leks whirled upon him and slashed his shoulder to the bone for three inches up and down. Forever after Buck avoided his blind side, and to the last of their comradeship had no more trouble. His only apparent ambition, like Dave's, was to be left alone, though, as Buck was afterward to learn, each of them possessed one other and even more vital ambition.

That night Buck faced the great problem of sleeping. The tent, illuminated by a candle, glowed warmly in the midst of the white plain; and when he, as a matter of course, entered it, both Perrault and François bombarded him with curses and cooking utensils, till he recovered from his consternation and fled ignominiously into the outer cold. A chill wind was blowing that nipped him sharply and bit with especial venom into his wounded shoulder. He lay down on the snow and attempted to sleep, but the frost soon drove him shivering to his feet. Miserable and disconsolate, he wandered about among the many tents, only to find that one place was as cold as another. Here and there savage dogs rushed upon him, but he bristled his neck-hair and snarled (for he was learning fast), and they let him go his way unmolested.

Finally an idea came to him. He would return and see how his own team mates were making out. To his astonishment, they had disappeared. Again he wandered about through the great camp, looking for them, and again he returned. Were they in the tent? No, that could not be, else he would not have been driven out. Then where could they possibly be? With drooping tail and shivering body, very forlorn indeed, he aimlessly circled the tent. Suddenly the snow gave way beneath his fore legs and he sank down. Something wriggled under his feet. He sprang back, bristling and snarling, fearful of the unseen and unknown. But a friendly little yelp reassured him, and he went back to investigate. A whiff of warm air ascended to his nostrils, and there, curled up under the snow in a snug ball, lay Billee. He whined placatingly, squirmed and wriggled to show his good will and intentions, and even ventured, as a bribe for peace, to lick Buck's face with his warm wet tongue.

Another lesson. So that was the way they did it, eh? Buck confidently selected a spot, and with much fuss and waste effort proceeded to dig a hole for himself. In a trice the heat from his body filled the confined space and he was asleep. The day had been long and arduous, and he slept soundly and comfortably, though he growled and barked and wrestled with bad dreams.

Nor did he open his eyes till roused by the noises of the waking camp. At first he did not know where he was. It had snowed during the night and he was completely buried. The snow walls pressed him on every side, and a great surge of fear swept through him—the fear of the wild thing for the trap. It was a token that he was harking back through his own life to the lives of his forebears, for he was a civilized dog, an unduly civilized dog and of his own experience knew no trap and so could not of himself fear it. The muscles of his whole body contracted spasmodically and instinctively, the hair on his neck and shoulders stood on end, and with a ferocious snarl he bounded straight up into the blinding day, the snow flying about him in a flashing cloud. Ere he landed on his feet, he saw the white camp spread out before him and knew where he was and remembered all that had passed from the time he went for a stroll with Manuel to the hole he had dug for himself the night before. A shout from François hailed his appearance. "Wot I say?" the dog driver cried to Perrault. "Dat Buck for sure learn queek as anyt'ing."

Perrault nodded gravely. As courier for the Canadian Government, bearing important despatches, he was anxious to secure the best dogs, and he was particularly gladdened by the possession of Buck.

Three more huskies were added to the team inside an hour, making a total of nine, and before another quarter of an hour had passed they were in harness and swinging up the trail toward the Dyea Cañon. Buck was glad to be gone, and though the work was hard he found he did not particularly despise it. He was surprised at the eagerness which animated the whole team and which was communicated to him; but still more surprising was the change wrought in Dave and Sol-leks. They were new dogs, utterly transformed by the harness. All passiveness and unconcern had dropped from them. They were alert and active, anxious that the work should go well, and fiercely irritable with whatever, by delay or confusion, retarded that work. The toil of the traces seemed the supreme expression of their being, and all that they lived for and the only thing in which they took delight.

Dave was wheeler or sled dog, pulling in front of him was Buck, then came Sol-leks; the rest of the team was strung out ahead, single file, to the leader, which position was filled by Spitz.

Buck had been purposely placed between Dave and Sol-leks so that he might receive instruction. Apt scholar that he was, they were equally apt teachers, never allowing him to linger long in error, and enforcing their teaching with their sharp teeth. Dave was fair and very wise. He never nipped Buck without cause, and he never failed to nip him when he stood in need of it. As François's whip backed him up, Buck found it to be cheaper to mend his ways than to retaliate. Once, during a brief halt, when he got tangled in the traces and delayed the start, both Dave and Sol-leks flew at him and administered a sound trouncing. The resulting tangle was even worse, but Buck took good care to keep the traces clear thereafter; and ere the day was done, so well had he mastered his work, his mates about ceased nagging him. Francois's whip snapped less frequently, and Perrault even honored Buck by lifting up his feet and carefully examining them.

It was a hard day's run, up the cañon, through Sheep Camp, past the Scales and the timber line, across glaciers and snowdrifts hundreds of feet deep, and over the great Chilkoot Divide, which stands between the salt water and the fresh and guards forbiddingly the sad and lonely North. They made good time down the chain of lakes which fills the craters of extinct volcanoes, and late that night pulled into the huge camp at the head of Lake Bennett, where thousands of goldseekers were building boats against the breakup of the ice in the spring. Buck made his hole in the snow and slept the sleep of the exhausted just, but all too early was routed out in the cold darkness and harnessed with his mates to the sled.

That day they made forty miles, the trail being packed; but the next day, and for many days to follow, they broke their own trail, worked harder, and made poorer time. As a rule, Perrault travelled ahead of the team, packing the snow with webbed shoes to make it easier for them. François, guiding the sled at the gee-pole, sometimes exchanged places with him but not often. Perrault was in a hurry, and he prided himself on his knowledge of ice, which knowledge was indispensable, for the fall ice was very thin, and where there was swift water, there was no ice at all.

Day after day, for days unending, Buck toiled in the traces. Always, they broke camp in the dark, and the first gray of dawn found them hitting the trail with fresh miles reeled off behind them. And always they pitched camp after dark, eating their bit of fish, and crawling to sleep into the snow. Buck was ravenous. The pound and a half of sun-dried salmon, which was his ration for each day, seemed to go nowhere. He never had enough, and suffered from perpetual hunger pangs. Yet the other dogs, because they weighed less and were born to the life, received a pound only of the fish and managed to keep in good condition.

He swiftly lost the fastidiousness which had characterized his old life. A dainty eater, he found that his mates, finishing first, robbed him of his unfinished ration. There was no defending it. While he was fighting off two or three, it was disappearing down the throats of the others. To remedy this, he ate as fast as they; and, so greatly did hunger compel him, he was not above taking what did not belong to him. He watched and learned. When he saw Pike, one of the new dogs, a clever malingerer and thief, slyly steal a slice of bacon when Perrault's back was turned, he duplicated the performance the following day, getting away with the whole chunk. A great uproar was raised, but he was unsuspected, while Dub, an awkward blunderer who was always getting caught, was punished for Buck's misdeed.

This first theft marked Buck as fit to survive in the hostile Northland environment. It marked his adaptability, his capacity to adjust himself to changing conditions, the lack of which would have meant swift and terrible death. It marked, further, the decay or going to pieces of his moral nature, a vain thing and a handicap in the ruthless struggle for existence. It was all well enough in the Southland, under the law of love and fellowship, to respect private property and personal feelings; but in the Northland, under the law of club and fang, whoso took such things into account was a fool, and in so far as he observed them he would fail to prosper.

Not that Buck reasoned it out. He was fit, that was all, and unconsciously he accommodated himself to the new mode of life. All his days, no matter what the odds, he had never run from a fight. But the club of the man in the red sweater had beaten into him a more fundamental and primitive code. Civilized, he could have died for a moral consideration, say the defence of Judge Miller's riding whip; but the completeness of his decivilization was now evidenced by his ability to flee from the defence of a moral consideration and so save his hide. He did not steal for joy of it, but because of the clamor of his stomach. He did not rob openly, but stole secretly and cunningly, out of respect for club and fang. In short, the things he did were done because it was easier to do them than not to do them.

His development (or retrogression) was rapid. His muscles became hard as iron and he grew callous to all ordinary pain. He achieved an internal as well as external economy. He could eat anything, no matter how loathsome or indigestible; and, once eaten, the juices of his stomach extracted the last particle of nutriment; and his blood carried it to the farthest reaches of his body, building it into the toughest and stoutest of tissues. Sight and scent became remarkably keen, while his hearing developed such acuteness that in his sleep he heard the faintest sound and knew whether it heralded peace or peril. He learned to bite the ice out with his teeth when it collected between his toes; and when he was thirsty and there was a thick scum of ice over the water hole, he would break it by rearing and striking it with stiff fore legs. His most conspicuous trait was an ability to scent the wind and forecast it a night in advance. No matter how breathless the air when he dug his nest by tree or bank, the wind that later blew inevitably found him to leeward, sheltered and snug.

And not only did he learn by experience, but instincts long dead became alive again. The domesticated generations fell from him. In vague ways he remembered back to the youth of the breed, to the time the wild dogs ranged in packs through the primeval forest, and killed their meat as they ran it down. It was no task for him to learn to fight with cut and slash and the quick wolf snap. In this manner had fought forgotten ancestors. They quickened the old life within him, and the old tricks which they had stamped into the heredity of the breed were his tricks. They came to him without effort or discovery, as though they had been his always. And when, on the still cold nights, he pointed his nose at a star and howled long and wolflike, it was his ancestors, dead and dust, pointing nose at star and howling down through the centuries and through him. And his cadences were their cadences, the cadences which voiced their woe and what to them was the meaning of the stillness, and the cold, and dark.

Thus, as token of what a puppet thing life is the ancient song surged through him and he came into his own again; and he came because men had found a yellow metal in the North, and because Manuel was a gardener's helper whose wages did not lap over the needs of his wife and divers small copies of himself.

# III
# The Dominant Primordial Beast

The dominant primordial beast was strong in Buck, and under the fierce conditions of trail life it grew and grew. Yet it was a secret growth. His new-born cunning gave him poise and control. He was too busy adjusting himself to the new life to feel at ease, and not only did he not pick fights, but he avoided them whenever possible. A certain deliberateness characterized his attitude. He was not prone to rashness and precipitate action; and in the bitter hatred between him and Spitz he betrayed no impatience, shunned all offensive acts.

On the other hand, possibly because he divined in Buck a dangerous rival, Spitz never lost an opportunity of showing his teeth. He even went out of his way to bully Buck, striving constantly to start the fight which could end only in the death of one or the other.

Early in the trip this might have taken place had it not been for an unwonted accident. At the end of this day they made a bleak and miserable camp on the shore of Lake Le Barge. Driving snow, a wind that cut like a white-hot knife, and darkness, had forced them to grope for a camping place. They could hardly have fared worse. At their backs rose a perpendicular wall of rock, and Perrault and François were compelled to make their fire and spread their sleeping robes on the ice of the lake itself. The tent they had discarded at Dyea in order to travel light. A few sticks of driftwood furnished them with a fire that thawed down through the ice and left them to eat supper in the dark.

Close in under the sheltering rock Buck made his nest. So snug and warm was it, that he was loath to leave it when François distributed the fish which he had first thawed over the fire. But

27

when Buck finished his ration and returned, he found his nest occupied. A warning snarl told him that the trespasser was Spitz. Till now Buck had avoided trouble with his enemy, but this was too much. The beast in him roared. He sprang upon Spitz with a fury which surprised them both, and Spitz particularly, for his whole experience with Buck had gone to teach him that his rival was an unusually timid dog, who managed to hold his own only because of his great weight and size.

François was surprised, too, when they shot out in a tangle from the disrupted nest and he divined the cause of the trouble. "A-a-ah!" he cried to Buck. "Gif it to heem, by Gar! Gif it to heem, the dirty t'eef!"

Spitz was equally willing. He was crying with sheer rage and eagerness as he circled back and forth for a chance to spring in. Buck was no less eager, and no less cautious, as he likewise circled back and forth for the advantage. But it was then that the unexpected happened, the thing which projected their struggle for supremacy far into the future, past many a weary mile of trail and toil.

An oath from Perrault, the resounding impact of a club upon a bony frame, and a shrill yelp of pain, heralded the breaking forth of pandemonium. The camp was suddenly discovered to be alive with skulking furry forms,—starving huskies, four or five score of them, who had scented the camp from some Indian village. They had crept in while Buck and Spitz were fighting, and when the two men sprang among them with stout clubs they showed their teeth and fought back. They were crazed by the smell of the food. Perrault found one with head buried in the grub-box. His club landed heavily on the gaunt ribs, and the grub-box was capsized on the ground. On the instant a score of the famished brutes were scrambling for the bread and bacon. The clubs fell upon them unheeded. They yelped and howled under the rain of blows, but struggled none the less madly till the last crumb had been devoured.

In the meantime the astonished team-dogs had burst out of their nests only to be set upon by the fierce invaders. Never had Buck seen such dogs. It seemed as though their bones would burst through their skins. They were mere skeletons, draped loosely in draggled hides, with blazing eyes and slavered fangs. But the hunger-madness made them terrifying, irresistible. There was no opposing them. The team-dogs were swept back against the cliff at the first onset. Buck was beset by three huskies, and in a trice his head and shoulders were ripped and slashed. The din was frightful. Billee was crying as usual. Dave and Sol-leks, dripping blood from a score of wounds, were fighting bravely side by side. Joe was snapping like a demon. Once, his teeth closed on the fore leg of a husky, and he crunched down through the bone. Pike, the malingerer, leaped upon the crippled animal, breaking its neck with a quick dash of teeth and a jerk. Buck got a frothing adversary by the throat, and was sprayed with blood when his teeth sank through the jugular. The warm taste of it in his mouth goaded him to greater fierceness. He flung himself upon another, and at the same time felt teeth sink into his own throat. It was Spitz treacherously attacking from the side.

Perrault and François, having cleaned out their part of the camp, hurried to save their sled-dogs. The wild wave of famished beasts rolled back before them, and Buck shook himself free. But it was only for a moment. The two men were compelled to run back to save the grub, upon which the huskies returned to the attack on the team. Billee, terrified into bravery, sprang through the savage circle and fled away over the ice. Pike and Dub followed on his heels, with the rest of the team behind. As Buck drew himself together to spring after them, out of the tail of his eye he saw Spitz rush upon him with the evident intention of overthrowing him. Once off his feet and under that mass of huskies, there was no hope for him. But he braced himself to the shock of Spitz's charge, then joined the flight out on the lake.

Later, the nine team-dogs gathered together and sought shelter in the forest. Though unpursued, they were in a sorry plight. There was not one who was not wounded in four or five places, while some were wounded grievously. Dub was badly injured in a hind leg; Dolly, the last husky added to the team at Dyea, had a badly torn throat; Joe had lost an eye; while Billee, the good-natured, with an ear chewed and rent to ribbons, cried and whimpered throughout the night. At daybreak they limped warily back to camp, to find the marauders gone and the two men in bad tempers. Fully half their grub supply was gone. The huskies had chewed through the sled lashings and canvas coverings. In fact, nothing, no matter how remotely eatable, had escaped them. They had eaten a pair of

Perrault's moose-hide moccasins, chunks out of the leather traces, and even two feet of lash from the end of François's whip. He broke from a mournful contemplation of it to look over his wounded dogs. "Ah, my frien's;" he said softly, "mebbe it mek you mad dog, dose many bites. Mebbe all mad dog, sacredam! Wot you t'ink, eh, Perrault?"

The courier shook his head dubiously. With four hundred miles of trail still between him and Dawson, he could ill afford to have madness break out among his dogs. Two hours of cursing and exertion got the harnesses into shape, and the wound-stiffened team was under way, struggling painfully over the hardest part of the trail they had yet encountered, and for that matter, the hardest between them and Dawson.

The Thirty Mile River was wide open. Its wild water defied the frost, and it was in the eddies only and in the quiet places that the ice held at all. Six days of exhausting toil were required to cover those thirty terrible miles. And terrible they were, for every foot of them was accomplished at the risk of life to dog and man. A dozen times, Perrault, nosing the way, broke through the ice bridges, being saved by the long pole he carried, which he so held that it fell each time across the hole made by his body. But a cold snap was on, the thermometer registering fifty below zero, and each time he broke through he was compelled for very life to build a fire and dry his garments.

Nothing daunted him. It was because nothing daunted him that he had been chosen for government courier. He took all manner of risks, resolutely thrusting his little weazened face into the frost and struggling on from dim dawn to dark. He skirted the frowning shores on rim ice that bent and crackled under foot and on which they dared not halt. Once, the sled broke through, with Dave and Buck, and they were half-frozen and all but drowned by the time they were dragged out. The usual fire was necessary to save them. They were coated solidly with ice, and the two men kept them on the run around the fire, sweating and thawing, so close that they were singed by the flames.

At another time Spitz went through, dragging the whole team after him up to Buck, who strained backward with all his strength, his fore paws on the slippery edge and the ice quivering and snapping all around. But behind him was Dave, likewise straining backward, and behind the sled was François, pulling till his tendons cracked.

Again, the rim ice broke away before and behind, and there was no escape except up the cliff. Perrault scaled it by a miracle, while François prayed for just that miracle; and with every thong and sled-lashing and the last bit of harness rove into a long rope, the dogs were hoisted, one by one, to the cliff crest. François came up last, after the sled and load. Then came the search for a place to descend, which decent was ultimately made by the aid of the rope, and night found them back on the river with a quarter of a mile to the day's credit.

By the time they made the Houtalinqua and good ice, Buck was played out. The rest of the dogs were in like condition; but Perrault, to make up lost time, pushed them late and early. The first day they covered thirty-five miles to the Big Salmon; the next day thirty-five more to the Little Salmon; the third day forty miles, which brought them well up toward the Five Fingers.

Buck's feet were not so compact and hard as the feet of the huskies. His had softened during the many generations since the day his last wild ancestor was tamed by a cave-dweller or river man. All day long he limped in agony, and camp once made, lay down like a dead dog. Hungry as he was, he would not move to receive his ration of fish, which François had to bring to him. Also, the dog-driver rubbed Buck's feet for half an hour each night after supper, and sacrificed the tops of his own moccasins to make four moccasins for Buck. This was a great relief, and Buck caused even the weazened face of Perrault to twist itself into a grin one morning, when François forgot the moccasins and Buck lay on his back, his four feet waving appealingly in the air, and refused to budge without them. Later his feet grew hard to the trail, and the worn-out footgear was thrown away.

At the Pelly one morning, as they were harnessing up, Dolly, who had never been conspicuous for anything, went suddenly mad. She announced her condition by a long, heartbreaking wolf howl that sent every dog bristling with fear, then sprang straight for Buck. He had never seen a dog go mad, nor did he have any reason to fear madness; yet he knew that here was horror, and fled away from it in panic. Straight away he raced, with Dolly, panting and frothing, one leap behind; nor could she gain on him, so great was his terror, nor could he leave her, so great was her madness. He plunged through the wooded breast of the island, flew down to the lower end, crossed a back channel filled with rough ice to another island, gained a third island, curved back to the main river, and in desperation started to cross it. And all the time, though he did not look, he could hear her snarling just one leap behind. François called to him a quarter of a mile away and he doubled back, still one leap ahead, gasping painfully for air and putting all his faith in that François would save him. The dog-driver held the axe poised in his hand, and as Buck shot past him the axe crashed down upon mad Dolly's head.

Buck staggered over against the sled, exhausted, sobbing for breath, helpless. This was Spitz's opportunity. He sprang upon Buck, and twice his teeth sank into his unresisting foe and ripped and tore the flesh to the bone. Then François's lash descended, and Buck had the satisfaction of watching Spitz receive the worst whipping as yet administered to any of the team.

"One devil, dat Spitz," remarked Perrault. "Some dam day heem keel dat Buck."

"Dat Buck two devils," was François's rejoinder. "All de tam I watch dat Buck I know for sure. Lissen: some dam fine day heem get mad lak hell an' den heem chew dat Spitz all up an' spit heem out on de snow. Sure. I know."

From then on it was war between them. Spitz, as lead-dog and acknowledged master of the team, felt his supremacy threatened by this strange Southland dog. And strange Buck was to him, for of the many Southland dogs he had known, not one had shown up worthily in camp and on the trail. They were all too soft, dying under the toil, the frost, and starvation. Buck was the exception. He alone endured and prospered, matching the husky in strength, savagery, and cunning. Then he was a masterful dog, and what made him dangerous was the fact that the club of the man in the red sweater had knocked all blind pluck and rashness out of his desire for mastery. He was preëminently cunning, and could bide his time with a patience that was nothing less than primitive.

It was inevitable that the clash for leadership should come. Buck wanted it. He wanted it because it was his nature, because he had been gripped tight by that nameless, incomprehensible pride of the trail and trace—that pride which holds dogs in the toil to the last gasp, which lures them to die joyfully in the harness, and breaks their hearts if they are cut out of the harness. This was the pride of Dave as wheel-dog, of Sol-leks as he pulled with all his strength; the pride that laid hold of them at break of camp, transforming them from sour and sullen brutes into straining, eager, ambitious creatures; the pride that spurred them on all day and dropped them at pitch of camp at night, letting them fall into gloomy unrest and uncontent. This was the pride that bore up Spitz and made him thrash the sled-dogs who blundered and shirked in the traces or hid away at harness-up time in the morning. Likewise it was this pride that made him fear Buck as a possible lead-dog. And this was Buck's pride, too.

He openly threatened the other's leadership. He came between him and the shirks he should have punished. And he did it deliberately. One night there was a heavy snowfall, and in the morning Pike, the malingerer, did not appear. He was securely hidden in his nest under a foot of snow. François called him and sought him in vain. Spitz was wild with wrath. He raged through the camp, smelling and digging in every likely place, snarling so frightfully that Pike heard and shivered in his hiding-place.

But when he was at last unearthed, and Spitz flew at him to punish him, Buck flew, with equal rage, in between. So unexpected was it, and so shrewdly managed, that Spitz was hurled backward and off his feet. Pike, who had been trembling abjectly, took heart at this open mutiny, and sprang upon his overthrown leader. Buck, to whom fair play was a forgotten code, likewise sprang upon Spitz. But François, chuckling at the incident while unswerving in the administration of justice, brought his lash down upon Buck with all his might. This failed to drive Buck from his prostrate rival, and the butt of the whip was brought into play. Half-stunned by the blow, Buck was knocked backward and the lash laid upon him again and again, while Spitz soundly punished the many times offending Pike.

In the days that followed, as Dawson grew closer and closer, Buck still continued to interfere between Spitz and the culprits; but he did it craftily, when François was not around. With the covert mutiny of Buck, a general insubordination sprang up and increased. Dave and Sol-leks were unaffected, but the rest of the team went from bad to worse. Things no longer went right. There was continual bickering and jangling. Trouble was always afoot, and at the bottom of it was Buck. He kept François busy, for the dog-driver was in constant apprehension of the life-and-death struggle between the two which he knew must take place sooner or later; and on more than one night the sounds of quarrelling and strife among the other dogs turned him out of his sleeping robe, fearful that Buck and Spitz were at it.

But the opportunity did not present itself, and they pulled into Dawson one dreary afternoon with the great fight still to come. Here were many men, and countless dogs, and Buck found them all at work. It seemed the ordained order of things that dogs should work. All day they swung up and down the main street in long teams, and in the night their jingling bells still went by. They hauled cabin logs and firewood, freighted up to the mines, and did all manner of work that horses did in the Santa Clara Valley. Here and there Buck met Southland dogs, but in the main they were the wild wolf husky breed. Every night, regularly, at nine, at twelve, at three, they lifted a nocturnal song, a weird and eerie chant, in which it was Buck's delight to join.

With the aurora borealis flaming coldly overhead, or the stars leaping in the frost dance, and the land numb and frozen under its pall of snow, this song of the huskies might have been the defiance of life, only it was pitched in minor key, with long-drawn wailings and half-sobs, and was more the pleading of life, the articulate travail of existence. It was an old song, old as the breed itself—one of the first songs of the younger world in a day when songs were sad. It was invested with the woe of unnumbered generations, this plaint by which Buck was so strangely stirred. When he moaned and sobbed, it was with the pain of living that was of old the pain of his wild fathers, and the fear and mystery of the cold and dark that was to them fear and mystery. And that he should be stirred by it marked the completeness with which he harked back through the ages of fire and roof to the raw beginnings of life in the howling ages.

Seven days from the time they pulled into Dawson, they dropped down the steep bank by the Barracks to the Yukon Trail, and pulled for Dyea and Salt Water. Perrault was carrying despatches if anything more urgent than those he had brought in; also, the travel pride had gripped him, and he purposed to make the record trip of the year. Several things favored him in this. The week's rest had recuperated the dogs and put them in thorough trim. The trail they had broken into the country was packed hard by later journeyers.

And further, the police had arranged in two or three places deposits of grub for dog and man, and he was travelling light.

They made Sixty Miles, which is a fifty-mile run, on the first day; and the second day saw them booming up the Yukon well on their way to Pelly. But such splendid running was achieved not without great trouble and vexation on the part of François. The insidious revolt led by Buck had destroyed the solidarity of the team. It no longer was as one dog leaping in the traces. The encouragement Buck gave the rebels led them into all kinds of petty misdemeanors. No more was Spitz a leader greatly to be feared. The old awe departed, and they grew equal to challenging his authority. Pike robbed him of half a fish one night, and gulped it down under the protection of Buck. Another night Dub and Joe fought Spitz and made him forego the punishment they deserved. And even Billee, the good-natured, was less good-natured, and whined not half so placatingly as in former days. Buck never came near Spitz without snarling and bristling menacingly. In fact, his conduct approached that of a bully, and he was given to swaggering up and down before Spitz's very nose.

The breaking down of discipline likewise affected the dogs in their relations with one another. They quarrelled and bickered more than ever among themselves, till at times the camp was a howling bedlam. Dave and Sol-leks alone were unaltered, though they were made irritable by the unending squabbling. François swore strange barbarous oaths, and stamped the snow in futile rage, and tore his hair. His lash was always singing among the dogs, but it was of small avail. Directly his back was turned they were at it again. He backed up Spitz with his whip, while Buck backed up the remainder of the team. François knew he was behind all the trouble, and Buck knew he knew; but Buck was too clever ever again to be caught red-handed. He worked faithfully in the harness, for the toil had become a delight to him; yet it was a greater delight slyly to precipitate a fight amongst his mates and tangle the traces.

At the mouth of the Tahkeena, one night after supper, Dub turned up a snowshoe rabbit, blundered it, and missed. In a second the whole team was in full cry. A hundred yards away was a camp of the Northwest Police, with fifty dogs, huskies all, who joined the chase. The rabbit sped down the river, turned off into a small creek, up the frozen bed of which it held steadily. It ran lightly on the surface of the snow, while the dogs ploughed through by main strength. Buck led the pack, sixty strong, around bend after bend, but he could not gain. He lay down low to the race, whining eagerly, his splendid body flashing forward, leap by leap, in the wan white moonlight. And leap by leap, like some pale frost wraith, the snowshoe rabbit flashed on ahead.

All that stirring of old instincts which at stated periods drives men out from the sounding cities to forest and plain to kill things by chemically propelled leaden pellets, the blood lust, the joy to kill—all this was Buck's, only it was infinitely more intimate. He was ranging at the head of the pack, running the wild thing down, the living meat, to kill with his own teeth and wash his muzzle to the eyes in warm blood.

There is an ecstasy that marks the summit of life, and beyond which life cannot rise. And such is the paradox of living, this ecstasy comes when one is most alive, and it comes as a complete forgetfulness that one is alive. This ecstasy, this forgetfulness of living, comes to the artist, caught up and out of himself in a sheet of flame; it comes to the soldier, war-mad on a stricken field and refusing quarter; and it came to Buck, leading the pack, sounding the old wolf-cry, straining after the food that was alive and that fled swiftly before him through the moonlight. He was sounding the deeps of his nature, and of the parts of his nature that were deeper than he, going back into the womb of Time. He was mastered by the sheer surging of life, the tidal wave of being, the perfect joy of each separate muscle, joint, and sinew and that it was everything that was not death, that it was aglow and rampant, expressing itself in movement, flying exultantly under the stars and over the face of dead matter that did not move.

But Spitz, cold and calculating even in his supreme moods, left the pack and cut across a narrow neck of land where the creek made a long bend around. Buck did not know of this, and as he rounded the bend, the frost wraith of a rabbit still flitting before him, he saw another and larger frost wraith leap from the overhanging bank in to the immediate path of the rabbit. It was Spitz. The rabbit could not turn, and as the white teeth broke its back in mid air it shrieked as loudly as a stricken man may shriek. At sound of this, the cry of Life plunging down from Life's apex in the grip of Death, the full pack at Buck's heels raised a hell's chorus of delight.

Buck did not cry out. He did not check himself, but drove in upon Spitz, shoulder to shoulder, so hard that he missed the throat. They rolled over and over in the powdery snow. Spitz gained his feet almost as though he had not been overthrown, slashing Buck down the shoulder and leaping clear. Twice his teeth clipped together, like the steel jaws of a trap, as he backed away for better footing, with lean and lifting lips that writhed and snarled.

In a flash Buck knew it. The time had come. It was to the death. As they circled about, snarling, ears laid back, keenly watchful for the advantage, the scene came to Buck with a sense of familiarity. He seemed to remember it all,—the white woods, and earth, and moonlight, and the thrill of battle. Over the whiteness and silence brooded a ghostly calm. There was not the the faintest whisper of air—nothing moved, not a leaf quivered, the visible breaths of the dogs rising slowly and lingering in the frosty air. They had made short work of the snowshoe rabbit, these dogs that were ill-tamed wolves; and they were now drawn up in an expectant circle. They, too, were silent, their eyes only gleaming and their breaths drifting slowly upward. To Buck it was nothing new or strange, this scene of old time. It was as though it had always been, the wonted way of things.

Spitz was a practised fighter. From Spitzbergen through the Arctic, and across Canada and the Barrens, he had held his own with all manner of dogs and achieved to mastery over them. Bitter rage was his, but never blind rage. In passion to rend and destroy, he never forgot that his enemy was in like passion to rend and destroy. He never rushed till he was prepared to receive a rush; never attacked till he had first defended that attack.

In vain Buck strove to sink his teeth in the neck of the big white dog. Wherever his fangs struck for the softer flesh, they were countered by the fangs of Spitz. Fang clashed fang, and lips were cut and bleeding, but Buck could not penetrate his enemy's guard. Then he warmed up and enveloped Spitz in a whirlwind of rushes. Time and time again he tried for the snow-white throat, where life bubbled near to the surface, and each time and every time Spitz slashed him and got away. Then Buck took to rushing, as though for the throat, when, suddenly drawing back his head and curving in from the side, he would drive his shoulder at the shoulder of Spitz, as a ram by which to overthrow him. But instead, Buck's shoulder was slashed down each time as Spitz leaped lightly away.

Spitz was untouched, while Buck was streaming with blood and panting hard. The fight was growing desperate. And all the while the silent and wolfish circle waited to finish off whichever dog went down. As Buck grew winded, Spitz took to rushing, and he kept him staggering for footing. Once Buck went over, and the whole circle of sixty dogs started up; but he recovered himself, almost in mid air, and the circle sank down again and waited.

But Buck possessed a quality that made for greatness— imagination. He fought by instinct, but he could fight by head as well. He rushed, as though attempting the old shoulder trick, but at the last instant swept low to the snow and in. His teeth closed on Spitz's left fore leg. There was a crunch of breaking bone, and the white dog faced him on three legs. Thrice he tried to knock him over, then repeated the trick and broke the right fore leg. Despite the pain and helplessness, Spitz struggled madly to keep up. He saw the silent circle, with gleaming eyes, lolling tongues, and silvery breaths drifting upward, closing in upon him as he had seen similar circles close in upon beaten antagonists in the past. Only this time he was the one who was beaten.

There was no hope for him. Buck was inexorable. Mercy was a thing reserved for gentler climes. He manoeuvred for the final rush. The circle had tightened till he could feel the breaths of the huskies on his flanks. He could see them, beyond Spitz and to either side, half crouching for the spring, their eyes fixed upon him. A pause seemed to fall. Every animal was motionless as though turned to stone. Only Spitz quivered and bristled as he staggered back and forth, snarling with horrible menace, as though to frighten off impending death. Then Buck sprang in and out, but while he was in, shoulder had at last squarely met shoulder. The dark circle became a dot on the moon-flooded snow as Spitz disappeared from view. Buck stood and looked on, the successful champion, the dominant primordial beast who had made his kill and found it good.

# IV
# Who Has Won to Mastership

"Eh? Wot I say? I spik true w'en I say dat Buck two devils."
This was François's speech next morning when he discovered
Spitz missing and Buck covered with wounds. He drew him to the
fire and by its light pointed them out.

"Dat Spitz fight lak hell," said Perrault, as he surveyed the
gaping rips and cuts.

"An' dat Buck fight lak two hells," was François's answer. "An'
now we make good time. No more Spitz, no more trouble, sure."

While Perrault packed the camp outfit and loaded the sled, the
dog-driver proceeded to harness the dogs. Buck trotted up to the
place Spitz would have occupied as leader; but François, not notic-
ing him, brought Sol-leks to the coveted position. In his judgment,
Sol-leks was the best lead-dog left. Buck sprang upon Sol-leks in a
fury, driving him back and standing in his place.

"Eh? eh?" François cried, slapping his thighs gleefully. "Look at
dat Buck. Heem keel dat Spitz, heem t'ink to take de job."

"Go 'way, Chook!" he cried, but Buck refused to budge.

He took Buck by the scruff of the neck, and though the dog
growled threateningly, dragged him to one side and replaced Sol-
leks. The old dog did not like it, and showed plainly that he was
afraid of Buck. François was obdurate, but when he turned his back
Buck again displaced Sol-leks, who was not at all unwilling to go.

François was angry. "Now, by Gar, I feex you!" he cried, coming
back with a heavy club in his hand.

Buck remembered the man in the red sweater, and retreated
slowly; nor did he attempt to charge in when Sol-leks was once more
brought forward. But he circled just beyond the range of the club,

snarling with bitterness and rage; and while he circled he watched the club so as to dodge it if thrown by François, for he was become wise in the way of clubs.

The driver went about his work, and he called to Buck when he was ready to put him in his old place in front of Dave. Buck retreated two or three steps. François followed him up, whereupon he again retreated. After some time of this, François threw down the club, thinking that Buck feared a thrashing. But Buck was in open revolt. He wanted, not to escape a clubbing, but to have the leadership. It was his by right. He had earned it, and he would not be content with less.

Perrault took a hand. Between them they ran him about for the better part of an hour. They threw clubs at him. He dodged. They cursed him, and his fathers and mothers before him, and all his seed to come after him down to the remotest generation, and every hair on his body and drop of blood in his veins; and he answered curse with snarl and kept out of their reach. He did not try to run away, but retreated around and around the camp, advertising plainly that when his desire was met, he would come in and be good.

François sat down and scratched his head. Perrault looked at his watch and swore. Time was flying, and they should have been on the trail an hour gone. François scratched his head again. He shook it and grinned sheepishly at the courier, who shrugged his shoulders in sign that they were beaten. Then François went up to where Sol-leks stood and called to Buck. Buck laughed, as dogs laugh, yet kept his distance. François unfastened Sol-leks's traces and put him back in his old place. The team stood harnessed to the sled in an unbroken line, ready for the trail. There was no place for Buck save at the front. Once more François called, and once more Buck laughed and kept away.

"T'row down de club," Perrault commanded.

François complied, whereupon Buck trotted in, laughing triumphantly, and swung around into position at the head of the team. His traces were fastened, the sled broken out, and with both men running they dashed out on to the river trail.

Highly as the dog-driver had forevalued Buck, with his two devils, he found, while the day was yet young, that he had undervalued. At a bound Buck took up the duties of leadership; and where judgment was required, and quick thinking and quick acting, he showed himself the superior even of Spitz, of whom François had never seen an equal.

But it was in giving the law and making his mates live up to it, that Buck excelled. Dave and Sol-leks did not mind the change in leadership. It was none of their business. Their business was to toil, and toil mightily, in the traces. So long as that were not interfered with, they did not care what happened. Billee, the good-natured, could lead for all they cared so long as he kept order. The rest of the team, however, had grown unruly during the last days of Spitz, and their surprise was great now that Buck proceeded to lick them into shape.

Pike, who pulled at Buck's heels, and who never put an ounce more of his weight against the breast band than he was compelled to do, was swiftly and repeatedly shaken for loafing, and ere the first day was done he was pulling more then ever before in his life. The first night in camp, Joe, the sour one, was punished roundly—a thing that Spitz had never succeeded in doing. Buck simply smothered him by virtue of superior weight, and cut him up till he ceased snapping and began to whine for mercy.

The general tone of the team picked up immediately. It recovered its old-time solidarity, and once more the dogs leaped as one dog in the traces. At the Rink Rapids two native huskies, Teek and Koona, were added; and the celerity with which Buck broke them in took away François's breath.

"Nevaire such a dog as dat Buck!" he cried. "No, nevaire! Heem worth one t'ousan' dollair, by Gar! Eh? Wot you say, Perrault?"

And Perrault nodded. He was ahead of the record then, and gaining day by day. The trail was in excellent condition, well packed and hard, and there was no new-fallen snow with which to contend. It was not too cold. The temperature dropped to fifty below zero and remained there the whole trip. The men rode and ran by turn, and the dogs were kept on the jump, with but infrequent stoppages.

The Thirty Mile River was comparatively coated with ice, and they covered in one day going out what had taken them ten days coming in. In one run they made a sixty-mile dash from the foot of Lake Le Barge to the White Horse Rapids. Across Marsh, Tagish, and Bennett (seventy miles of lakes), they flew so fast that the man whose turn it was to run towed behind the sled at the end of a rope.

And on the last night of the second week they topped White Pass and dropped down the sea slope with the lights of Skagway and of the shipping at their feet.

It was a record run. Each day for fourteen days they had averaged forty miles. For three days Perrault and François threw chests up and down the main street of Skagway and were deluged with invitations to drink, while the team was the constant centre of a worshipful crowd of dog-busters and mushers. Then three or four Western bad men aspired to clean out the town, were riddled like timber boxes for their pains, and public interest turned to other idols. Next came official orders. François called Buck to him, threw his arms around him, wept over him. And that was the last of François and Perrault. Like other men, they passed out of Buck's life for good.

A Scotch half-breed took charge of him and his mates, and in company with a dozen other dog-teams he started back over the weary trail to Dawson. It was no light running now, nor record time, but heavy toil each day, with a heavy load behind; for this was the mail train, carrying word from the world to the men who sought gold under the shadow of the Pole.

Buck did not like it, but he bore up well to the work, taking pride in it after the manner of Dave and Sol-leks, and seeing that his mates, whether they prided in it or not, did their fair share. It was a monotonous life, operating with machine-like regularity. One day was very like another. At a certain time each morning the cooks turned out, fires were built, and breakfast was eaten. Then while some broke camp, others harnessed the dogs, and they were under way an hour or so before the darkness which gave warning of dawn. At night, camp was made. Some pitched the flies, others cut firewood and pine boughs for the beds, and still others carried water or ice for the cooks. Also, the dogs were fed. To them, this was the one feature of the day, though it was good to loaf around, after the fish was eaten, for an hour or so with the other dogs, of which there were fivescore and odd. There were fierce fighters among them, but three battles with the fiercest brought Buck to mastery, so that when he bristled and showed his teeth they got out of his way.

Best of all, perhaps, he loved to lie near the fire, hind legs crouched under him, fore legs stretched out in front, head raised, and eyes blinking dreamily at the flames. Sometimes he thought of

Judge Miller's big house in the sun-kissed Santa Clara Valley, and
of the cement swimming-tank, and Ysabel, the Mexican hairless,
and Toots, the Japanese pug; but oftener he remembered the man in
the red sweater, the death of Curly, the great fight with Spitz, and
the good things he had eaten or would like to eat. He was not
homesick. The Sunland was very dim and distant, and such memories had no power over him. Far more potent were the memories of
his heredity that gave things he had never seen before a seeming
familiarity; the instincts (which were but the memories of his ancestors become habits) which had lapsed in later days, and still later, in
him, quickened and became alive again.

Sometimes as he crouched there, blinking dreamily at the flames,
it seemed that the flames were of another fire, and that as he
crouched by this other fire he saw another and different man from
the half-breed cook before him. This other man was shorter of leg
and longer of arm, with muscles that were stringy and knotty rather
than rounded and swelling. The hair of this man was long and
matted, and his head slanted back under it from the eyes. He
uttered strange sounds, and seemed very much afraid of the darkness, into which he peered continually, clutching in his hand, which
hung midway between knee and foot, a stick with a heavy stone
made fast to the end. He was all but naked, a ragged and fire-
scorched skin hanging part way down his back, but on his body there
was much hair. In some places, across the chest and shoulders and
down the outside of the arms and thighs, it was matted into almost a
thick fur. He did not stand erect, but with trunk inclined forward
from the hips, on legs that bent at the knees. About his body there
was a peculiar springiness, or resiliency, almost catlike, and a quick
alertness as of one who lived in perpetual fear of things seen and
unseen.

At other times this hairy man squatted by the fire with head
between his legs and slept. On such occasions his elbows were on his
knees, his hands clasped above his head as though to shed rain by
the hairy arms. And beyond that fire, in the circling darkness, Buck
could see many gleaming coals, two by two, always two by two,
which he knew to be the eyes of great beasts of prey. And he could
hear the crashing of their bodies through the undergrowth, and the
noises they made in the night. And dreaming there by the Yukon
bank, with lazy eyes blinking at the fire, these sounds and sights of

another world would make the hair to rise along his back and stand on end across his shoulders and up his neck, till he whimpered low and suppressedly, or growled softly, and the half-breed cook shouted at him, "Hey, you Buck, wake up!" Whereupon the other world would vanish and the real world come into his eyes, and he would get up and yawn and stretch as though he had been asleep.

It was a hard trip, with the mail behind them, and the heavy work wore them down. They were short of weight and in poor condition when they made Dawson, and should have had a ten days' or a week's rest at least. But in two days' time they dropped down the Yukon bank from the Barracks, loaded with letters for the outside. The dogs were tired, the drivers grumbling, and to make matters worse, it snowed every day. This meant a soft trail, greater friction on the runners, and heavier pulling for the dogs; yet the drivers were fair through it all, and did their best for the animals.

Each night the dogs were attended to first. They ate before the drivers ate, and no man sought his sleeping-robe till he had seen to the feet of the dogs he drove. Still, their strength went down. Since the beginning of the winter they had travelled eighteen hundred miles, dragging sleds the whole weary distance; and eighteen hundred miles will tell upon life of the toughest. Buck stood it, keeping his mates up to their work and maintaining discipline, though he too was very tired. Billee cried and whimpered regularly in his sleep each night. Joe was sourer than ever, and Sol-leks was unapproachable, blind side or other side.

But it was Dave who suffered most of all. Something had gone wrong with him. He became more morose and irritable, and when camp was pitched at once made his nest, where his driver fed him. Once out of the harness and down, he did not get on his feet again till harness-up time in the morning. Sometimes, in the traces, when jerked by a sudden stoppage of the sled, or by straining to start it, he would cry out with pain. The driver examined him, but could find nothing. All the drivers became interested in his case. They talked it over at meal-time, and over their last pipes before going to bed, and one night they held a consultation. He was brought from his nest to the fire and was pressed and prodded till he cried out many times. Something was wrong inside, but they could locate no broken bones, could not make it out.

By the time Cassiar Bar was reached, he was so weak that he was falling repeatedly in the traces. The Scotch half-breed called a halt and took him out of the team, making the next dog, Sol-leks, fast to the sled. His intention was to rest Dave, letting him run free behind the sled. Sick as he was, Dave resented being taken out, grunting and growling while the traces were unfastened, and whimpering broken-heartedly when he saw Sol-leks in the position he had held and served so long. For the pride of trace and trail was his, and sick unto death, he could not bear that another dog should do his work.

When the sled started, he floundered in the soft snow alongside the beaten trail, attacking Sol-leks with his teeth, rushing against him and trying to thrust him off into the soft snow on the other side, striving to leap inside his traces and get between him and the sled, and all the while whining and yelping and crying with grief and pain. The half-breed tried to drive him away with the whip; but he paid no heed to the stinging lash, and the man had not the heart to strike harder. Dave refused to run quietly on the trail behind the sled, where the going was easy, but continued to flounder alongside in the soft snow, where the going was most difficult, till exhausted, then he fell, and lay where he fell, howling lugubriously as the long train of sleds churned by.

With the last remnant of his strength he managed to stagger along behind till the train made another stop, when he floundered past the sleds to his own, where he stood alongside Sol-leks. His driver lingered a moment to get a light for his pipe from the man behind. Then he returned and started his dogs. They swung out on the trail with remarkable lack of exertion, turned their heads uneasily, and stopped in surprise. The driver was surprised, too; the sled had not moved. He called his comrades to witness the sight. Dave had bitten through both of Sol-leks's traces, and was standing directly in front of the sled in his proper place.

He pleaded with his eyes to remain there. The driver was perplexed. His comrades talked of how a dog could break its heart through being denied the work that killed it, and recalled instances they had known, where dogs, too old for the toil, or injured, had died because they were cut out of the traces. Also, they held it a mercy, since Dave was to die anyway, that he should die in the traces, heart-easy and content. So he was harnessed in again, and proudly he pulled as of old, though more than once he cried out involuntarily from the bite of his inward hurt. Several times he fell down and was dragged in the traces, and once the sled ran upon him so that he limped thereafter on one of his hind legs.

But he held out till camp was reached, when his driver made a place for him by the fire. Morning found him too weak to travel. At harness-up time he tried to crawl to his driver. By convulsive efforts he got on his feet, staggered, and fell. Then he wormed his way forward slowly toward where the harnesses were being put on his mates. He would advance his fore legs and drag up his body with a sort of hitching movement, when he would advance his fore legs and hitch ahead again for a few more inches. His strength left him, and the last his mates saw of him he lay gasping in the snow and yearning toward them. But they could hear him mournfully howling till they passed out of sight behind a belt of river timber.

Here the train was halted. The Scotch half-breed slowly retraced his steps to the camp they had left. The men ceased talking. A revolver-shot rang out. The man came back hurriedly. The whips snapped, the bells tinkled merrily, the sleds churned along the trail; but Buck knew, and every dog knew, what had taken place behind the belt of river trees.

# V
# The Toil of Trace and Trail

Thirty days from the time it left Dawson, the Salt Water Mail, with Buck and his mates at the fore, arrived at Skagway. They were in a wretched state, worn out and worn down. Buck's one hundred and forty pounds had dwindled to one hundred and fifteen. The rest of his mates, though lighter dogs, had relatively lost more weight than he. Pike, the malingerer, who, in his lifetime of deceit, had often successfully feigned a hurt leg, was now limping in earnest. Sol-leks was limping, and Dub was suffering from a wrenched shoulder blade.

They were all terribly footsore. No spring or rebound was left in them. Their feet fell heavily on the trail, jarring their bodies and doubling the fatigue of a day's travel. There was nothing the matter with them except that they were dead tired. It was not the dead-tiredness that comes through brief and excessive effort, from which recovery is a matter of hours; but it was the dead-tiredness that comes through the slow and prolonged strength drainage of months of toil. There was no power of recuperation left, no reserve strength to call upon. It had been all used, the last least bit of it. Every muscle, every fibre, every cell, was tired, dead tired. And there was reason for it. In less than five months they had travelled twenty-five hundred miles, during the last eighteen hundred of which they had had but five days' rest. When they arrived at Skagway they were apparently on their last legs. They could barely keep the traces taut, and on the down grades just managed to keep out of the way of the sled.

"Mush on, poor sore feets," the driver encouraged them as they tottered down the main street of Skagway. "Dis is de las'. Den we get one long res'. Eh? For sure. One bully long res'."

The drivers confidently expected a long stop-over. Themselves, they had covered twelve hundred miles with two days' rest, and in the nature of reason and common justice they deserved an interval of loafing. But so many were the men who had rushed into the Klondike, and so many were the sweethearts, wives, and kin that had not rushed in, that the congested mail was taking on Alpine proportions; also, there were official orders. Fresh batches of Hudson Bay dogs were to take the places of those worthless for the trail. The worthless ones were to be got rid of, and, since dogs count for little against dollars, they were to be sold.

Three days passed, by which time Buck and his mates found how really tired and weak they were. Then, on the morning of the fourth day, two men from the States came along and bought them, harness and all, for a song. The men addressed each other as "Hal" and "Charles." Charles was a middle-aged, lightish-colored man, with weak and watery eyes and a mustache that twisted fiercely and vigorously up, giving the lie to the limply drooping lip it concealed. Hal was a youngster of nineteen or twenty, with a big Colt's revolver and a hunting-knife strapped about him on a belt that fairly bristled with cartridges. This belt was the most salient thing about him. It advertised his callowness—a callowness sheer and unutterable. Both men were manifestly out of place, and why such as they should adventure the North is part of the mystery of things that passes understanding.

Buck heard the chaffering, saw the money pass between the man and the Government agent, and knew that the Scotch half-breed and the mail-train drivers were passing out of his life on the heels of Perrault and François and the others who had gone before. When driven with his mates to the new owners' camp, Buck saw a slipshod and slovenly affair, tent half stretched, dishes unwashed, everything in disorder; also, he saw a woman. "Mercedes" the men called her. She was Charles's wife and Hal's sister—a nice family party.

Buck watched them apprehensively as they proceeded to take down the tent and load the sled. There was a great deal of effort about their manner, but no businesslike method. The tent was rolled into an awkward bundle three times as large as it should have been. The tin dishes were packed away unwashed. Mercedes continually fluttered in the way of her men and kept up an unbroken chattering of remonstrance and advice. When they put a clothes-sack on the front of the sled, she suggested it should go on the back; and when they had it put on the back, and covered it over with a couple of other bundles, she discovered overlooked articles which could abide nowhere else but in that very sack, and they unloaded again.

Three men from a neighboring tent came out and looked on, grinning and winking at one another.

"You've got a right smart load as it is," said one of them; "and it's not me should tell you your business, but I wouldn't tote that tent along if I was you."

"Undreamed of!" cried Mercedes, throwing up her hands in dainty dismay. "However in the world could I manage without a tent?"

"It's springtime, and you won't get any more cold weather," the man replied.

She shook her head decidedly, and Charles and Hal put the last odds and ends on top the mountainous load.

"Think it'll ride?" one of the men asked.

"Why shouldn't it?" Charles demanded rather shortly.

"Oh, that's all right, that's all right," the man hastened meekly to say. "I was just a-wonderin', that is all. It seemed a mite top-heavy."

Charles turned his back and drew the lashings down as well as he could, which was not in the least well.

"An' of course the dogs can hike along all day with that contraption behind them," affirmed a second of the men.

"Certainly," said Hal, with freezing politeness, taking hold of the gee-pole with one hand and swinging his whip from the other. "Mush!" he shouted. "Mush on there!"

The dogs sprang against the breastbands, strained hard for a few moments, then relaxed. They were unable to move the sled.

"The lazy brutes, I'll show them," he cried, preparing to lash out at them with the whip.

But Mercedes interfered, crying, "Oh, Hal, you mustn't," as she caught hold of the whip and wrenched it from him. "The poor dears! Now you must promise you won't be harsh with them for the rest of the trip, or I won't go a step."

"Precious lot you know about dogs," her brother sneered; "and I wish you'd leave me alone. They're lazy, I tell you, and you've got to whip them to get anything out of them. That's their way. You ask any one. Ask one of those men."

Mercedes looked at them imploringly, untold repugnance at sight of pain written in her pretty face.

"They're weak as water, if you want to know," came the reply from one of the men. "Plumb tuckered out, that's what's the matter. They need a rest."

"Rest be blanked," said Hal, with his beardless lips; and Mercedes said, "Oh!" in pain and sorrow at the oath.

But she was a clannish creature, and rushed at once to the defence of her brother. "Never mind that man," she said pointedly. "You're driving our dogs and you do what you think best with them."

Again Hal's whip fell upon the dogs. They threw themselves against the breastbands, dug their feet into the packed snow, got down low to it, and put forth all their strength. The sled held as though it were an anchor. After two efforts, they stood still, panting. The whip was whistling savagely, when once more Mercedes interfered. She dropped on her knees before Buck, with tears in her eyes, and put her arms around his neck.

"You poor, poor dears," she cried sympathetically, "why don't you pull hard?—then you wouldn't be whipped." Buck did not like her, but he was feeling too miserable to resist her, taking it as part of the day's miserable work.

One of the onlookers, who had been clenching his teeth to suppress hot speech, now spoke up:—

"It's not that I care a whoop what becomes of you, but for the dogs' sakes I just want to tell you, you can help them a mighty lot by breaking out that sled. The runners are froze fast. Throw your weight against the gee-pole, right and left, and break it out."

A third time the attempt was made, but this time, following the advice, Hal broke out the runners which had been frozen to the snow. The overloaded and unwieldy sled forged ahead, Buck and his mates struggling frantically under the rain of blows. A hundred yards ahead the path turned and sloped steeply into the main street. It would have required an experienced man to keep the top-heavy sled upright, and Hal was not such a man. As they swung on the turn the sled went over, spilling half its load through the loose lashings. The dogs never stopped. The lightened sled bounded on its side behind them. They were angry because of the ill treatment they had received and the unjust load. Buck was raging. He broke into a run, the team following his lead. Hal cried, "Whoa! whoa!" but they gave no heed. He tripped and was pulled off his feet. The capsized sled ground over him, and the dogs dashed on up the street, adding to the gayety of Skagway as they scattered the remainder of the outfit along its chief thoroughfare.

Kind-hearted citizens caught the dogs and gathered up the scattered belongings. Also, they gave advice. Half the load and twice the dogs, if they ever expected to reach Dawson, was what was said. Hal and his sister and brother-in-law listened unwillingly, pitched tent, and overhauled the outfit, canned goods were turned out that made men laugh, for canned goods on the Long Trail is a thing to dream about. "Blankets for a hotel," quoth one of the men who laughed and helped. "Half as many is too much; get rid of them. Throw away that tent, and all those dishes—who's going to wash them anyway? Good Lord, do you think you're travelling on a Pullman?"

And so it went, the inexorable elimination of the superfluous. Mercedes cried when her clothes-bags were dumped on the ground and article after article was thrown out. She cried in general, and she cried in particular over each discarded thing. She clasped hands about knees, rocking back and forth broken-heartedly. She averred she would not go an inch, not for a dozen Charleses. She appealed to everybody and to everything, finally wiping her eyes and proceeding to cast out even articles of apparel that were imperative necessaries. And in her zeal, when she had finished with her own, she attacked the belongings of her men and went through them like a tornado.

This accomplished, the outfit, though cut in half, was still a formidable bulk. Charles and Hal went out in the evening and bought six Outside dogs. These, added to the six of the original team, and Teek and Koona, the huskies obtained at the Rink Rapids on the record trip, brought the team up to fourteen. But the Outside dogs, though practically broken in since their landing, did not amount to much. Three were short-haired pointers, one was a Newfoundland, and the other two were mongrels of indeterminate breed. They did not seem to know anything, these newcomers. Buck and his comrades looked upon them with disgust, and though he speedily taught them their places and what not to do, he could not teach them what to do. They did not take kindly to trace and trail. With the exception of the two mongrels, they were bewildered and spirit-broken by the strange savage environment in which they found themselves and by ill treatment they had received. The two mongrels were without spirit at all; bones were the only things breakable about them.

With the newcomers hopeless and forlorn, and the old team worn out by twenty-five hundred miles of continuous trail, the outlook was anything but bright. The two men, however, were quite cheerful. And they were proud, too. They were doing the thing in style, with fourteen dogs. They had seen other sleds depart over the Pass for Dawson or come in from Dawson, but never had they seen a sled with so many as fourteen dogs. In the nature of Arctic travel there was a reason why fourteen dogs should not drag one sled, and that was that one sled could not carry the food for fourteen dogs. But Charles and Hal did not know this. They had worked the trip out with a pencil, so much to a dog, so many dogs, and so many days, Q.E.D. Mercedes looked over their shoulders and nodded comprehensively, it was all so very simple.

Late next morning Buck led the long team up the street. There was nothing lively about it, no snap or go in him and his fellows. They were starting dead weary. Four times he had covered the distance between Salt Water and Dawson, and the knowledge that, jaded and tired, he was facing the same trail once more, made him bitter. His heart was not in the work, nor was the heart of any dog. The Outsides were timid and frightened, the Insides without confidence in their masters.

Buck felt vaguely that there was no depending upon these two men and the woman. They did not know how to do anything, and as the days went by it became apparent that they could not learn. They were slack in all things, without order or discipline. It took them half the night to pitch a slovenly camp, and half the morning to break that camp and get the sled loaded in fashion so slovenly that for the rest of the day they were occupied in stopping and rearranging the load. Some days they did not make ten miles. On other days they were unable to get started at all. And on no day did they succeed in making more than half the distance used by the men as a basis in their dog-food computation.

It was inevitable that they should go short on dog-food. But they hastened it by overfeeding, bringing the day nearer when under-feeding would commence. The Outside dogs, whose digestions had not been trained by chronic famine to make the most of little, had voracious appetites. And when, in addition to this, the worn-out huskies pulled weakly, Hal decided that the orthodox ration was too small. He doubled it. And to cap it all, when Mercedes, with tears in her pretty eyes and a quaver in her throat, could not cajole him into giving the dogs still more, she stole from the fish-sacks and fed them slyly. But it was not food that Buck and the huskies needed, but rest. And though they were making poor time, the heavy load they dragged sapped their strength severely.

Then came the underfeeding. Hal awoke one day to the fact that his dog-food was half gone and the distance only quarter covered; further, that for love or money no additional dog-food was to be obtained. So he cut down even the orthodox ration and tried to increase the day's travel. His sister and brother-in-law seconded him; but they were frustrated by their heavy outfit and their own incompetence. It was a simple matter to give the dogs less food; but it was impossible to make the dogs travel faster, while their own inability to get under way earlier in the morning prevented them from travelling longer hours. Not only did they not know how to work dogs, but they did not know how to work themselves.

The first to go was Dub. Poor blundering thief that he was, always getting caught and punished, he had none the less been a faithful worker. His wrenched shoulder-blade, untreated and unrested, went from bad to worse, till finally Hal shot him with the big Colt's revolver. It is a saying of the country that an Outside dog starves to death on the ration of the husky, so the six Outside dogs under Buck could do no less than die on half the ration of the husky. The Newfoundland went first, followed by the three short-haired pointers, the two mongrels hanging more grittily on to life, but going in the end.

By this time all the amenities and gentlenesses of the Southland had fallen away from the three people. Shorn of its glamour and romance, Arctic travel became to them a reality too harsh for their manhood and womanhood. Mercedes ceased weeping over the dogs, being too occupied with weeping over herself and with quarrelling with her husband and brother. To quarrel was the one thing they were never too weary to do. Their irritability arose out of their misery, increased with it, doubled upon it, outdistanced it. The wonderful patience of the trail which comes to men who toil hard and suffer sore, and remain sweet of speech and kindly, did not come to these two men and the woman. They had no inkling of such a patience. They were stiff and in pain; their muscles ached, their bones ached, their very hearts ached; and because of this they became sharp of speech, and hard words were first on their lips in the morning and last at night.

Charles and Hal wrangled whenever Mercedes gave them a chance. It was the cherished belief of each that he did more than his share of the work, and neither forbore to speak this belief at every opportunity. Sometimes Mercedes sided with her husband, sometimes with her brother. The result was a beautiful and unending family quarrel. Starting from a dispute as to which should chop a few sticks for the fire (a dispute which concerned only Charles and Hal), presently would be lugged in the rest of the family, fathers, mothers, uncles, cousins, people thousands of miles away, and some of them dead. That Hal's views on art, or the sort of society plays his mother's brother wrote, should have anything to do with the chopping of a few sticks of firewood, passes comprehension; nevertheless the quarrel was as likely to tend in that direction as in the direction of Charles's political prejudices. And that Charles's sister's tale-bearing tongue should be relevant to the building of a Yukon fire, was apparent only to Mercedes, who disburdened herself of copious opinions upon that topic, and incidentally upon a few other traits unpleasantly peculiar to her husband's family. In the meantime the fire remained unbuilt, the camp half pitched, and the dogs unfed.

Mercedes nursed a special grievance—the grievance of sex. She was pretty and soft, and had been chivalrously treated all her days. But the present treatment by her husband and brother was everything save chivalrous. It was her custom to be helpless. They complained. Upon which impeachment of what to her was her most essential sex prerogative, she made their lives unendurable. She no longer considered the dogs, and because she was sore and tired, she persisted in riding on the sled. She was pretty and soft, but she weighed one hundred and twenty pounds—a lusty last straw to the load dragged by the weak and starving animals. She rode for days, till they fell in the traces and the sled stood still. Charles and Hal begged her to get off and walk, pleaded with her, entreated, the while she wept and importuned Heaven with a recital of their brutality.

On one occasion they took her off the sled by main strength. They never did it again. She let her legs go limp like a spoiled child, and sat down on the trail. They went on their way, but she did not move. After they had travelled three miles they unloaded the sled, came back for her, and by main strength put her on the sled again.

In the excess of their own misery they were callous to the suffering of their animals. Hal's theory, which he practised on others, was that one must get hardened. He had started out preaching it to his sister and brother-in-law. Failing there, he hammered it into the dogs with a club. At the Five Fingers the dog-food gave out, and a toothless old squaw offered to trade them a few pounds of frozen horse hide for the Colt's revolver that kept the big hunting-knife company at Hal's hip. A poor substitute for food was this hide, just as it had been stripped from the starved horses of the cattlemen six months back. In its frozen state it was more like strips of galvanized iron, and when a dog wrestled it into his stomach it thawed into thin and innutritious leathery strings and into a mass of short hair, irritating and indigestible.

And through it all Buck staggered along at the head of the team as in a nightmare. He pulled when he could; when he could no longer pull, he fell down and remained down till blows from whip or club drove him to his feet again. All the stiffness and gloss had gone out of his beautiful furry coat. The hair hung down, limp and draggled, or matted with dried blood where Hal's club had bruised him. His muscles had wasted away to knotty strings, and the flesh pads had disappeared, so that each rib and every bone in his frame were outlined cleanly through the loose hide that was wrinkled in folds of emptiness. It was heartbreaking, only Buck's heart was unbreakable. The man in the red sweater had proved that.

As it was with Buck, so was it with his mates. They were perambulating skeletons. There were seven all together, including him. In their very great misery they had become insensible to the bite of the lash or the bruise of the club. The pain of the beating was dull and distant, just as the things their eyes saw and their ears heard seemed dull and distant. They were not half living, or quarter living. They were simply so many bags of bones in which sparks of life fluttered faintly. When a halt was made, they dropped down in the traces like dead dogs, and the spark dimmed and paled and seemed to go out. And when the club or whip fell upon them, the spark fluttered feebly up, and they tottered to their feet and staggered on.

There came a day when Billee, the good-natured, fell and could not rise. Hal had traded off his revolver, so he took the axe and knocked Billee on the head as he lay in the traces, then cut the carcass out of the harness and dragged it to one side. Buck saw, and his mates saw, and they knew that this thing was very close to them. In the next day Koona went, and but five of them remained; Joe, too far gone to be malignant; Pike, crippled and limping, only half conscious and not conscious enough longer to malinger; Sol-leks, the one-eyed, still faithful to the toil of trace and trail, and mournful in that he had so little strength with which to pull; Teek, who had not travelled so far that winter and who was now beaten more than the others because he was fresher; and Buck, still at the head of the team, but no longer enforcing discipline or striving to enforce it, blind with weakness half the time and keeping the trail by the loom of it and by the dim feel of his feet.

It was beautiful spring weather, but neither dogs nor humans were aware of it. Each day the sun rose earlier and set later. It was dawn by three in the morning, and twilight lingered till nine at night. The whole long day was a blaze of sunshine. The ghostly winter silence had given way to the great spring murmur of awakening life. This murmur arose from all the land, fraught with the joy of living. It came from the things that lived and moved again, things which had been as dead and which had not moved during the long months of frost. The sap was rising in the pines. The willows and aspens were bursting out in young buds. Shrubs and vines were putting on fresh garbs of green. Crickets sang in the nights, and in the days all manner of creeping, crawling things rustled forth into the sun. Partridges and woodpeckers were booming and knocking in the forest. Squirrels were chattering, birds singing, and overhead honked the wild-fowl driving up from the South in cunning wedges that split the air.

From every hill slope came the trickle of running water, the music of unseen fountains. All things were thawing, bending, snapping.

The Yukon was straining to break loose the ice that bound it down. It ate away from beneath; the sun ate from above. Air-holes formed, fissures sprang and spread apart, while thin sections of ice fell through bodily into the river. And amid all this bursting, rending, throbbing, of awakening life, under the blazing sun and through the soft-sighing breezes, like wayfarers to death, staggered the two men, the woman, and the huskies.

With the dogs falling, Mercedes weeping and riding, Hal swearing innocuously, and Charles's eyes wistfully watering, they staggered into John Thornton's camp at the mouth of White River. When they halted, the dogs dropped down as though they had all been struck dead. Mercedes dried her eyes and looked at John Thornton. Charles sat down on a log to rest. He sat down very slowly and painstakingly what of his great stiffness. Hal did the talking. John Thornton was whittling the last touches on the axe-handle he had made from a stick of birch. He whittled and listened, gave monosyllabic replies, and, when it was asked, terse advice. He knew the breed, and he gave his advice in the certainty that it would not be followed.

"They told us up above that the bottom was dropping out of the trail and that the best thing for us to do was to lay over," Hal said in response to Thornton's warning to take no more chances on the rotten ice. "They told us we couldn't make White River, and here we are." This last with a sneering ring of triumph in it.

"And they told you true," John Thornton answered. "The bottom's likely to drop out at any moment. Only fools, with the blind luck of fools, could have made it. I tell you straight, I wouldn't risk my carcass on that ice for all the gold in Alaska."

"That's because you're not a fool, I suppose," said Hal. "All the same, we'll go on to Dawson." He uncoiled his whip. "Get up there, Buck! Hi! Get up there! Mush on!"

Thornton went on whittling. It was idle, he knew, to get between a fool and his folly; while two or three fools more or less would not alter the scheme of things.

But the team did not get up at the command. It had long since passed into the stage where blows were required to rouse it. The whip flashed out, here and there, on its merciless errands. John Thornton compressed his lips. Sol-leks was the first to crawl to his feet. Teek followed. Joe came next, yelping with pain. Pike made painful efforts. Twice he fell over, when half up, and on the third attempt managed to rise. Buck made no effort. He lay quietly where he had fallen. The lash bit into him again and again, but he neither whined nor struggled. Several times Thornton started, as though to speak, but changed his mind. A moisture came into his eyes, and, as the whipping continued, he arose and walked irresolutely up and down.

This was the first time Buck had failed, in itself a sufficient reason to drive Hal into a rage. He exchanged the whip for the customary club. Buck refused to move under the rain of heavier blows which now fell upon him. Like his mates, he was barely able to get up, but, unlike them, he had made up his mind not to get up. He had a vague feeling of impending doom. This had been strong upon him when he pulled into the bank, and it had not departed from him. What of the thin and rotten ice he had felt under his feet all day, it seemed that he sensed disaster close at hand, out there ahead on the ice where his master was trying to drive him. He refused to stir. So greatly had he suffered, and so far gone was he, that the blows did not hurt much. And as they continued to fall upon him, the spark of life within flickered and went down. It was nearly out. He felt strangely numb. As though from a great distance, he was aware that he was being beaten. The last sensations of pain left him. He no longer felt anything, though very faintly he could hear the impact of the club upon his body. But it was no longer his body, it seemed so far away.

And then, suddenly, without warning, uttering a cry that was inarticulate and more like the cry of an animal, John Thornton sprang upon the man who wielded the club. Hal was hurled backward, as though struck by a falling tree. Mercedes screamed. Charles looked on wistfully, wiped his watery eyes, but did not get up because of his stiffness.

John Thornton stood over Buck, struggling to control himself, too convulsed with rage to speak.

"If you strike that dog again, I'll kill you," he at last managed to say in a choking voice.

"It's my dog," Hal replied, wiping the blood from his mouth as he came back. "Get out of my way, or I'll fix you. I'm going to Dawson."

Thornton stood between him and Buck and evinced no intention of getting out of the way. Hal drew his long hunting-knife. Mercedes screamed, cried, laughed, and manifested the chaotic abandonment of hysteria. Thornton rapped Hal's knuckles with the axe-handle, knocking the knife to the ground. He rapped his knuckles again as he tried to pick it up. Then he stooped, picked it up himself, and with two strokes cut Buck's traces.

Hal had no fight left in him. Besides, his hands were full with his sister, or his arms, rather; while Buck was too near dead to be of further use in hauling the sled. A few minutes later they pulled out from the bank and down the river. Buck heard them go and raised his head to see. Pike was leading. Sol-leks was at the wheel, and between were Joe and Teek. They were limping and staggering. Mercedes was riding the loaded sled. Hal guided at the gee-pole, and Charles stumbled along in the rear.

As Buck watched them, Thornton knelt beside him and with rough, kindly hands searched for broken bones. By the time his search had disclosed nothing more than many bruises and a state of terrible starvation, the sled was a quarter of a mile away. Dog and man watched it crawling along over the ice. Suddenly, they saw its back end drop down, as into a rut, and the gee-pole, with Hal clinging to it, jerk into the air. Mercedes's scream came to their ears. They saw Charles turn and make one step to run back, and then a whole section of ice give way and dogs and humans disappear. A yawning hole was all that was to be seen. The bottom had dropped out of the trail.

John Thornton and Buck looked at each other.

"You poor devil," said John Thornton and Buck licked his hand.

# VI
# For the Love of a Man

When John Thornton froze his feet in the previous December, his partners had made him comfortable and left him to get well, going on themselves up the river to get out a raft of saw-logs for Dawson. He was still limping slightly at the time he rescued Buck, but with the continued warm weather even the slight limp left him. And here, lying by the river bank through the long spring days, watching the running water, listening lazily to the songs of birds and the hum of nature, Buck slowly won back his strength.

A rest comes very good after one has travelled three thousand miles, and it must be confessed that Buck waxed lazy as his wounds healed, his muscles swelled out, and the flesh came back to cover his bones. For that matter, they were all loafing—Buck, John Thornton, and Skeet and Nig—waiting for the raft to come that was to carry them down to Dawson. Skeet was a little Irish setter who early made friends with Buck, who in a dying condition, was unable to resent her first advances. She had the doctor trait which some dogs possess, and as a mother cat washes her kittens, so she washed and cleansed Buck's wounds. Regularly, each morning after he had finished his breakfast, she performed her self-appointed task, till he came to look for her ministrations as much as he did for Thornton's. Nig, equally friendly though less demonstrative, was a huge black dog, half bloodhound and half deerhound, with eyes that laughed and a boundless good nature.

To Buck's surprise these dogs manifested no jealousy toward him. They seemed to share the kindliness and largeness of John Thornton. As Buck grew stronger they enticed him into all sorts of ridiculous games, in which Thornton himself could not forbear to join, and in this fashion Buck romped through his convalescence and into a new existence. Love, genuine passionate love, was his for the first time.

61

This he had never experienced at Judge Miller's down in the sun-kissed Santa Clara Valley. With the Judge's sons, hunting and tramping, it had been a working partnership; with the Judge's grandsons, a sort of pompous guardianship; and with the Judge himself, a stately and dignified friendship. But love that was fever-ish and burning, that was adoration, that was madness, it had taken John Thornton to arouse.

This man had saved his life, which was something; but, further, he was the ideal master. Other men saw to the welfare of their dogs from a sense of duty and business expediency; he saw to the welfare of his as if they were his own children, because he could not help it. And he saw further. He never forgot a kindly greeting or a cheering word, and to sit down for a long talk with them ("gas" he called it) was as much his delight as theirs. He had a way of taking Buck's head roughly between his hands, and resting his own head upon Buck's, of shaking him back and forth, the while calling him ill names that to Buck were love names. Buck knew no greater joy than that rough embrace and the sound of murmured oaths, and at each jerk back and forth it seemed that his heart would be shaken out of his body so great was its ecstasy. And when, released, he sprang to his feet, his mouth laughing, his eyes eloquent, his throat vibrant with unuttered sound, and in that fashion remained without movement, John Thornton would reverently exclaim, "God! you can all but speak!"

Buck had a trick of love expression that was akin to hurt. He would often seize Thornton's hand in his mouth and close so fiercely that the flesh bore the impress of his teeth for some time afterward. And as Buck understood the oaths to be love words, so the man understood this feigned bite for a caress.

For the most part, however, Buck's love was expressed in adora-tion. While he went wild with happiness when Thornton touched him or spoke to him, he did not seek these tokens. Unlike Skeet, who was wont to shove her nose under Thornton's hand and nudge and nudge till petted, or Nig, who would stalk up and rest his great head on Thornton's knee, Buck was content to adore at a distance. He would lie by the hour, eager, alert, at Thornton's feet, looking up into his face, dwelling upon it, studying it, following with keenest interest each fleeting expression, every movement or change of feature. Or, as chance might have it, he would lie farther away, to the side or rear, watching the outlines of the man and the occasional movements of his body. And often, such was the communion in which they lived, the strength of Buck's gaze would draw John Thornton's head around, and he would return the gaze, without speech, his heart shining out of his eyes as Buck's heart shone out.

For a long time after his rescue, Buck did not like Thornton to get out of his sight. From the moment he left the tent to when he entered it again, Buck would follow at his heels. His transient masters since he had come into the Northland had bred in him a fear that no master could be permanent. He was afraid that Thornton would pass out of his life as Perrault and François and the Scotch half-breed had passed out. Even in the night, in his dreams, he was haunted by this fear. At such times he would shake off sleep and creep through the chill to the flap of the tent, where he would stand and listen to the sound of his master's breathing.

But in spite of this great love he bore John Thornton, which seemed to bespeak the soft civilizing influence, the strain of the primitive, which the Northland had aroused in him, remained alive and active. Faithfulness and devotion, things born of fire and roof, were his; yet he retained his wildness and wiliness. He was a thing of the wild, come in from the wild to sit by John Thornton's fire, rather than a dog of the soft Southland stamped with the marks of generations of civilization. Because of his very great love, he could not steal from this man, but from any other man, in any other camp, he did not hesitate an instant, while the cunning with which he stole enabled him to escape detection.

His face and body were scored by the teeth of many dogs, and he fought as fiercely as ever and more shrewdly. Skeet and Nig were too good-natured for quarrelling—besides, they belonged to John Thornton; but the strange dog, no matter what the breed or valor, swiftly acknowledged Buck's supremacy or found himself struggling for life with a terrible antagonist. And Buck was merciless. He had learned well the law of club and fang, and he never forewent an advantage or drew back from a foe he had started on the way to Death. He had lessoned from Spitz, and from the chief fighting dogs of the police and mail, and knew there was no middle course. He must master or be mastered; while to show mercy was a weakness. Mercy did not exist in the primordial life. It was misunderstood for fear, and such misunderstandings made for death. Kill or be killed, eat or be eaten, was the law; and this mandate, down out of the depths of Time, he obeyed.

He was older than the days he had seen and the breaths he had drawn. He linked the past with the present, and the eternity behind him throbbed through him in a mighty rhythm to which he swayed as the tides and seasons swayed. He sat by John Thornton's fire, a broad-breasted dog, white-fanged and long-furred; but behind him were the shades of all manner of dogs, half-wolves and wild wolves, urgent and prompting, tasting the savor of the meat he ate, thirsting for the water he drank, scenting the wind with him, listening with him and telling him the sounds made by the wild life in the forest, dictating his moods, directing his actions, lying down to sleep with him when he lay down, and dreaming with him and beyond him and becoming themselves the stuff of his dreams.

So peremptorily did these shades beckon him, that each day mankind and the claims of mankind slipped farther from him. Deep in the forest a call was sounding, and as often as he heard this call, mysteriously thrilling and luring, he felt compelled to turn his back upon the fire and the beaten earth around it, and to plunge into the forest, and on and on, he knew not where or why; nor did he wonder where or why, the call sounding imperiously, deep in the forest. But as often as he gained the soft unbroken earth and the green shade, the love for John Thornton drew him back to the fire again.

Thornton alone held him. The rest of mankind was as nothing. Chance travellers might praise or pet him; but he was cold under it all, and from a too demonstrative man he would get up and walk away. When Thornton's partners, Hans and Pete, arrived on the long-expected raft, Buck refused to notice them till he learned they were close to Thornton; after that he tolerated them in a passive sort of way, accepting favors from them as though he favored them by accepting. They were of the same large type as Thornton, living close to the earth, thinking simply and seeing clearly; and ere they swung the raft into the big eddy by the saw-mill at Dawson, they understood Buck and his ways, and did not insist upon an intimacy such as obtained with Skeet and Nig.

For Thornton, however, his love seemed to grow and grow. He alone among men could put a pack upon Buck's back in the summer travelling. Nothing was too great for Buck to do, when Thornton commanded. One day (they had grub-staked themselves from the proceeds of the raft and left Dawson for the head-waters of the Tanana) the men and dogs were sitting on the crest of a cliff which fell away, straight down, to naked bed-rock three hundred feet below. John Thornton was sitting near the edge, Buck at his shoulder. A thoughtless whim seized Thornton, and he drew the attention of Hans and Pete to the experiment he had in mind. "Jump, Buck!" he commanded, sweeping his arm out and over the chasm. The next instant he was grappling with Buck on the extreme edge, while Hans and Pete were dragging them back into safety.

"It's uncanny," Pete said, after it was over and they had caught their speech.

Thornton shook his head. "No, it is splendid, and it is terrible, too. Do you know, it sometimes makes me afraid."

"I'm not hankering to be the man that lays hands on you while he's around," Pete announced conclusively, nodding his head toward Buck.

"Py Jingo!" was Hans's contribution. "Not mineself either."

It was at Circle City, ere the year was out, that Pete's apprehensions were realized. "Black" Burton, a man evil-tempered and malicious, had been picking a quarrel with a tenderfoot at the bar, when Thornton stepped good-naturedly between. Buck, as was his custom, was lying in a corner, head on paws, watching his master's every action. Burton struck out, without warning, straight from the shoulder. Thornton was sent spinning, and saved himself from falling only by clutching the rail of the bar.

Those who were looking on heard what was neither bark nor yelp, but a something which is best described as a roar, and they saw Buck's body rise up in the air as he left the floor for Burton's throat. The man saved his life by instinctively throwing out his arm, but was hurled backward to the floor with Buck on top of him. Buck loosed his teeth from the flesh of the arm and drove in again for the throat. This time the man succeeded only in partly blocking, and his throat was torn open. Then the crowd was upon Buck, and he was driven off; but while a surgeon checked the bleeding, he prowled up and down, growling furiously, attempting to rush in, and being forced back by an array of hostile clubs. A "miners' meeting," called on the spot, decided that the dog had sufficient provocation, and Buck was discharged. But his reputation was made, and from that day his name spread through every camp in Alaska.

Later on, in the fall of the year, he saved John Thornton's life in quite another fashion. The three partners were lining a long and narrow poling-boat down a bad stretch of rapids on the Forty Mile Creek. Hans and Pete moved along the bank, snubbing with a thin manila rope from tree to tree, while Thornton remained in the boat, helping its descent by means of a pole, and shouting directions to the shore. Buck, on the bank, worried and anxious, kept abreast of the boat, his eyes never off his master.

At a particularly bad spot, where a ledge of barely submerged rocks jutted out into the river, Hans cast off the rope, and, while Thornton poled the boat out into the stream, ran down the bank with the end in his hand to snub the boat when it had cleared the ledge. This it did, and was flying down-stream in a current as swift as a mill-race, when Hans checked it with the rope and checked too suddenly. The boat flirted over and snubbed in to the bank bottom up, while Thornton, flung sheer out of it, was carried down-stream toward the worst part of the rapids, a stretch of wild water in which no swimmer could live.

Buck had sprung in on the instant; and at the end of three hundred yards, amid a mad swirl of water, he overhauled Thornton. When he felt him grasp his tail, Buck headed for the bank, swimming with all his splendid strength. But the progress shoreward was slow; the progress down-stream amazingly rapid. From below came the fatal roaring where the wild current went wilder and was rent in shreds and spray by the rocks which thrust through like the teeth of an enormous comb. The suck of the water as it took the beginning of the last steep pitch was frightful, and Thornton knew that the shore was impossible. He scraped furiously over a rock, bruised across a second, and struck a third with crushing force. He clutched its slippery top with both hands, releasing Buck, and above the roar of the churning water shouted: "Go, Buck! Go!"

Buck could not hold his own, and swept on downstream, struggling desperately, but unable to win back. When he heard Thornton's command repeated, he partly reared out of the water, throwing his head high, as though for a last look, then turned obediently toward the bank. He swam powerfully and was dragged ashore by Pete and Hans at the very point where swimming ceased to be possible and destruction began.

They knew that the time a man could cling to a slippery rock in the face of that driving current was a matter of minutes, and they ran as fast as they could up the bank to a point far above where Thornton was hanging on. They attached the line with which they had been snubbing the boat to Buck's neck and shoulders, being careful that it should neither strangle him nor impede his swimming, and launched him into the stream. He struck out boldly, but not straight enough into the stream. He discovered the mistake too late, when Thornton was abreast of him and a bare half-dozen strokes away while he was being carried helplessly past.

Hans promptly snubbed with the rope, as though Buck were a boat. The rope thus tightening on him in the sweep of the current, he was jerked under the surface, and under the surface he remained till his body struck against the bank and he was hauled out. He was half-drowned, and Hans and Pete threw themselves upon him, pounding the breath into him and the water out of him. He staggered to his feet and fell down. The faint sound of Thornton's voice came to them, and though they could not make out the words of it, they knew that he was in his extremity. His master's voice acted on Buck like an electric shock. He sprang to his feet and ran up the bank ahead of the men to the point of his previous departure.

Again the rope was attached and he was launched, and again he struck out, but this time straight into the stream. He had miscalculated once, but he would not be guilty of it a second time. Hans paid out the rope, permitting no slack, while Pete kept it clear of coils. Buck held on till he was on a line straight above Thornton; then he turned, and with the speed of an express train headed down upon him. Thornton saw him coming, and, as Buck struck him like a battering ram, with the whole force of the current behind him, he reached up and closed with both arms around the shaggy neck. Hans snubbed the rope around the tree, and Buck and Thornton were jerked under the water. Strangling, suffocating, sometimes one upper-most and sometimes the other, dragging over the jagged bottom, smashing against rocks and snags, they veered in to the bank.

Thornton came to, belly downward and being violently propelled back and forth across a drift log by Hans and Pete. His first glance was for Buck, over whose limp and apparently lifeless body Nig was setting up a howl, while Skeet was licking the wet face and closed eyes. Thornton was himself bruised and battered, and he went carefully over Buck's body, when he had been brought around, finding three broken ribs.

"That settles it," he announced. "We camp right here." And camp they did, till Buck's ribs knitted and he was able to travel.

That winter, at Dawson, Buck performed another exploit, not so heroic, perhaps, but one that put his name many notches higher on the totem-pole of Alaskan fame. This exploit was particularly gratifying to the three men; for they stood in need of the outfit which it furnished, and were enabled to make a long-desired trip into the virgin East, where miners had not yet appeared. It was brought about by a conversation in the Eldorado Saloon, in which men waxed boastful of their favorite dogs. Buck, because of his record, was the target for these men, and Thornton was driven stoutly to defend him. At the end of half an hour one man stated that his dog could start a sled with five hundred pounds and walk off with it; a second bragged six hundred for his dog; and a third, seven hundred.

"Pooh! Pooh!" said John Thornton, "Buck can start a thousand pounds."

"And break it out? and walk off with it for a hundred yards?" demanded Matthewson, a Bonanza king, he of the seven hundred vaunt.

"And break it out, and walk off with it for a hundred yards," John Thornton said coolly.

"Well," Matthewson said, slowly and deliberately, so that all could hear, "I've got a thousand dollars that says he can't. And there it is." So saying, he slammed a sack of gold dust of the size of a bologna sausage down upon the bar.

Nobody spoke. Thornton's bluff, if bluff it was, had been called. He could feel a flush of warm blood creeping up his face. His tongue had tricked him. He did not know whether Buck could start a thousand pounds. Half a ton! The enormousness of it appalled him. He had great faith in Buck's strength and had often thought him capable of starting such a load; but never, as now, had he faced the possibility of it, the eyes of a dozen men fixed upon him, silent and waiting. Further, he had no thousand dollars; nor had Hans or Pete.

"I've got a sled standing outside now, with twenty fifty-pound sacks of flour on it," Matthewson went on with brutal directness, "so don't let that hinder you."

Thornton did not reply. He did not know what to say. He glanced from face to face in the absent way of a man who has lost the power of thought and is seeking somewhere to find the thing that will start it going again. The face of Jim O'Brien, a Mastodon king and old-time comrade, caught his eyes. It was a cue to him, seeming to rouse him to do what he would never have dreamed of doing.

"Can you lend me a thousand?" he asked, almost in a whisper.

"Sure," answered O'Brien, thumping down a plethoric sack by the side of Matthewson's. "Though it's little faith I'm having, John, that the beast can do the trick."

The Eldorado emptied its occupants into the street to see the test. The tables were deserted, and the dealers and gamekeepers came forth to see the outcome of the wager and to lay odds. Several hundred men, furred and mittened, banked around the sled within easy distance. Matthewson's sled, loaded with a thousand pounds of flour, had been standing for a couple of hours, and in the intense cold (it was sixty below zero) the runners had frozen fast to the hard-packed snow. Men offered odds of two to one that Buck could not budge the sled. A quibble arose concerning the phrase "break out." O'Brien contended it was Thornton's privilege to knock the runners loose, leaving Buck to "break it out" from a dead stand-still. Matthewson insisted that the phrase included breaking the runners from the frozen grip of the snow. A majority of the men who had witnessed the making of the bet decided in his favor, whereat the odds went up to three to one against Buck. There were no takers. Not a man believed him capable of the feat. Thornton had been hurried into the wager, heavy with doubt; and now that he looked at the sled itself, the concrete fact, with the regular team of ten dogs curled up in the snow before it, the more impossible the task appeared. Matthewson waxed jubilant.

"Three to one!" he proclaimed. "I'll lay you another thousand at that figure, Thornton. What d'ye say?"

Thornton's doubt was strong in his face, but his fighting spirit was aroused—the fighting spirit that soars above odds, fails to recognize the impossible, and is deaf to all save the clamor for battle. He called Hans and Pete to him. Their sacks were slim, and with his own the three partners could rake together only two hundred dollars. In the ebb of their fortunes, this sum was their total capital; yet they laid it unhesitatingly against Matthewson's six hundred.

The team of ten dogs was unhitched, and Buck, with his own harness, was put into the sled. He had caught the contagion of the excitement, and he felt that in some way he must do a great thing for John Thornton. Murmurs of admiration at his splendid appearance went up. He was in perfect condition, without an ounce of superfluous flesh, and the one hundred and fifty pounds that he weighed were so many pounds of grit and virility. His furry coat shone with the sheen of silk. Down the neck and across the shoulders, his mane, in repose as it was, half bristled and seemed to lift with every movement, as though excess of vigor made each particular hair alive and active. The great breast and heavy fore legs were no more than in proportion with the rest of the body where the muscles showed in tight rolls underneath the skin. Men felt these muscles and proclaimed them hard as iron, and the odds went down to two to one.

"Gad, sir! Gad, sir!" stuttered a member of the latest dynasty, a king of the Skookum Benches. "I offer you eight hundred for him, sir, before the test, sir; eight hundred just as he stands."

Thornton shook his head and stepped to Buck's side.

"You must stand off from him," Matthewson protested. "Free play and plenty of room."

The crowd fell silent; only could be heard the voices of the gamblers vainly offering two to one. Everybody acknowledged Buck a magnificent animal, but twenty fifty-pound sacks of flour bulked too large in their eyes for them to loosen their pouch-strings.

Thornton knelt down by Buck's side. He took his head in his two hands and rested cheek on cheek. He did not playfully shake him, as was his wont, or murmur soft love curses; but he whispered in his ear. "As you love me, Buck. As you love me," was what he whispered. Buck whined with suppressed eagerness.

The crowd was watching curiously. The affair was growing mysterious. It seemed like a conjuration. As Thornton got to his feet, Buck seized his mittened hand between his jaws, pressing in with his teeth and releasing slowly, half-reluctantly. It was the answer, in terms, not of speech, but of love. Thornton stepped well back.

"Now, Buck," he said.

Buck tightened the traces, then slacked them for a matter of several inches. It was the way he had learned.

"Gee!" Thornton's voice rang out, sharp in the tense silence.

Buck swung to the right, ending the movement in a plunge that took up the slack and with a sudden jerk arrested his one hundred and fifty pounds. The load quivered, and from under the runners arose a crisp crackling.

"Haw!" Thornton commanded.

Buck duplicated the manoeuvre, this time to the left. The crackling turned into a snapping, the sled pivoting and the runners slipping and grating several inches to the side. The sled was broken out. Men were holding their breaths, intensely unconscious of the fact.

"Now, MUSH!"

Thornton's command cracked out like a pistol-shot. Buck threw himself forward, tightening the traces with a jarring lunge. His whole body was gathered compactly together in the tremendous effort, the muscles writhing and knotting like live things under the silky fur. His great chest was low to the ground, his head forward and down, while his feet were flying like mad, the claws scarring the hard-packed snow in parallel grooves. The sled swayed and trembled, half-started forward. One of his feet slipped, and one man groaned aloud. Then the sled lurched ahead in what appeared a rapid succession of jerks, though it never really came to a dead stop again...half an inch...an inch...two inches....The jerks perceptibly diminished; as the sled gained momentum, he caught them up, till it was moving steadily along.

Men gasped and began to breathe again, unaware that for a moment they had ceased to breathe. Thornton was running behind, encouraging Buck with short, cheery words. The distance had been measured off, and as he neared the pile of firewood which marked the end of the hundred yards, a cheer began to grow and grow, which burst into a roar as he passed the firewood and halted at command. Every man was tearing himself loose, even Matthewson. Hats and mittens were flying in the air. Men were shaking hands, it did not matter with whom, and bubbling over in a general incoherent babel.

But Thornton fell on his knees beside Buck. Head was against head, and he was shaking him back and forth. Those who hurried up heard him cursing Buck, and he cursed him long and fervently, and softly and lovingly.

"Gad, sir! Gad, sir!" spluttered the Skookum Bench king. "I'll give you a thousand for him, sir, a thousand, sir—twelve hundred, sir."

Thornton rose to his feet. His eyes were wet. The tears were streaming frankly down his cheeks. "Sir," he said to the Skookum Bench king, "no, sir. You can go to hell, sir. It's the best I can do for you, sir."

Buck seized Thornton's hand in his teeth. Thornton shook him back and forth. As though animated by a common impulse, the onlookers drew back to a respectful distance, nor were they again indiscreet enough to interrupt.

# VII
# The Sounding of the Call

When Buck earned sixteen hundred dollars in five minutes for John Thornton, he made it possible for his master to pay-off certain debts and to journey with his partners into the East after a fabled lost mine, the history of which was as old as the history of the country. Many men had sought it; few had found it; and more than a few there were who had never returned from the quest. This lost mine was steeped in tragedy and shrouded in mystery. No one knew of the first man. The oldest tradition stopped before it got back to him. From the beginning there had been an ancient and ramshackle cabin. Dying men had sworn to it, and to the mine the site of which it marked, clinching their testimony with nuggets that were unlike any known grade of gold in the Northland.

But no living man had looted this treasure house, and the dead were dead; wherefore John Thornton and Pete and Hans, with Buck and half a dozen other dogs, faced into the East on an unknown trail to achieve where men and dogs as good as themselves had failed. They sledded seventy miles up the Yukon, swung to the left into the Stewart River, passed the Mayo and the McQueston, and held on until the Stewart itself became a streamlet, threading the upstanding peaks which marked the backbone of the continent.

John Thornton asked little of man or nature. He was unafraid of the wild. With a handful of salt and a rifle he could plunge into the wilderness and fare wherever he pleased and as long as he pleased. Being in no haste, Indian fashion, he hunted his dinner in the course of the day's travel; and if he failed to find it, like the Indian, he kept on travelling, secure in the knowledge that sooner or later he would come to it. So, on this great journey into the East, straight meat was the bill of fare, ammunition and tools principally made up the load on the sled, and the time-card was drawn upon the limitless future.

To Buck it was boundless delight, this hunting, fishing, and indefinite wandering through strange places. For weeks at a time they would hold on steadily, day after day; and for weeks upon end they would camp, here and there, the dogs loafing and the men burning holes through frozen muck and gravel and washing countless pans of dirt by the heat of the fire. Sometimes they went hungry, sometimes they feasted riotously, all according to the abundance of game and the fortune of hunting. Summer arrived, and dogs and men packed on their backs, rafted across blue mountain lakes, and descended or ascended unknown rivers in slender boats whipsawed from the standing forest.

The months came and went, and back and forth they twisted through the uncharted vastness, where no men were and yet where men had been if the Lost Cabin were true. They went across divides in summer blizzards, shivered under the midnight sun on naked mountains between the timber line and the eternal snows, dropped into summer valleys amid swarming gnats and flies, and in the shadows of glaciers picked strawberries and flowers as ripe and fair as any the Southland could boast. In the fall of the year they penetrated a weird lake country, sad and silent, where wild-fowl had been, but where then there was no life nor sign of life—only the blowing of chill winds, the forming of ice in sheltered places, and the melancholy rippling of waves on lonely beaches.

And through another winter they wandered on the obliterated trails of men who had gone before. Once, they came upon a path blazed through the forest, an ancient path, and the Lost Cabin seemed very near. But the path began nowhere and ended nowhere, and it remained mystery, as the man who made it and the reason he made it remained mystery. Another time they chanced upon the time-graven wreckage of a hunting lodge, and amid the shreds of rotted blankets John Thornton found a long-barrelled flint-lock. He knew it for a Hudson Bay Company gun of the young days in the Northwest, when such a gun was worth its height in beaver skins packed flat. And that was all—no hint as to the man who in an early day had reared the lodge and left the gun among the blankets.

Spring came on once more, and at the end of all their wandering they found, not the Lost Cabin, but a shallow placer in a broad valley where the gold showed like yellow butter across the bottom of the washing-pan. They sought no farther. Each day they worked earned them thousands of dollars in clean dust and nuggets, and they worked every day. The gold was sacked in moose-hide bags, fifty pounds to the bag, and piled like so much fire-wood outside the spruce-bough lodge. Like giants they toiled, days flashing on the heels of days like dreams as they heaped the treasure up.

There was nothing for the dogs to do save the hauling in of meat now and again that Thornton killed, and Buck spent long hours musing by the fire. The vision of the short-legged hairy man came to him more frequently, now that there was little work to be done; and often, blinking by the fire, Buck wandered with him in that other world which he remembered.

The salient thing of this other world seemed fear. When he watched the hairy man sleeping by the fire, head between his knees and hands clasped above, Buck saw that he slept restlessly, with many starts and awakenings, at which times he would peer fearfully into the darkness and fling more wood upon the fire. Did they walk by the beach of a sea, where the hairy man gathered shell-fish and ate them as he gathered, it was with eyes that roved everywhere for hidden danger and with legs prepared to run like the wind at its first appearance. Through the forest they crept noiselessly, Buck at the hairy man's heels; and they were alert and vigilant, the pair of them, ears twitching and moving and nostrils quivering, for the man heard and smelled as keenly as Buck. The hairy man could spring up into the trees and travel ahead as fast as on the ground, swinging by the arms from limb to limb, sometimes a dozen feet apart, letting go and catching, never falling, never missing his grip. In fact, he seemed as much at home among the trees as on the ground; and Buck had memories of nights of vigil spent beneath trees wherein the hairy man roosted, holding on tightly as he slept.

And closely akin to the visions of the hairy man was the call still sounding in the depths of the forest. It filled him with a great unrest and strange desires. It caused him to feel a vague, sweet gladness, and he was aware of wild yearnings and stirrings for he knew not what. Sometimes he pursued the call into the forest, looking for it as though it were a tangible thing, barking softly or defiantly, as the mood might dictate. He would thrust his nose into the cool wood moss, or into the black soil where long grasses grew, and snort with joy at the fat earth smells; or he would crouch for hours, as if in concealment, behind fungus-covered trunks of fallen trees, wide-eyed and wide-eared to all that moved and sounded about him. It might be, lying thus, that he hoped to surprise this call he could not understand. But he did not know why he did these various things. He was impelled to do them, and did not reason about them at all. Irresistible impulses seized him. He would be lying in camp, dozing lazily in the heat of the day, when suddenly his head would lift and his ears cock up, intent and listening, and he would spring to his feet and dash away, and on and on, for hours, through the forest aisles and across the open spaces where the niggerheads bunched. He loved to run down dry watercourses, and to creep and spy upon the bird life in the woods. For a day at a time he would lie in the underbrush where he could watch the partridges drumming and strutting up and down. But especially he loved to run in the dim twilight of the summer midnights, listening to the subdued and sleepy murmurs of the forest, reading signs and sounds as man may read a book, and seeking for the mysterious something that called—called, waking or sleeping, at all times, for him to come.

One night he sprang from sleep with a start, eager-eyed, nostrils quivering and scenting, his mane bristling in recurrent waves. From the forest came the call (or one note of it, for the call was many-noted), distinct and definite as never before—a long-drawn howl, like, yet unlike, any noise made by a husky dog. And he knew it, in the old familiar way, as a sound heard before. He sprang through the sleeping camp and in swift silence dashed through the woods. As he drew closer to the cry he went more slowly, with caution in every movement, till he came to an open place among the trees, and looking out saw, erect on haunches, with nose pointed to the sky, a long, lean, timber wolf.

He had made no noise, yet it ceased from its howling and tried to sense his presence. Buck stalked into the open, half crouching, body gathered compactly together, tail straight and stiff, feet falling with unwonted care. Every movement advertised commingled threatening and overture of friendliness. It was the menacing truce that marks the meeting of wild beasts that prey. But the wolf fled at sight of him. He followed, with wild leapings, in a frenzy to overtake. He ran him into a blind channel, in the bed of the creek, where a timber jam barred the way. The wolf whirled about, pivoting on his hind legs after the fashion of Joe and of all cornered husky dogs, snarling and bristling, clipping his teeth together in a continuous and rapid succession of snaps.

Buck did not attack, but circled him about and hedged him in with friendly advances. The wolf was suspicious and afraid; for Buck made three of him in weight, while his head barely reached Buck's shoulder. Watching his chance, he darted away, and the chase was resumed. Time and again he was cornered and the thing repeated, though he was in poor condition or Buck could not so easily have overtaken him. He would run till Buck's head was even with his flank, when he would whirl around at bay, only to dash away again at the first opportunity.

But in the end Buck's pertinacity was rewarded; for the wolf, finding that no harm was intended, finally sniffed noses with him. Then they became friendly, and played about in the nervous, half-coy way with which fierce beasts belie their fierceness. After some time of this the wolf started off at an easy lope in a manner that plainly showed he was going somewhere. He made it clear to Buck that he was to come, and they ran side by side through the sombre twilight, straight up the creek bed, into the gorge from which it issued, and across the bleak divide where it took its rise.

On the opposite slope of the watershed they came down into a level country where were great stretches of forest and many streams, and through these great stretches they ran steadily, hour after hour, the sun rising higher and the day growing warmer. Buck was wildly glad. He knew he was at last answering the call, running by the side of his wood brother toward the place from where the call surely came. Old memories were coming upon him fast, and he was stirring to them as of old he stirred to the realities of which they were the shadows. He had done this thing before, somewhere in that other and dimly remembered world, and he was doing it again now, running free in the open, the unpacked earth underfoot, the wide sky overhead.

They stopped by a running stream to drink, and, stopping, Buck remembered John Thornton. He sat down. The wolf started on toward the place from where the call surely came, then returned to him, sniffing noses and making actions as though to encourage him. But Buck turned about and started slowly on the back track. For the better part of an hour the wild brother ran by his side, whining softly. Then he sat down, pointed his nose upward, and howled. It was a mournful howl, and as Buck held steadily on his way he heard it grow faint and fainter until it was lost in the distance.

John Thornton was eating dinner when Buck dashed into camp and sprang upon him, in a frenzy of affection, overturning him, scrambling upon him, licking his face, biting his hand—"playing the general tom-fool," as John Thornton characterized it, the while he shook Buck back and forth and cursed him lovingly.

For two days and nights Buck never left camp, never let Thornton out of his sight. He followed him about at his work, watched him while he ate, saw him into his blankets at night and out of them in the morning. But after two days the call in the forest began to sound more imperiously than ever. Buck's restlessness came back on him, and he was haunted by recollections of the wild brother, and of the smiling land beyond the divide and the run side by side through the wide forest stretches. Once again he took to wandering in the woods, but the wild brother came no more; and though he listened through long vigils, the mournful howl was never raised.

He began to sleep out at night, staying away from camp for days at a time; and once he crossed the divide at the head of the creek and went down into the land of timber and streams. There he wandered for a week, seeking vainly for fresh sign of the wild brother, killing his meat as he travelled and travelling with the long, easy lope that seems never to tire. He fished for salmon in a broad stream that emptied somewhere into the sea, and by this stream he killed a large black bear, blinded by the mosquitoes while likewise fishing, and raging through the forest helpless and terrible. Even so, it was a hard fight, and it aroused the last latent remnants of Buck's ferocity. And two days later, when he returned to his kill and found a dozen wolverenes quarrelling over the spoil, he scattered them like chaff; and those that fled left two behind who would quarrel no more.

The blood-longing became stronger than ever before. He was a killer, a thing that preyed, living on the things that lived, unaided, alone, by virtue of his own strength and prowess, surviving triumphantly in a hostile environment where only the strong survive. Because of all this he became possessed of a great pride in himself, which communicated itself like a contagion to his physical being. It advertised itself in all his movements, was apparent in the play of every muscle, spoke plainly as speech in the way he carried himself, and made his glorious furry coat if anything more glorious. But for the stray brown on his muzzle and above his eyes, and for the splash of white hair that ran midmost down his chest, he might well have been mistaken for a gigantic wolf, larger than the largest of the breed. From his St. Bernard father he had inherited size and weight, but it was his shepherd mother who had given shape to that size and weight. His muzzle was the long wolf muzzle, save that it was larger than the muzzle of any wolf; and his head, somewhat broader, was the wolf head on a massive scale.

His cunning was wolf cunning, and wild cunning; his intelligence, shepherd intelligence and St. Bernard intelligence; and all this, plus an experience gained in the fiercest of schools, made him as formidable a creature as any that roamed the wild. A carnivorous animal, living on a straight meat diet, he was in full flower, at the high tide of his life, overspilling with vigor and virility. When Thornton passed a caressing hand along his back, a snapping and crackling followed the hand, each hair discharging its pent magnetism at the contact. Every part, brain and body, nerve tissue and fibre, was keyed to the most exquisite pitch; and between all the parts there was a perfect equilibrium or adjustment. To sights and sounds and events which required action, he responded with lightning-like rapidity. Quickly as a husky dog could leap to defend from attack or to attack, he could leap twice as quickly. He saw the movement, or heard sound, and responded in less time than another dog required to compass the mere seeing or hearing. He perceived and determined and responded in the same instant. In point of fact the three actions of perceiving, determining, and responding were sequential; but so infinitesimal were the intervals of time between them that they appeared simultaneous. His muscles were surcharged with vitality, and snapped into play sharply, like steel springs. Life streamed through him in splendid flood, glad and rampant, until it seemed that it would burst him asunder in sheer ecstasy and pour forth generously over the world.

"Never was there such a dog," said John Thornton one day, as the partners watched Buck marching out of camp.

"When he was made, the mould was broke," said Pete.

"Py jingo! I t'ink so mineself," Hans affirmed.

They saw him marching out of camp, but they did not see the instant and terrible transformation which took place as soon as he was within the secrecy of the forest. He no longer marched. At once he became a thing of the wild, stealing along softly, cat-footed, a passing shadow that appeared and disappeared among the shadows. He knew how to take advantage of every cover, to crawl on his belly like a snake, and like a snake to leap and strike. He could take a ptarmigan from its nest, kill a rabbit as it slept, and snap in mid air the little chipmunks fleeing a second too late for the trees. Fish, in open pools, were not too quick for him; nor were beaver, mending their dams, too wary. He killed to eat, not from wantonness; but he preferred to eat what he killed himself. So a lurking humor ran through his deeds, and it was his delight to steal upon the squirrels, and, when he all but had them, to let them go, chattering in mortal fear to the tree-tops.

As the fall of the year came on, the moose appeared in greater abundance, moving slowly down to meet the winter in the lower and less rigorous valleys. Buck had already dragged down a stray part-grown calf; but he wished strongly for larger and more formidable quarry, and he came upon it one day on the divide at the head of the creek. A band of twenty moose had crossed over from the land of streams and timber, and chief among them was a great bull. He was in a savage temper, and, standing over six feet from the ground, was as formidable an antagonist as ever Buck could desire. Back and forth the bull tossed his great palmated antlers, branching to fourteen points and embracing seven feet within the tips. His small eyes burned with a vicious and bitter light, while he roared with fury at sight of Buck.

From the bull's side, just forward of the flank, protruded a feathered arrow-end, which accounted for his savageness. Guided by that instinct which came from the old hunting days of the primordial world, Buck proceeded to cut the bull out from the herd. It was no slight task. He would bark and dance about in front of the bull, just out of reach of the great antlers and of the terrible splay hoofs which could have stamped his life out with a single blow. Unable to turn his back on the fanged danger and go on, the bull would be driven into paroxysms of rage. At such moments he charged Buck, who retreated craftily, luring him on by a simulated inability to escape. But when he was thus separated from his fellows, two or three of the younger bulls would charge back upon Buck and enable the wounded bull to rejoin the herd.

There is a patience of the wild—dogged, tireless, persistent as life itself—that holds motionless for endless hours the spider in its web, the snake in its coils, the panther in its ambuscade; this patience belongs peculiarly to life when it hunts its living food; and it belonged to Buck as he clung to the flank of the herd, retarding its march, irritating the young bulls, worrying the cows with their half-grown calves, and driving the wounded bull mad with helpless rage. For half a day this continued. Buck multiplied himself, attacking from all sides, enveloping the herd in a whirlwind of menace, cutting out his victim as fast as it could rejoin its mates, wearing out the patience of creatures preyed upon, which is a lesser patience than that of creatures preying.

As the day wore along and the sun dropped to its bed in the northwest (the darkness had come back and the fall nights were six hours long), the young bulls retraced their steps more and more reluctantly to the aid of their beset leader. The down-coming winter was harrying them on to the lower levels, and it seemed they could never shake off this tireless creature that held them back. Besides, it was not the life of the herd, or of the young bulls, that was threatened. The life of only one member was demanded, which was a remoter interest than their lives, and in the end they were content to pay the toll.

As twilight fell the old bull stood with lowered head, watching his mates—the cows he had known, the calves he had fathered, the bulls he had mastered—as they shambled on at a rapid pace through the fading light. He could not follow, for before his nose leaped the merciless fanged terror that would not let him go. Three hundred-weight more than half a ton he weighed; he had lived a long, strong life, full of fight and struggle, and at the end he faced death at the teeth of a creature whose head did not reach beyond his great knuckled knees.

From then on, night and day, Buck never left his prey, never gave it a moment's rest, never permitted it to browse the leaves of trees or the shoots of young birch and willow. Nor did he give the wounded bull opportunity to slake his burning thirst in the slender trickling streams they crossed. Often, in desperation, he burst into long stretches of flight. At such times Buck did not attempt to stay him, but loped easily at his heels, satisfied with the way the game was played, lying down when the moose stood still, attacking him fiercely when he strove to eat or drink.

The great head drooped more and more under its tree of horns, and the shambling trot grew weaker and weaker. He took to standing for long periods, with nose to the ground and dejected ears dropped limply; and Buck found more time in which to get water for himself and in which to rest. At such moments, panting with red lolling tongue and with eyes fixed upon the big bull, it appeared to Buck that a change was coming over the face of things. He could feel a new stir in the land. As the moose were coming into the land, other kinds of life were coming in. Forest and stream and air seemed palpitant with their presence. The news of it was borne in upon him, not by sight or sound, or smell, but by some other and subtler sense. He heard nothing, saw nothing, yet knew that the land was somehow different; that through it strange things were afoot and ranging; and he resolved to investigate after he had finished the business in hand.

At last, at the end of the fourth day, he pulled the great moose down. For a day and a night he remained by the kill, eating and sleeping, turn and turn about. Then, rested, refreshed and strong, he turned his face toward camp and John Thornton. He broke into the long easy lope, and went on, hour after hour, never at loss for the tangled way, heading straight home through strange country with a certitude of direction that put man and his magnetic needle to shame.

As he held on he became more and more conscious of the new stir in the land. There was life abroad in it different from the life which had been there throughout the summer. No longer was this fact borne in upon him in some subtle, mysterious way. The birds talked of it, the squirrels chattered about it, the very breeze whispered of it. Several times he stopped and drew in the fresh morning air in great sniffs, reading a message which made him leap on with greater speed. He was oppressed with a sense of calamity happening, if it were not calamity already happened; and as he crossed the last watershed and dropped down into the valley toward camp, he proceeded with greater caution.

Three miles away he came upon a fresh trail that sent his neck hair rippling and bristling. It led straight toward camp and John

Thornton. Buck hurried on, swiftly and stealthily, every nerve straining and tense, alert to the multitudinous details which told a story—all but the end. His nose gave him a varying description of the passage of the life on the heels of which he was travelling. He remarked the pregnant silence of the forest. The bird life had flitted. The squirrels were in hiding. One only he saw,—a sleek gray fellow, flattened against a gray dead limb so that he seemed a part of it, a woody excrescence upon the wood itself.

As Buck slid along with the obscureness of a gliding shadow, his nose was jerked suddenly to the side as though a positive force had gripped and pulled it. He followed the new scent into a thicket and found Nig. He was lying on his side, dead where he had dragged himself, an arrow protruding, head and feathers, from either side of his body.

A hundred yards farther on, Buck came upon one of the sled-dogs Thornton had bought in Dawson. This dog was thrashing about in a death-struggle, directly on the trail, and Buck passed around him without stopping. From the camp came the faint sound of many voices, rising and falling in a sing-song chant. Bellying forward to the edge of the clearing, he found Hans, lying on his face, feathered with arrows like a porcupine. At the same instant Buck peered out where the spruce-bough lodge had been and saw what made his hair leap straight up on his neck and shoulders. A gust of overpowering rage swept over him. He did not know that he growled, but he growled aloud with a terrible ferocity. For the last time in his life he allowed passion to usurp cunning and reason, and it was because of his great love for John Thornton that he lost his head.

The Yeehats were dancing about the wreckage of the spruce-bough lodge when they heard a fearful roaring and saw rushing upon them an animal the like of which they had never seen before. It was Buck, a live hurricane of fury, hurling himself upon them in a frenzy to destroy. He sprang at the foremost man (it was the chief of the Yeehats), ripping the throat wide open till the rent jugular spouted a fountain of blood. He did not pause to worry the victim, but ripped in passing, with the next bound tearing wide the throat of a second man. There was no withstanding him. He plunged about in their very midst, tearing, rending, destroying, in constant and terrific motion which defied the arrows they discharged at him. In fact, so inconceivably rapid were his movements, and so closely were the Indians tangled together, that they shot one another with the arrows; and one young hunter, hurling a spear at Buck in mid air, drove it through the chest of another hunter with such force that the point broke through the skin of the back and stood out beyond. Then a panic seized the Yeehats, and they fled in terror to the woods, proclaiming as they fled the advent of the Evil Spirit.

And truly Buck was the Fiend incarnate, raging at their heels and dragging them down like deer as they raced through the trees. It was a fateful day for the Yeehats. They scattered far and wide over the country, and it was not till a week later that the last of the survivors gathered together in a lower valley and counted their losses. As for Buck, wearying of the pursuit, he returned to the desolated camp. He found Pete where he had been killed in his blankets in the first moment of surprise. Thornton's desperate struggle was fresh-written on the earth, and Buck scented every detail of it down to the edge of a deep pool. By the edge, head and fore feet in the water, lay Skeet, faithful to the last. The pool itself, muddy and discolored from the sluice boxes, effectually hid what it contained, and it contained John Thornton; for Buck followed his trace into the water, from which no trace led away.

All day Buck brooded by the pool or roamed restlessly above the camp. Death, as a cessation of movement, as a passing out and away from the lives of the living, he knew, and he knew John Thornton was dead. It left a great void in him, somewhat akin to hunger, but a void which ached and ached, and which food could not fill. At times, when he paused to contemplate the carcasses of the Yeehats, he forgot the pain of it; and at such times he was aware of a great pride in himself—a pride greater than any he had yet experienced. He had killed man, the noblest game of all, and he had killed in the face of the law of club and fang. He sniffed the bodies curiously. They had died so easily. It was harder to kill a husky dog than them. They were no match at all, were it not for their arrows and spears and clubs. Thenceforward he would be unafraid of them except when they bore in their hands their arrows, spears, and clubs.

Night came on, and a full moon rose high over the trees into the sky, lighting the land till it lay bathed in ghostly day. And with the coming of the night, brooding and mourning by the pool, Buck became alive to a stirring of the new life in the forest other than that which the Yeehats had made. He stood up, listening and scenting.

From far away drifted a faint, sharp yelp, followed by a chorus of similar sharp yelps. As the moments passed the yelps grew closer and louder. Again Buck knew them as things heard in that other world which persisted in his memory. He walked to the centre of the open space and listened. It was the call, the many-noted call, sounding more luringly and compelling than ever before. And as never before, he was ready to obey. John Thornton was dead. The last tie was broken. Man and the claims of man no longer bound him.

Hunting their living meat, as the Yeehats were hunting it, on the flanks of the migrating moose, the wolf pack had at last crossed over from the land of streams and timber and invaded Buck's valley. Into the clearing where the moonlight streamed, they poured in a silvery flood; and in the centre of the clearing stood Buck, motionless as a statue, waiting their coming. They were awed, so still and large he stood, and a moment's pause fell, till the boldest one leaped straight for him. Like a flash Buck struck, breaking the neck. Then he stood, without movement, as before, the stricken wolf rolling in agony behind him. Three others tried it in sharp succession; and one after the other they drew back, streaming blood from slashed throats or shoulders.

This was sufficient to fling the whole pack forward, pellmell, crowded together, blocked and confused by its eagerness to pull down the prey. Buck's marvellous quickness and agility stood him in good stead. Pivoting on his hind legs, and snapping and gashing, he was everywhere at once, presenting a front which was apparently unbroken so swiftly did he whirl and guard from side to side. But to prevent them from getting behind him, he was forced back, down past the pool and into a creek bed, till he brought up against a high gravel bank. He worked along to a right angle in the bank which the men had made in the course of mining, and in this angle he came to bay, protected on three sides and with nothing to do but face the front.

And so well did he face it, that at the end of half an hour the wolves drew back discomfited. The tongues of all were out and lolling, the white fangs showing cruelly white in the moonlight. Some were lying down with heads raised and ears pricked forward; other stood on their feet, watching him; and still others were lapping water from the pool. One wolf, long and lean and gray, advanced cautiously, in a friendly manner, and Buck recognized the wild brother with whom he had run for a night and a day. He was whining softly, and, as Buck whined, they touched noses.

Then an old wolf, gaunt and battle-scarred, came forward. Buck writhed his lips into the preliminary of a snarl, but sniffed noses with him. Whereupon the old wolf sat down, pointed nose at the moon, and broke out the long wolf howl. The others sat down and howled. And now the call came to Buck in unmistakable accents. He, too, sat down and howled. This over, he came out of his angle and the pack crowded around him, sniffing in half-friendly, half-savage manner. The leaders lifted the yelp of the pack and sprang away into the woods. The wolves swung in behind, yelping in chorus. And Buck ran with them, side by side with the wild brother, yelping as he ran.

And here may well end the story of Buck. The years were not many when the Yeehats noted a change in the breed of timber wolves; for some were seen with splashes of brown on head and nuzzle, and with a rift of white centering down the chest. But more remarkable than this, the Yeehats tell of a Ghost Dog that runs at the head of the pack. They are afraid of this Ghost Dog, for it has cunning greater than they, stealing from their camps in fierce winters, robbing their traps, slaying their dogs, and defying their bravest hunters.

Nay, the tale grows worse. Hunters there are who fail to return to the camp, and hunters there have been whom their tribesmen found with throats slashed cruelly open and with wolf prints about them in the snow greater than the prints of any wolf. Each fall, when the Yeehats follow the movement of the moose, there is a certain valley which they never enter. And women there are who become sad when the word goes over the fire of how the Evil Spirit came to select that valley for an abiding-place.

In the summers there is one visitor, however, to that valley, of which the Yeehats do not know. It is a great, gloriously coated wolf, like, and yet unlike, all other wolves. He crosses alone from the smiling timber land and comes down into an open space among the trees. Here a yellow stream flows from rotted moose-hide sacks and sinks into the ground, with long grasses growing through it and vegetable mould overruning it and hiding its yellow from the sun;

and here he muses for a time, howling once, long and mournfully, ere he departs.

But he is not always alone. When the long winter nights come on and the wolves follow their meat into the lower valleys, he may be seen running at the head of the pack through the pale moonlight or glimmering borealis, leaping gigantic above his fellows, his great throat a-bellow as he sings a song of the younger world, which is the song of the pack.

---

# Chapter 3

---

# Bâtard

---

# by Jack London

Bâtard was a devil. This was recognized throughout the Northland. "Hell's Spawn" he was called by many men, but his master, Black Leclère, chose for him the shameful name "Bâtard." Now Black Leclère was also a devil, and the twain were well matched. There is a saying that when two devils come together, hell is to pay. This is to be expected, and this certainly was to be expected when Bâtard and Black Leclère came together. The first time they met, Bâtard was a part-grown puppy, lean and hungry, with bitter eyes; and they met with a snap and snarl, and wicked looks, for Leclère's upper lip had a wolfish way of lifting and showing the white, cruel teeth. And it lifted then, and his eyes glinted viciously, as he reached for Bâtard and dragged him out from the squirming litter. It was certain that they divined each other, for on the instant Bâtard had buried his puppy fangs in Leclère's hand, and Leclère, thumb and finger, was coolly choking his young life out of him.

"*Sacredam,*" the Frenchman said softly, flirting the quick blood from his bitten hand and gazing down on the little puppy choking and gasping in the snow.

Leclère turned to John Hamlin, storekeeper of the Sixty Mile Post. "Dat fo' w'at Ah lak heem. 'Ow moch, eh, you, *M'sieu'*? 'Ow moch? Ah buy heem, now; Ah buy heem queek."

And because he hated him with an exceeding bitter hate, Leclère bought Bâtard and gave him his shameful name. And for five years the twain adventured across the Northland, from St. Michael's and the Yukon delta to the headreaches of the Pelly and even so far as the Peace River, Athabasca, and the Great Slave. And they acquired a reputation for uncompromising wickedness, the like of which never before attached itself to man and dog.

Bâtard did not know his father,—hence his name,—but, as John Hamlin knew, his father was a great grey timber wolf. But the mother of Bâtard, as he dimly remembered her, was snarling, bickering, obscene, husky, full-fronted and heavy-chested, with a malign eye, a cat-like grip on life, and a genius for trickery and evil. There was neither faith nor trust in her. Her treachery alone could be relied upon, and her wild-wood amours attested her general depravity. Much of evil and much of strength were there in these, Bâtard's progenitors, and, bone and flesh of their bone and flesh, he had inherited it all. And then came Black Leclère, to lay his heavy hand on the bit of pulsating puppy life, to press and prod and mould till it became a big bristling beast, acute in knavery, overspilling with hate, sinister, malignant, diabolical. With a proper master Bâtard might have made an ordinary, fairly efficient sled-dog. He never got the chance: Leclère but confirmed him in his congenital iniquity.

The history of Bâtard and Leclère is a history of war—of five cruel, relentless years, of which their first meeting is fit summary. To begin with, it was Leclère's fault, for he hated with understanding and intelligence, while the long-legged, ungainly puppy hated only blindly, instinctively, without reason or method. At first there were no refinements of cruelty (these were to come later), but simple beatings and crude brutalities. In one of these Bâtard had an ear injured. He never regained control of the riven muscles, and ever after the ear drooped limply down to keep keen the memory of his tormentor. And he never forgot.

His puppyhood was a period of foolish rebellion. He was always worsted, but he fought back because it was his nature to fight back. And he was unconquerable. Yelping shrilly from the pain of lash and club, he none the less contrived always to throw in the defiant snarl, the bitter vindictive menace of his soul which fetched without fail more blows and beatings. But his was his mother's tenacious grip on life. Nothing could kill him. He flourished under misfortune, grew fat with famine, and out of his terrible struggle for life developed a preternatural intelligence. His were the stealth and cunning of the husky, his mother, and the fierceness and valour of the wolf, his father.

Possibly it was because of his father that he never wailed. His puppy yelps passed with his lanky legs, so that he became grim and taciturn, quick to strike, slow to warn. He answered curse with snarl, and blow with snap, grinning the while his implacable hatred; but never again, under the extremest agony, did Leclère bring from him the cry of fear nor of pain. This unconquerableness but fanned Leclère's wrath and stirred him to greater deviltries.

Did Leclère give Bâtard half a fish and to his mates whole ones, Bâtard went forth to rob other dogs of their fish. Also he robbed caches and expressed himself in a thousand rogueries, till he became a terror to all dogs and masters of dogs. Did Leclère beat Bâtard and fondle Babette—Babette who was not half the worker he was,—why Bâtard threw her down in the snow and broke her hind leg in his heavy jaws, so that Leclère was forced to shoot her. Likewise, in bloody battles, Bâtard mastered all his team-mates, set them the law of trail and forage, and made them live to the law he set.

In five years he heard but one kind word, received but one soft stroke of a hand, and then he did not know what manner of things they were. He leaped like the untamed thing he was, and his jaws were together in a flash. It was the missionary at Sunrise, a newcomer in the country, who spoke the kind word and gave the soft stroke of the hand. And for six months after, he wrote no letters home to the States, and the surgeon at McQuestion travelled two hundred miles on the ice to save him from blood-poisoning.

Men and dogs looked askance at Bâtard when he drifted into their camps and posts. The men greeted him with feet threateningly lifted for the kick, the dogs with bristling manes and bared fangs. Once a man did kick Bâtard, and Bâtard, with quick wolf snap, closed his jaws like a steel trap on the man's calf and crunched down to the bone. Whereat the man was determined to have his life, only Black Leclère, with ominous eyes and naked hunting-knife, stepped in between. The killing of Bâtard—ah, *sacredam, that* was a pleasure Leclère reserved for himself. Some day it would happen, or else—bah! who was to know? Anyway, the problem would be solved.

For they had become problems to each other. The very breath each drew was a challenge and a menace to the other. Their hate bound them together as love could never bind. Leclère was bent on the coming of the day when Bâtard should wilt in spirit and cringe and whimper at his feet. And Bâtard—Leclère knew what was in Bâtard's mind, and more than once had read it in Bâtard's eyes. And so clearly had he read that, when Bâtard was at his back, he made it a point to glance often over his shoulder.

Men marvelled when Leclère refused large money for the dog. "Some day you will kill him and be out his price," said John Hamlin once, when Bâtard lay panting in the snow where Leclère had kicked him, and no one knew whether his ribs were broken, and no one dared look to see.

"Dat," said Leclère, dryly, "dat is my biz'ness, M'sieu'." And the men marvelled that Bâtard did not run away. They did not understand. But Leclère understood. He was a man who lived much in the open, beyond the sound of human tongue, and he had learned the voices of wind and storm, the sigh of night, the whisper of dawn, the clash of day. In a dim way he could hear the green things growing, the running of the sap, the bursting of the bud. And he knew the subtle speech of the things that moved, of the rabbit in the snare, the moody raven beating the air with hollow wing, the baldface shuffling under the moon, the wolf like a grey shadow gliding betwixt the twilight and the dark. And to him Bâtard spoke clear and direct. Full well he understood why Bâtard did not run away, and he looked more often over his shoulder.

When in anger, Bâtard was not nice to look upon, and more than once he had leapt for Leclere's throat, to be stretched quivering and senseless in the snow, by the butt of the ever ready dogwhip. And so Bâtard learned to bide his time. When he reached his full strength and prime of youth, he thought the time had come. He was broad-chested, powerfully muscled, of far more than ordinary size, and his neck from head to shoulders was a mass of bristling hair—to all appearances a full-blooded wolf. Leclère was lying asleep in his furs when Bâtard deemed the time to be ripe. He crept upon him stealthily, head low to earth and lone ear laid back, with a feline softness of tread. Bâtard breathed gently, very gently, and not till he was close at hand did he raise his head. He paused for a moment, and looked at the bronzed full throat, naked and knotty, and swelling to a deep steady pulse. The slaver dripped down his fangs and slid off his tongue at the sight, and in that moment he remembered his drooping ear, his uncounted blows and prodigious wrongs, and without a sound sprang on the sleeping man.

Leclère awoke to the pang of the fangs in his throat, and, perfect animal that he was, he awoke clear-headed and with full comprehension. He closed on Bâtard's windpipe with both his hands, and rolled out of his furs to get his weight uppermost. But the thousands of Bâtard's ancestors had clung at the throats of unnumbered moose and caribou and dragged them down, and the wisdom of those ancestors was his. When Leclère's weight came on top of him, he drove his hind legs upwards and in, and clawed down chest and abdomen, ripping and tearing through skin and muscle. And when he felt the man's body wince above him and lift, he worried and shook at the man's throat. His teammates closed around in a snarling circle, and Bâtard, with failing breath and fading sense,

knew that their jaws were hungry for him. But that did not matter—it was the man, the man above him, and he ripped and clawed,
and shook and worried, to the last ounce of his strength. But
Leclère choked him with both his hands, till Bâtard's chest heaved
and writhed for the air denied, and his eyes glazed and set, and his
jaws slowly loosened, and his tongue protruded black and swollen.

"Eh? *Bon,* you devil!" Leclère gurgled, mouth and throat clogged
with his own blood, as he shoved the dizzy dog from him.

And then Leclère cursed the other dogs off as they fell upon
Bâtard. They drew back into a wider circle, squatting alertly on
their haunches and licking their chops, the hair on every neck
bristling and erect.

Bâtard recovered quickly, and at sound of Leclère's voice, tottered to his feet and swayed weakly back and forth.

"A-h-ah! You beeg devil!" Leclère spluttered. "Ah fix you; Ah fix
you plentee, by *Gar!*"

Bâtard, the air biting into his exhausted lungs like wine, flashed
full into the man's face, his jaws missing and coming together with a
metallic clip. They rolled over and over on the snow, Leclère
striking madly with his fists. Then they separated, face to face, and
circled back and forth before each other. Leclère could have drawn
his knife. His rifle was at his feet. But the beast in him was up and
raging. He would do the thing with his hands—and his teeth.
Bâtard sprang in, but Leclère knocked him over with a blow of the
fist, fell upon him, and buried his teeth to the bone in the dog's
shoulder.

It was a primordial setting and a primordial scene, such as might
have been in the savage youth of the world. An open space in a dark
forest, a ring of grinning wolf-dogs, and in the centre two beasts,
locked in combat, snapping and snarling, raging madly about, panting, sobbing, cursing, straining, wild with passion, in a fury of
murder, ripping and tearing and clawing in elemental brutishness.

But Leclère caught Bâtard behind the ear, with a blow from his
fist, knocking him over, and, for the instant, stunning him. Then
Leclère leaped upon him with his feet, and sprang up and down,
striving to grind him into the earth. Both Bâtard's hind legs were
broken ere Leclère ceased that he might catch breath.

"A-a-ah! A-a-ah!" he screamed, incapable of speech, shaking his
fist, through sheer impotence of throat and larynx.

But Bâtard was indomitable. He lay there in a helpless welter, his lip feebly lifting and writhing to the snarl he had not the strength to utter. Leclère kicked him, and the tired jaws closed on the ankle, but could not break the skin.

Then Leclère picked up the whip and proceeded almost to cut him to pieces, at each stroke of the lash crying: "Dis taim Ah break you! Eh? By *Gar*! Ah break you!"

In the end, exhausted, fainting from loss of blood, he crumpled up and fell by his victim, and when the wolf-dogs closed in to take their vengeance, with his last consciousness dragged his body on top of Bâtard to shield him from their fangs.

This occurred not far from Sunrise, and the missionary, opening the door to Leclère a few hours later, was surprised to note the absence of Bâtard from the team. Nor did his surprise lessen when Leclère threw back the robes from the sled, gathered Bâtard into his arms and staggered across the threshold. It happened that the surgeon of McQuestion, who was something of a gadabout, was up on a gossip, and between them they proceeded to repair Leclère.

"*Merci, non,*" said he. "Do you fix firs' de dog. To die? *Non.* Eet is not good. Becos' heem Ah mus' yet break. Dat fo' w'at he mus' not die."

The surgeon called it a marvel, the missionary a miracle, that Leclère pulled through at all; and so weakened was he, that in the spring the fever got him, and he went on his back again. Bâtard had been in even worse plight, but his grip on life prevailed, and the bones of his hind legs knit, and his organs righted themselves, during the several weeks he lay strapped to the floor. And by the time Leclère, finally convalescent, sallow and shaky, took the sun by the cabin door, Bâtard had reasserted his supremacy among his kind, and brought not only his own team-mates but the missionary's dogs into subjection.

He moved never a muscle, nor twitched a hair, when, for the first time, Leclère tottered out on the missionary's arm, and sank down slowly and with infinite caution on the three-legged stool.

"*Bon!*" he said. "Bon! De good sun!" And he stretched out his wasted hands and washed them in the warmth.

Then his gaze fell on the dog, and the old light blazed back in his eyes. He touched the missionary lightly on the arm. "*Mon père,* dat is one beeg devil, dat Bâtard. You will bring me one pistol, so, dat Ah drink de sun in peace."

And thenceforth for many days he sat in the sun before the cabin door. He never dozed, and the pistol lay always across his knees. Bâtard had a way, the first thing each day, of looking for the weapon in its wonted place. At sight of it he would lift his lip faintly in token that he understood, and Leclère would lift his own lip in an answering grin. One day the missionary took note of the trick. "Bless me!" he said. "I really believe the brute comprehends." Leclère laughed softly. "Look you, *mon père*. Dat w'at Ah now spik, to dat does he lissen."

As if in confirmation, Bâtard just perceptibly wriggled his lone ear up to catch the sound.

"Ah say 'keel'."

Bâtard growled deep down in his throat, the hair bristled along his neck, and every muscle went tense and expectant.

"Ah lift de gun, so, like dat." And suiting action to word, he sighted the pistol at Bâtard.

Bâtard, with a single leap, sideways, landed around the corner of the cabin out of sight.

"Bless me!" he repeated at intervals.

Leclère grinned proudly.

"But why does he not run away?"

The Frenchman's shoulders went up in the racial shrug that means all things from total ignorance to infinite understanding.

"Then why do you not kill him?"

Again the shoulders went up.

*"Mon pere,"* he said after a pause, "de taim is not yet. He is one beeg devil. Some taim Ah break heem, so, an' so, all to leetle bits. Hey? some taim. *Bon!"*

A day came when Leclère gathered his dogs together and floated down in a bateau to Forty Mile, and so on to the Porcupine, where he took a commission from the P. C. Company, and went exploring for the better part of a year. After that he poled up the Koyokuk to deserted Arctic City, and later came drifting back, from camp to camp, along the Yukon. And during the long months Bâtard was well lessoned. He learned many tortures, and, notably, the torture of hunger, the torture of thirst, the torture of fire, and, worst of all, the torture of music.

Like the rest of his kind, he did not enjoy music. It gave him exquisite anguish, racking him nerve by nerve, and ripping apart every fibre of his being. It made him howl, long and wolf-like, as when the wolves bay the stars on frosty nights. He could not help howling. It was his one weakness in the contest with Leclère, and it was his shame. Leclère, on the other hand, passionately loved music—as passionately as he loved strong drink. And when his soul clamoured for expression, it usually uttered itself in one or the other of the two ways, and more usually in both ways. And when he had drunk, his brain a-lilt with unsung song and the devil in him aroused and rampant, his soul found its supreme utterance in torturing Bâtard.

"Now we will haf a leetle museek," he would say. "Eh? W'at you t'ink, Bâtard?"

It was only an old and battered harmonica, tenderly treasured and patiently repaired; but it was the best that money could buy, and out of its silver reeds he drew weird vagrant airs that men had never heard before. Then Bâtard, dumb of throat, with teeth tight clenched, would back away, inch by inch, to the farthest cabin corner. And Leclère, playing, playing, a stout club tucked under his arm, followed the animal up, inch by inch, step by step, till there was no further retreat.

At first Bâtard would crowd himself into the smallest possible space, groveling close to the floor; but as the music came nearer and nearer, he was forced to uprear, his back jammed into the logs, his fore legs fanning the air as though to beat off the rippling waves of sound. He still kept his teeth together, but severe muscular contractions attacked his body, strange twitchings and jerkings, till he was all a-quiver and writhing in silent torment. As he lost control, his jaws spasmodically wrenched apart, and deep throaty vibrations issued forth, too low in the register of sound for human ear to catch. And then, nostrils distended, eyes dilated, hair bristling in helpless rage, arose the long wolf howl. It came with a slurring rush upward, swelling to a great heart-breaking burst of sound, and dying away in sadly cadenced woe—then the next rush upward, octave upon octave; the bursting heart; and the infinite sorrow and misery, fainting, fading, falling, and dying slowly away.

It was fit for hell. And Leclère, with fiendish ken, seemed to divine each particular nerve and heartstring, and with long wails and tremblings and sobbing minors to make it yield up its last shred of grief. It was frightful, and for twenty-four hours after, Bâtard was nervous and unstrung, starting at common sounds, tripping over his own shadow, but, withal, vicious and masterful with his team-mates. Nor did he show signs of a breaking spirit. Rather did he grow more grim and taciturn, biding his time with an inscrutable patience that began to puzzle and weigh upon Leclère. The dog would lie in the firelight, motionless, for hours, gazing straight before him at Leclère, and hating him with his bitter eyes.

Often the man felt that he had bucked against the very essence of life—the unconquerable essence that swept the hawk down out of the sky like a feathered thunderbolt, that drove the great grey goose across the zones, that hurled the spawning salmon through two thousand miles of boiling Yukon flood. At such times he felt impelled to express his own unconquerable essence; and with strong drink, wild music, and Bâtard, he indulged in vast orgies, wherein he pitted his puny strength in the face of things, and challenged all that was, and had been, and was yet to be.

"Dere is somet'ing dere," he affirmed, when the rhymed vagaries of his mind touched the secret chords of Bâtard's being and brought forth the long lugubrious howl. "Ah pool eet out wid bot' my han's, so, an' so. Ha! Ha! Eet is fonee! Eet is ver' fonee! De priest chant, de womans pray, de mans swear, de leetle bird go *peep-peep,* Bâtard, heem go *yow-yow*—an' eet is all de ver' same t'ing. Ha! Ha!"

Father Gautier, a worthy priest, once reproved him with instances of concrete perdition. He never reproved him again.

"Eet may be so, *mon père,*" he made answer. "An' Ah t'ink Ah go troo hell a-snappin', lak de hemlock troo de fire. Eh, *mon père?*"

But all bad things come to an end as well as good, and so with Black Leclère. On the summer low water, in a poling boat, he left McDougall for Sunrise. He left McDougall in company with Timothy Brown, and arrived at Sunrise by himself. Further, it was known that they had quarrelled just previous to pulling out; for the *Lizzie,* a wheezy ten-ton stern-wheeler, twenty-four hours behind, beat Leclère in by three days. And when he did get in, it was with a clean-drilled bullet hole through his shoulder muscle, and a tale of ambush and murder.

A strike had been made at Sunrise, and things had changed considerably. With the infusion of several hundred gold-seekers, a deal of whisky, and half-a-dozen equipped gamblers, the missionary had seen the page of his years of labour with the Indians wiped clean. When the squaws became preoccupied with cooking beans and keeping the fire going for the wifeless miners, and the bucks with swapping their warm furs for black bottles and broken timepieces, he took to his bed, said "Bless me" several times, and departed to his final accounting in a rough-hewn, oblong box. Whereupon the gamblers moved their roulette and faro tables into the mission house, and the click of chips and clink of glasses went up from dawn till dark and to dawn again.

Now Timothy Brown was well beloved among these adventurers of the North. The one thing against him was his quick temper and ready fist,—a little thing, for which his kind heart and forgiving hand more than atoned. On the other hand, there was nothing to atone for Black Leclère. He was "black," as more than one remembered deed bore witness, while he was as well hated as the other was beloved. So the men of Sunrise put an antiseptic dressing on his shoulder and hauled him before Judge Lynch.

It was a simple affair. He had quarrelled with Timothy Brown at McDougall. With Timothy Brown he had left McDougall. Without Timothy Brown he had arrived at Sunrise. Considered in the light of his evilness, the unanimous conclusion was that he had killed Timothy Brown. On the other hand, Leclère acknowledged their facts, but challenged their conclusion, and gave his own explanation. Twenty miles out of Sunrise he and Timothy Brown were poling the boat along the rocky shore. From that shore two rifle-shots rang out. Timothy Brown pitched out of the boat and went down bubbling red, and that was the last of Timothy Brown. He, Leclère, pitched into the bottom of the boat with a stinging shoulder. He lay very quiet, peeping at the shore. After a time two Indians stuck up their heads and came out to the water's edge, carrying between them a birch-bark canoe. As they launched it, Leclère let fly. He potted one, who went over the side after the manner of Timothy Brown. The other dropped into the bottom of the canoe, and then canoe and poling boat went down the stream in a drifting battle. After that they hung up on a split current, and the canoe passed on one side of an island, the poling boat on the other. That was the last of the canoe, and he came on into Sunrise. Yes, from the way the Indian in the canoe jumped, he was sure he had potted him. That was all. This explanation was not deemed adequate. They gave him ten hours' grace while the *Lizzie* steamed down to investigate. Ten hours later she came wheezing back to Sunrise. There had been nothing to investigate. No evidence had been found to back up his statements. They told him to make his will, for he possessed a fifty-thousand-dollar Sunrise claim, and they were a law-abiding as well as a law-giving breed.

Leclère shrugged his shoulders. "Bot one t'ing," he said; "a leetle w'at you call, favour—a leetle favour, dat is eet. I gif my feefty t'ousan' dollair to de church. I gif my husky dog, Bâtard, to de devil. De leetle favour? Firs' you hang heem, an' den you hang me. Eet is good, eh?"

Good it was, they agreed, that Hell's Spawn should break trail for his master across the last divide, and the court was adjourned down to the river bank, where a big spruce tree stood by itself. Slackwater Charley put a hangman's knot in the end of a hauling-line, and the noose was slipped over Leclère's head and pulled tight around his neck. His hands were tied behind his back, and he was assisted to the top of a cracker box. Then the running end of the line was passed over an overhanging branch, drawn taut, and made fast. To kick the box out from under would leave him dancing on the air.

"Now for the dog," said Webster Shaw, sometime mining engineer. "You'll have to rope him, Slackwater."

Leclère grinned. Slackwater took a chew of tobacco, rove a running noose, and proceeded leisurely to coil a few turns in his hand. He paused once or twice to brush particularly offensive mosquitoes from off his face. Everybody was brushing mosquitoes, except Leclère, about whose head a small cloud was visible. Even Bâtard, lying full-stretched on the ground, with his fore paws rubbed the pests away from eyes and mouth.

But while Slackwater waited for Bâtard to lift his head, a faint call came from the quiet air, and a man was seen waving his arms and running across the flat from Sunrise. It was the storekeeper.

"C-call 'er off, boys," he panted, as he came in among them.

"Little Sandy and Bernadotte's jes' got in," he explained with returning breath. "Landed down below an' come up by the short cut. Got the Beaver with 'm. Picked 'm up in his canoe, stuck in a back channel, with a couple of bullet-holes in 'm. Other buck was Klok-Kutz, the one that knocked spots out of his squaw and dusted."

"Eh? W'at Ah say? Eh?" Leclère cried exultantly. "Dat de one fo' sure! Ah know. Ah spik true."

"The thing to do is to teach these damned Siwashes a little manners," spoke Webster Shaw. "They're getting fat and sassy, and we'll have to bring them down a peg. Round in all the bucks and string up the Beaver for an object lesson. That's the programme. Come on and let's see what he's got to say for himself."

"Heh, *M'sieu*!" Leclère called, as the crowd began to melt away through the twilight in the direction of Sunrise. "Ah lak ver' moch to see de fon."

"Oh, we'll turn you loose when we come back," Webster Shaw shouted over his shoulder. "In the meantime meditate on your sins and the ways of providence. It will do you good, so be grateful."

As is the way with men who are accustomed to great hazards, whose nerves are healthy and trained in patience, so it was with Leclère, who settled himself to the long wait—which is to say that he reconciled his mind to it. There was no settling of the body, for the taut rope forced him to stand rigidly erect. The least relaxation of the leg muscles pressed the rough-fibred noose into his neck, while the upright position caused him much pain in his wounded shoulder. He projected his under lip and expelled his breath upwards along his face, to blow the mosquitoes away from his eyes. But the situation had its compensation. To be snatched from the maw of death was well worth a little bodily suffering, only it was unfortunate that he should miss the hanging of the Beaver.

And so he mused, till his eyes chanced to fall upon Bâtard, head between fore paws and stretched on the ground asleep. And then Leclère ceased to muse. He studied the animal closely, striving to sense if the sleep were real or feigned. Bâtard's sides were heaving regularly, but Leclère felt that the breath came and went a shade too quickly; also he felt that there was a vigilance or alertness to every hair that belied unshackling sleep. He would have given his Sunrise claim to be assured that the dog was not awake, and once, when one of his joints cracked, he looked quickly and guiltily at Bâtard to see if he roused. He did not rouse then but a few minutes later he got up slowly and lazily, stretched, and looked carefully about him.

*"Sacredam,"* said Leclère under his breath. Assured that no one was in sight or hearing, Bâtard sat down, curled his upper lip almost into a smile, looked up at Leclère, and licked his chops.

"Ah see my feenish," the man said, and laughed sardonically aloud.

Bâtard came nearer, the useless ear wabbling, the good ear cocked forward with devilish comprehension. He thrust his head on one side quizzically, and advanced with mincing, playful steps. He rubbed his body gently against the box till it shook and shook again. Leclère teetered carefully to maintain his equilibrium.

"Bâtard," he said calmly, "look out. Ah keel you."

Bâtard snarled at the word, and shook the box with greater force. Then he upreared, and with his fore paws threw his weight against it higher up. Leclère kicked out with one foot, but the rope bit into his neck and checked so abruptly as nearly to overbalance him.

"Hi, ya! *Chook! Mush-on!"* he screamed.

Bâtard retreated, for twenty feet or so, with a fiendish levity in his bearing that Leclère could not mistake. He remembered the dog often breaking the scum of ice on the water hole by lifting up and throwing his weight upon it; and remembering, he understood what he now had in mind. Bâtard faced about and paused. He showed his white teeth in a grin, which Leclère answered; and then hurled his body through the air, in full charge, straight for the box.

Fifteen minutes later, Slackwater Charley and Webster Shaw, returning, caught a glimpse of a ghostly pendulum swinging back and forth in the dim light. As they hurriedly drew in closer, they made out the man's inert body, and a live thing that clung to it, and shook and worried, and gave to it the swaying motion.

"Hi ya! *Chook!* you Spawn of Hell," yelled Webster Shaw.

But Bâtard glared at him, and snarled threateningly, without loosing his jaws.

Slackwater Charley got out his revolver, but his hand was shaking, as with a chill, and he fumbled.

"Here, you take it," he said, passing the weapon over.

Webster Shaw laughed shortly, drew a sight between the gleaming eyes, and pressed the trigger. Bâtard's body twitched with the shock, threshed the ground spasmodically for a moment, and went suddenly limp. But his teeth still held fast locked.

# Chapter 4

## Letters From Jack London

The letters presented in this brief collection in general catalog Jack London's "rise to fame." Since London himself never wrote an autobiography, perhaps these early letters will also suggest his own assessment of both how and why he came to write. In the process one sees London's sources for some of his ideas, including those with which he deals in *The Call of the Wild*.

All letters used in this chapter are from *Letters from Jack London,* edited by King Hendricks and Irving Shepard (New York: Odyssey Press, 1965), and are reprinted with permission of Western Publishing Co.

## To Anna Strunsky

Oakland, Calif.

Jan. 21, 1900

Dear Miss Strunsky:—

O Pshaw!

Dear Anna:—

There! Let's get our friendship down to a comfortable basis. The superscription, "Miss Strunsky," is as disagreeable as the putting on of a white collar, and both are equally detestable. I did not read your last till Friday morning, and the day and evening were taken up. But at last I am free. My visitors are gone, the one back to his desert hermitage, and the other to his own country. And I have much work to make up. Do you know, I have the fatal faculty of making friends, and lack the blessed trait of being able to quarrel with them. And they are constantly turning up. My home is the Mecca of every returned Klondiker, sailor, or soldier of fortune I ever met. Some day I shall build an establishment, invite them all, and turn them loose upon each other. Such a mingling of castes and creeds and characters could not be duplicated. The destruction would be great.

However, I am so overjoyed at being free that I cannot be anything but foolish. I shall, with pitfall and with gin, beset the road my visitors do wander in; and among other things, erect a Maxim rapid-fire gun just within my front door. The sanctity of my fireside shall be inviolate. Or, should my heart fail me, I'll run away to the other side of the world.

Find enclosed, review of Mary Antin's book. Had I not known you I could not have understood the little which I do. Somehow we must ever build upon the concrete. To illustrate: do you notice the same in excerpt from her, beginning, "I thought of tempests and shipwrecks." How I would like to know the girl, to see her, to talk with her, to do a little toward cherishing her imagination. I sometimes weep at the grave of mine. It was sown on arid soil, gave vague promises of budding, but was crushed out by the harshness of things—a mixed metaphor, I believe.

"Like most modern Jewesses who have written, she is, I fear, destined to spiritual suffering." How that haunts one!

Ho! ho! I have just returned from the window. Turmoil and strife called me from the machine, and behold! My nephew [Johnny Miller], into whom it is my wish to inculcate some of the saltiness of the earth, had closed in combat with an ancient enemy in the form of a truculent Irish boy. There they were, hard at it, boxing gloves of course, and it certainly did me good to see the way in which he stood up to it. Only, alas, I see I shall have to soon give him instructions, especially in defense—all powder and flash and snappy in attack, but forgetful of guarding himself. "For life is strife," and a physical coward is the most unutterable of abominations.

Tell me what you think of Ms. It was the work of my golden youth. When I look upon it I feel very old. It has knocked from pillar to post and reposed in all manner of places. When my soul waxes riotous, I bring it forth, and lo! I am again a lamb. It cures all ills of the ego and is a sovereign remedy for self-conceit. "Mistake" is writ broad in fiery letters. The influences at work in me, from Zangwill to Marx, are obvious. I would have portrayed types and ideals of which I knew nothing, and so, trusted myself to false wings. You showed me your earliest printed production last night; reciprocating, I show you one written at the time I first knew Hamilton. I felt I had something there, but I certainly missed it. Some day, putting it at the bottom of the deepest of chests, I shall reattempt it.

Tell me the weak points, not of course in diction, etc. Tell me what rings false to you. And be unsparing, else shall I have to class you with the rest of my friends, and it is not complimentary to them if they only knew it.

One has so much to say that the best course is to not say anything. Paper was made for business correspondence and for invitations; while the tongue is too often geared at too high a pitch to adequately carry on its labors.

Very sincerely,
Jack London

P.S. Your Stanford address? I have forgotten it. Is it "Stanford University," or "Palo Alto"?

## To Houghton Mifflin Company

Oakland, Calif.
Jan. 31, 1900

Gentlemen:

In reply to yours of January 25th. requesting additional biographical data. I see I shall have to piece out my previous narrative, which, in turn, will make this choppy.

My father was Pennsylvania-born, a soldier, scout, backwoodsman, trapper, and wanderer. My mother was born in Ohio. Both came west independently, meeting and marrying in San Francisco, where I was born January 12, 1876. What little city life I then passed was in my babyhood. My life, from my fourth to my ninth years, was spent upon Californian ranches. I learned to read and write about my fifth year, though I do not remember anything about it. I always could read and write, and have no recollection antedating such a condition. Folks say I simply insisted upon being taught. Was an omnivorous reader, principally because reading matter was scarce and I had to be grateful for whatever fell into my hands. Remember reading some of Trowbridge's works for boys at six years of age. At seven I was reading Paul du Chaillu's *Travels,* Captain Cook's *Voyages,* and *Life of Garfield.* All through this period I devoured what Seaside Library novels I could borrow from the womenfolk and dime novels from the farm hands. At eight I was deep in Ouida and Washington Irving. Also during this period read a great deal of American History. Also, life on a Californian ranch is not very nourishing to the imagination.

Somewhere around my ninth year we removed to Oakland, which, today, I believe, is a town of about eighty thousand, and is removed by thirty minutes from the heart of San Francisco. Here, most precious to me was a free library. Since that time Oakland has been my home seat. Here my father died, and here I yet live with my mother. I have not married—the world is too large and its call too insistent.

However, from my ninth year, with the exception of the hours spent at school (and I earned them by hard labor), my life has been one of toil. It is worthless to give the long sordid list of occupations, none of them trades, all heavy manual labor. Of course I continued to read. Was never without a book. My education was popular, graduating from the grammar school at about fourteen. Took a taste for the water. At fifteen left home and went upon a Bay life. San Francisco Bay is no mill pond by the way. I was a salmon fisher, an oyster pirate, a schooner sailor, a fish patrolman, a longshoreman, and a general sort of bay-faring adventurer—a boy in years and a man amongst men. Always a book, and always reading when the rest were asleep; when they were awake I was one with them, for I was always a good comrade.

Within a week of my seventeenth birthday I shipped before the mast as sailor on a three top-mast sealing schooner. We went to Japan and hunted along the coast north to the Russian side of Bering Sea. This was my longest voyage; I could not again endure one of such length; not because it was tedious or long, but because life was so short. However, I have made short voyages, too brief to mention, and today am at home in any forecastle or stokehold—good comradeship, you know. I believe this comprises my travels; for I spoke at length in previous letter concerning my tramping and Klondiking. Have been all over Canada, Northwest Ty., Alaska, etc., etc., at different times, besides mining, prospecting and wandering through the Sierra Nevadas.

I have outlined my education. In the main I am self-educated; have had no mentor but myself. High school or college curriculums I simply selected from, finding it impossible to follow the rut—life and pocket book were both too short. I attended the first year of high school (Oakland), then stayed at home, without coaching, and crammed the next two years into three months and took the entrance examination, and entered the University of California at Berkeley. Was forced, much against my inclinations, to give this over just prior to the completion of my Freshman Year.

My father died while I was in the Klondike, and I returned home to take up the reins.

As to literary work: My first magazine article (I had done no newspaper work), was published in January, 1899; it is now the fifth story in the *"Son of the Wolf."* Since then I have done work for *The Overland Monthly, The Atlantic, The Wave, The Arena, The Youth's Companion, The Review of Reviews,* etc., etc., besides a host of lesser publications, and to say nothing of newspaper and syndicate work. Hackwork all, or nearly so, from a comic joke or triolet to pseudoscientific disquisitions upon things about which I knew nothing. Hackwork for dollars, that's all, setting aside practically all ambitious efforts to some future period of less financial stringence. Thus, my literary life is just thirteen months old today.

Naturally, my reading early bred in me a desire to write, but my manner of life prevented me attempting it. I have had no literary help or advice of any kind—just been sort of hammering around in the dark till I knocked holes through here and there and caught glimpses of daylight. Common knowledge of magazine methods, etc., came to me as revelation. Not a soul to say here you are and there you mistake.

Of course, during my revolutionary period I perpetrated my opinions upon the public through the medium of the local papers, gratis. But that was years ago when I went to high school and was more notorious than esteemed. Once, by the way, returned from my sealing voyage, I won a prize essay* of twenty-five dollars from a San Francisco paper over the heads of Stanford and California Universities, both of which were represented by second and third place through their undergraduates. This gave me hope for achieving something ultimately.

After my tramping trip I started to high school in 1895. I entered the University of California in 1896. Thus, had I continued, I would be just now preparing to take my sheepskin.

As to studies: I am always studying. The aim of the university is simply to prepare one for a whole future life of study. I have been denied this advantage, but am knocking along somehow. Never a night (whether I have gone out or not), but the last several hours are spent in bed with my books. All things interest me—the world is so very good. Principal studies are, scientific, sociological, and ethical—these, of course, including biology, economics, psychology, physiology, history, etc., etc., without end. And I strive, also, to not neglect literature.

Am healthy, love exercise, and take little. Shall pay the penalty some day.

There, I can't think of anything else. I know what data I have furnished is wretched, but autobiography is not entertaining to a narrator who is sick of it. Should you require further information, just specify, and I shall be pleased to supply it. Also, I shall be grateful for the privilege of looking over the biographical note before it is printed.

Very truly yours,
Jack London

---

*"Typhoon off the Coast of Japan," San Francisco *Morning Call,* 1893.

*To Cloudesley Johns*

Oakland, Calif.,
Jan. 6, 1902

Dear Cloudesley:—

But after all, what squirming, anywhere, damned or otherwise, means anything? That's the question I am always prone to put: What's this chemical ferment called life all about? Small wonder that small men down the ages have conjured gods in answer. A little god is a snug little possession and explains it all. But how about you and me, who have no god?

I have at last discovered what I am. I am a materialistic monist, and there's damn little satisfaction in it.

I am at work on a short story that no self-respecting bourgeois magazine will ever have anything to do with. In conception it is really one of your stories. It's a crackerjack. If it's ever published I'll let you know. If not, we'll wait until you come west again.

As regards "effete respectability," I haven't any, and I don't have anything to do with any who have . . . except magazines. Nevertheless I shall be impelled to strong drink if something exciting doesn't happen along pretty soon.

My dear boy, nobody can help himself in anything, and heaven helps no one. Man is not a free agent, and free will is a fallacy exploded by science long ago. Here is what we are: —or, better still, I'll give you Fish's definition: "Philosophical materialism holds that matter and the motion of matter make up the sum total of existence, and that what we know as psychical phenomena in man and other animals are to be interpreted in an ultimate analysis as simply the peculiar aspect which is assumed by certain enormously complicated motions of matter." That is what we are, and we move along the line of least resistance. Whatever we do, we do because it is easier to than not to. No man ever lived who didn't do the easiest thing (for him).

Or, as Pascal puts it: "In the just and the unjust we find hardly anything which does not change its character in changing its climate. Three degrees of an elevation of the pole reverses the whole jurisprudence. A meridian is decisive of truth; and a few years, of possession. Fundamental laws change. Right has its epochs. A pleasant justice which a river or a mountain limits. Truth this side the Pyrenees; error on the other."

Nay, nay. We are what we are, and we cannot help ourselves. No man is to be blamed, and no man praised.

Yes, (W.H.) Cosgrave* wrote me instanter about the letters. I am afraid they're not for him. They would be utter Greek. Say, Cloudesley, did you ever reflect on the yellow magazinism of the magazines? Cosgrave says I ought not to write for the *Examiner*. And in same breath he says he will take what I write if I write what he wants. O ye gods! Neither the *Examiner* nor *Everybody's* wants masterpieces, art, and where's the difference in the sacrifice on my part?

You mention Sedgewick of *Leslie's*. Do you mean weekly or monthly *Leslie's?* And what are his initials?

Well, in six days I shall be twenty-six years old, and in nine days Joan will be one year old. Did you know we named her Joan?

Jack London


*To George P. Brett****

Piedmont, Calif.
March 10, 1903

Dear Mr. Brett:—

I am glad you like the *Call of the Wild,* but, unfortunately, I cannot accept your offer for all rights in it. You see, the *Saturday*

---

*An editor of *Everybody's* magazine.

**President of the Macmillan Co.

*Evening Post* bought the American serial rights of it, and already have sent me over half of the proof-sheets; while Watt & Son are handling the English serial sale of it.

The whole history of this story has been very rapid. On my return from England I sat down to write it into a 4000 word yarn, but it got away from me & I was forced to expand it to its present length. I was working on it when you came to see me in January. At the time I had made up my mind to let you carry the uncompleted duplicate away with you; but somehow the conversation did not lead up to it & I became diffident. Then I sent a copy to the *Saturday Evening Post* and they at once accepted it.

They have paid me three cents a word for the American serial rights. This was the money I intended dividing between my debts and my South Sea trip. But when it arrived last week, my debts loomed so large & the South Seas loomed so expensive, that I compromised matters and bought a sloop-yacht [*The Spray*] for San Francisco Bay. It is now hauled out & being fitted up. I shall live on it a great deal, and on it I shall write the greater part of my sea-novel. The sloop is old, but it is roomy & fast. I can stand upright in the cabin which is quite large. I'll send you a picture of her some time.

I did not like the title, *The Call of the Wild,* and neither did the *Saturday Evening Post.* I racked my brains for a better title, & suggested *The Sleeping Wolf.* They, however, if in the meantime they do not hit upon a better title, are going to publish it in the *Post* under *The Wolf.** This I do not like so well as *The Sleeping Wolf,* which I do not like very much either. There is a good title somewhere, if we can only lay hold of it.

The *Saturday Evening Post,* as first buyer, reserved the right of setting date for simultaneous serial publication in England & America, so they would be the ones to write to in this connection. Of course, they will illustrate it.

I should have been glad to close with your offer, both for the sake of the cash & of the experiment you mention; but, as I have explained, the serial right has passed out of my hands. As a book, however, under the circumstances as they are, you may succeed in getting a fair sale out of it.

---

*\*The Saturday Evening Post* used the title *Call of the Wild.*

I shall shortly make a rough sketch of the map for the frontispiece of *Fish Patrol Stories*. The difficulty with *Youth's Companion* is that they may not publish it serially for a good time to come.

Will you please send me five copies of *Children of the Frost* (if they have not already been sent), and also, one copy of *Guns, Ammunition, and Tackle*, & charge to my account.

Sincerely yours,
Jack London

## To George P. Brett

Piedmont, Calif.
March 25, 1903

Dear Mr. Brett:—

I have telegraphed you today accepting your offer for *The Call of the Wild*.*

I had thought, previous to receiving this last letter from you, that my already having disposed of serial rights had knocked in the head whatever plan you had entertained for the publishing of the book. I cannot tell how glad I am that I was mistaken.

I am sure that pushing the book in the manner you mention will be of the utmost value to me, giving me, as you say, an audience for subsequent books. It is the audience already gathered, as I do hope you will gather in this case, that counts.

Concerning title, I must confess to a sneaking preference for *The Call of the Wild*. But, under any circumstance, I want the decision

---

*Brett offered London $2,000 for publishing rights (outright sale), no royalties. London received $700 from *The Saturday Evening Post*. So for a book that has sold nearly 2 million copies, London received $2,700.

of the title to rest with you. You know the publishing end of it, and the market value of titles, as I could not dream to know.

You may send the contract along at your convenience for me to sign. And I cannot convey to you the greatness of my pleasure at knowing that the book has struck you favorably; for I feel, therefore, that it is an earnest of the work I hope to do for you when I find myself. And find myself I will, some day.

Concerning the *Kempton-Wace Letters,* I am rushing the proofs through as fast as they arrive.

The covers you mention sending will probably arrive in this afternoon's mail, when I shall at once state my preference.

As the *Letters* come out anonymously, they should not collide with the dog story at all.

Sincerely yours,<br>Jack London

P.S. Do you remember what I told you of the nationality of Joseph Conrad? It is correct. He was a Polish boy who ran away to sea from Poland.

## To Anna Strunsky

Oakland, Calif.<br>Oct. 13, 1904

Dear Anna:—

The movement of this is too rapid and sketchy. It is too much in the form of a narrative, and narrative, in a short story, is only good when it is in the first person.

The subject merits greater length. Make longer scenes, dialogues, between them.

And then you quit too suddenly, too abruptly. It is not rounded to its end, but chopped off with a hatchet.

You should elaborate the development of his apparent madness, his own psychology, the psychology of the cruelty of the East Side idealists—as you did for me by word of mouth.

My criticism is, in short, that you have taken a splendid subject and not extracted its full splendor. You have mastery of it (the subject), full mastery,—you *understand;* yet you have not so expressed your understanding as to make the reader understand. And this same criticism I would make in general of all your short stories.

Remember this—confine a short story within the shortest possible time-limit—a day, an hour, if possible—or, if, as sometimes with the best of short stories, a long period of time must be covered,—months—merely hint or sketch (incidentally) the passage of time, and tell the story only in its crucial moments.

Really, you know, development does not belong in the short story, but in the novel.

The short story is a rounded fragment from life, a single mood, situation, or action.

Now don't think me egotistical because I refer you to my stories—I have them at the ends of my fingers, so I save time by mentioning them. Take down and open *Son of the Wolf.*

The first eight deal with single situations, though several of them cover fairly long periods of time—the time is sketched and made subordinate to the final situation. You see, the situation is considered primarily— "The Son of the Wolf" in beginning is hungry for woman, he goes to get one; the situation is how he got one.

"The Priestly Prerogative" is the scene in the cabin—the rest is introductory, preliminary.

"The Wife of a King"—not a good short story in any sense.

"The Odyssey of the North"—covering a long period of time, in first person, so that long period of time (the whole life of Naass) is exploited in an hour and a half in Malemute Kid's cabin.

Take down and open *God of His Fathers.*

First story, single situation.

"Great Interrogation"—single situation in cabin where whole past history of man and woman is exploited. And so on, to the last story,

"Scorn of Women"—see in it how time is always sketched and situation is exploited—yet it is not a short story.

And so forth and so forth.

Am sending you "The Nose" ("A Nose for the King") for a wee bit of a smile.

Jack London

## To George P. Brett

Oakland, Calif.
Dec. 5, 1904

Dear Mr. Brett:—

I'm dropping you a line hot with the idea. I have the idea for the next book I shall write—along the first part of next year.

Not a sequel to    *Call of the Wild.*

But a companion to   "   "   "   "

I'm going to reverse the process.

Instead of devolution or decivilization of a dog, I'm going to give the evolution, the civilization of a dog—development of domesticity, faithfulness, love, morality, and all the amenities and virtues.

And it will be a *proper* companion-book—in the same style, grasp, concrete way. Have already mapped part of it out. A complete antithesis to the *Call of the Wild.* And with that book as a forerunner, it should make a hit.

What d' ye think?*

Jack London

---

*The letter refers to *White Fang.*

## To C. F. Lowrie

Los Angeles, Calif.
Jan. 13, 1911

Dear Comrade Lowrie:

In reply to yours of Jan. 5. I certainly must have met Miss Dopp, because she says so, and I see my mistake of mixing her up with Mary E. Marcy; but if Miss Dopp could only realize that in the course of the year I meet several thousand people whom I never meet again, she would understand how impossible it is for me to remember her.

I wrote *Before Adam* because I quarreled with the science of Stanley Waterloo in his *Story of Ab*. In one generation he had his primitive men discover fire, domesticate the dog and the horse, invent the bow and arrow and the spear, and achieve an intricate tribal development. To myself, I said this was impossible. Primitive man developed very slowly. Therefore I wrote *Before Adam* to show two things, (1) the mistakes and lost off-shoots in the process of biologic evolution; and (2) that in a single generation the only device primitive man, in my story, invented, was the carrying of water and berries in gourds. Gosh—if you knew all my troubles with persons of the Miss Dopp variety, you would not soothingly suggest to me that I should not lose "any more sleep over the matter." Believe me, I sleep like a babe, these people jump into me, I slam back, and the thing is forgotten the next instant.

Yours for the Revolution,
Jack London

## To Ralph Kasper*

Glen Ellen, Calif.
June 25, 1914

Dear Ralph Kasper:—

Just a rush line to you. I have come back from Mexico, and at present time am catching up, as usual, with my correspondence, and in addition recovering from an attack of rotten bacillary dysentary, hence, my inevitable, as usual, rush.

I have always inclined toward Haeckel's position. In fact, "incline" is too weak a word. I am a hopeless materialist. I see the soul as nothing else than the sum of the activities of the organism plus personal habits, memories, and experiences of the organism, plus inherited habits, memories, experiences, of the organism. *I believe that when I am dead, I am dead. I believe that with my death I am just as much obliterated as the last mosquito you or I smashed.*

I have no patience with fly-by-night philosophers such as Bergson. I have no patience with the metaphysical philosophers. With them, always, the wish is parent to the thought, and their wish is parent to their profoundest philosophical conclusions. I join with Haeckel in being what, in lieu of any other phrase, I am compelled to call "a positive scientific thinker."

Please forgive rush,

Sincerely yours,
Jack London

---

*Member of the International Typographical Union, Socialist, and a close friend of London's.

# Chapter 5

# Gold Creek
# and
# Gold Town*

*From *Jack London and the Klondike,* by Franklin Walker (San Marino, Calif: The Huntington Library, 1966, pp. 101-24). Reprinted courtesy of the Henry E. Huntington Library and Art Gallery.

Gold is what they had come for, and, if they wished to do any prospecting before deep winter set in, it was now or never. Plans to search for a strike up the Stewart were quickly abandoned when an old-timer assured the new party that the Stewart was half-frozen and that for some days to come movement up it would be impractical. More promising hunting lay in the opposite direction. Some three or four miles down the Yukon a small stream, Henderson Creek, flowed into the river from the right; rumour had it that there might be gold in its sands. On Monday, October 11, Jim Goodman, the only experienced placer miner in the group, set out to see if he could find any likely ground on the Henderson. By evening he was back with word that he had got some good colours.

Tuesday bright and early Jim Goodman and Jack London, accompanied by two other gold-seekers referred to by Thompson as "Charles and Elma," set out for the Henderson, where they spent three days prospecting. Thompson and Sloper remained at the cabin, baking yeast bread, biscuits, and pies, sharpening tools, making a sled. Their domesticity was given a note of excitement when, on Wednesday the thirteenth of October, so much slush ice came in from the Stewart that Thompson felt it likely the Yukon was freezing up and that boat traffic downriver was at an end for the season. This was the date which tradition had set as a likely one for the closing. But boats continued on that day, the next, and the next—in fact, in 1897 boats continued to get through to Dawson until early November. By the time the boys returned from Henderson, Thompson and his companions were ready to take their chances on getting down to Dawson by boat and returning later on the ice. They could thus file gold claims, see old friends, and get the lay of the land.

How much gold London and Goodman found on the Henderson during those October days is hard to say. They had some success, according to Thompson's diary. "Boys got back from Henderson, staked 8 claims." How the claims were to be divided up is not clear. But we do know from the mining records in Dawson that Jack London filed papers for a claim, "more particularly described as placer mining claim No. 54 on the Left Fork ascending Henderson Creek in the aforesaid Mining Division."[1] "I solemnly swear that I have discovered therein a deposit of Gold," London was to affirm before the Gold Commissioner in Dawson.

How much of a thrill was it to see that gold, how much of a pan did he wash out? Did he actually find only "fool's gold," as one persistent yarn maintains? Certainly the story told by Thompson in his old age to Irving Stone that London had been so misled is not very persuasive. In the first place, stories of this sort are stock-in-trade for making famous men look like fools. In addition, Thompson was not with London when he staked on the Henderson, and the experienced Goodman, who was, was not likely to make such an error. Later on in the winter London was to lie grinning in his bunk while Thompson would daydream about how much wealth they would get from the creek in the following summer. He probably grinned because he knew that, though there was pay dirt there, it was not rich enough to make strenuous effort pay off. Two years later, after London had returned to Oakland, he wrote to a friend in the Klondike asking about Thompson, who was still pursuing the will-o'-the-wisp in the Northland: he imagined him "with wilder schemes than ever in his head: and smoking good cigars while doing nothing."[2]

Still, there must have been a thrill even in the act of panning for gold in the wilderness, and the sight of a streak was enough to make the world seem rosy. In his fiction, London has his hero in *Burning Daylight* enjoy the thrill of discovery to the fullest.

One day in December Daylight filled a pan from bedrock on his own claim and carried it into his cabin. Here a fire burned and enabled him to keep water unfrozen in a canvas tank. He squatted over the tank and began to wash. Earth and gravel seemed to fill the pan. As he imparted to it a circular movement, the lighter, coarser particles washed out over the edge. At times he combed the surface with his fingers, raking out handfuls of gravel. The contents of the pan diminished. As it drew near to the bottom, for the purpose of fleeting and tentative examination, he gave the pan a sudden sloshing movement, emptying it of water. And the whole bottom showed as if covered with butter. Thus the yellow gold flashed up as the muddy water was flirted away. It was gold—gold-dust, coarse, gold nuggets, large nuggets. He was all alone. He set the pan down for a moment and thought long thoughts. Then he finished the washing, and weighed the results in his scales. At the rate of sixteen dollars to the ounce, the pan had contained seven hundred and odd dollars. It was beyond anything that even he had dreamed.

No such reality for London. The job for the moment was to stake, then to file in Dawson, and then decide whether to work the claim or not. To set or blaze the two centre stakes and four corner stakes was not a difficult matter, and a notice assured those to come after him that London laid claim to five hundred feet of stream bed, from rimrock to rimrock, "260,000 square feet," as he was to estimate in Dawson.

London's gold claim may not have been based, however, on any extensive prospecting or panning for colours. London may not, in fact, have seen any colour in his pan at all. As Harold A. Innis has pointed out in *Settlement and the Mining Frontier,* with the proliferation of claims on the Yukon much land was staked on pure speculation. The saying went, "All the prospecting tools a man needs now is an axe and a lead-pencil," and the phrase "pool-room prospecting" became a commonplace. In June, 1897, there were eight hundred claims on record in Dawson; by January, 1898, there were five thousand; and that number had increased to seventeen thousand by September, 1898. The majority of these claims were forfeited because of failure to work on them. This was the case with London's claim; the records show it reverted to the Crown after his departure, was taken out again by a man named Ritchie in 1901, who kept it registered until 1904, when he in turn abandoned it. Today the area where the claim lay is being profitably worked by gold dredges.

Innis points out some of the reasons that very few Klondikers became successful miners; London was certainly one of the vast majority.

The rich creeks were staked in the main by miners who were in the Yukon before the strike at Bonanza and who had the advantage of experience with the peculiar problems of the district. The art of handling frozen ground and of sinking shafts to the bedrock of creeks and drifting across the channel to discover the pay streak had been developed, as we have seen, before the discovery of the Klondike. On the other hand, "so much more is being learned that it may truthfully be said that it has taken the second year at Klondike to develop the Yukon placer expert." Work began as soon as the frost dried up the surface water of the creeks. Wood to the extent of possibly 30 cords of pine, spruce, and birch was cut during the summer in preparation for burning and thawing. The upper layer of muck was picked or thawed and shovelled out. When the shaft of about 4 feet x 6 feet reached an inconvenient depth for shovelling, a rope windlass was erected and the dirt hoisted up by bucket. By placing the windlass at the top of cribbing above the shaft labour in disposing the dump was reduced, the latter being gradually piled up around the cribbing. After penetration through the muck, gravel was reached and it was necessary to depend on thawing. Dry and green wood were hauled to the shaft on dog sleds, split to a required fineness and taken to the bottom. A layer of finely split dry spruce was covered by heavier pieces of very dry wood and in turn by green wood. The latter was intended to lengthen the time of burning and to hold in heat. Candles were necessary to raise the temperature of the pine and to light it.

And so the story goes. It took a month to cut down to bedrock, perhaps another month to drift across the streak. Thawed earth had to be panned for gold to see if you were on the right trail. (Twenty-five cents a pan was considered very rich gravel, while ten cents a pan corresponded to an adequate wage in the States.) These operations were restricted to four or five months, say November to March. After that, the moderation of temperature made the mining unsafe. When warm weather finally arrived, you washed your dump in sluice boxes, if you were fortunate enough to have the use of a good stream of water. Usually this involved going in with others to build a diversion dam and flume. All this took a good deal of faith, confidence in one's luck, and persistence. What chance that it would be done by amateurs on soil showing poor picking a few miles up the Henderson?

The boys were back from their prospecting by Friday evening, and on Saturday afternoon at 1:45 P.M., October 16, 1897, Thompson, London, "Charles and Elma" started downriver by boat for Dawson. They had with them enough stores to last for about three weeks, together with tent, blankets, and other camping equipment. "Went to get news, mail, etc. and post ourselves on the country in general, also to file our claims on Henderson," Thompson noted. They made twenty two miles before stopping for the night at the old station of Sixtymile, at the mouth of the tributary by that name which flowed into the West side of the Yukon; here were many empty cabins, a post store with no food to sell, and a good many boats headed for Dawson pulled up for the night.

Saturday, with two additional passengers, they made the final fifty-mile run to Dawson, stopping en route to cut some firewood, knowing that wood was scarce in the boom-town. They camped that night three miles short of their goal so that they would reach their destination in the morning with a day to get settled in. On Monday, October 18, they floated around a bend to see the famous Klondike flow in from their right. Klondike City, better known as Louse Town, lay before them just short of the noted tributary. Dawson City was on a spongy flat below a slide-scarred mountain on the far side of the shallow gold stream. The Yukon, unconcerned with man's paltry efforts, continued to move with majesty between steep hills as it swept past Dawson towards its big bend above the Arctic Circle.

They beached the *Yukon Belle* at Louse Town, where Thompson stayed with the outfits, while London and his new companions crossed the Klondike by ferry, climbed up the sixteen-foot bank which formed the south edge of Dawson, and set out to look for a camping place. While he waited, Thompson ran across some of the travellers from the *Belle of the Yukon* (Charles Rand, Dave Sullivan, and William Odette) and learned that Tarwater had nearly drowned "crossing the Klondyke River with his pack on his back." That pack did not contain much food, and Dawson was far from hospitable to men without outfits. Already, along with many others, Tarwater had been urged to continue downriver to Fort Yukon. By evening the party had encountered Louis W. Bond, who was known to some of them, and had set up camp by the Bond cabin.

London was to remain in Dawson somewhat over six weeks, leaving for Split-up Island on the third of December and arriving there on the seventh of December. During this period he had plenty of opportunity to get impressions of the gold city, which was to appear frequently in his fiction. His movements can no longer be followed in Thompson's diary, which ends on October 18. His reactions can, however, be built up to some extent from his fiction.

Dawson City that fall was no place to pick up one's spirits. It was cold, often shrouded in fog, its ramshackle shanties and leaky cabins inhabited by some five thousand restless and nearly panic-stricken sourdoughs and cheechakos. The shortage of food, which had created many rumours on the Chilkoot trail and which had driven Tarwater downriver, was the most pressing topic of the moment. As early as August, Inspector Charles Constantine of the North-west Mounted Police had written Ottawa, ". . . the outlook for grub is not assuring for the number of people here—about four thousand crazy or lazy men, chiefly American miners and toughs from the coast towns."[3] The prospect had got worse rather than better since then. River steamboats bringing food to the Klondike had first been shoaled in slack water and then frozen in at Fort Yukon, three hundred and fifty miles downriver; two steamboats that had got past Fort Yukon had been held up at Circle City and robbed of their supplies by desperate men even worse off than those in Dawson. About two weeks before London arrived, Inspector Constantine had posted a notice on Front Street:

> For those who have not laid in a winter's supply to remain longer is to court death from starvation, or at least the certainty of sickness from scurvy and other troubles. Starvation now stares everyone in the face who is hoping and waiting for outside relief. . . .[4]

In *A Daughter of the Snows* London pictures a tense Dawson City, the authorities fearful of the food shortage, making plans for getting as many people as possible out of town. The head of one of the big trading companies has just issued orders to scale down filling of warehouse requisitions to half the amount stipulated so that the food would last longer. A steamer is about to set off downriver with three hundred Klondikers willing to face short rations at Fort Yukon rather than starve in Dawson, where newcomers who had packed over the Chilkoot were frantically selling their outfits to buy dogs to trek back up again as soon as the ice was firm. Distressed Klondikers had posted many notices on the front of the big warehouse building: "Dogs lost, found, and for sale occupied some space, but the rest was devoted to notices of sales of outfits. The timid were already growing frightened. Outfits of five hundred pounds were offering at a dollar a pound, without flour; others, with flour, at a dollar and a half."

During the six weeks London spent in Dawson matters seemed at a standstill, with everyone awaiting the closing of the river. The weather of late October was fitful and changeable; finally, when the freeze, which would make sledding possible both to the mines and upriver to the Stewart and on to the Chilkoot and Dyea, seemed about at hand, a warm Chinook came along to prolong the suspense. The birches and aspens along the Yukon and on the slopes of Moosehide Mountain back of Dawson had long since turned fiery yellow-red and dropped their leaves; their ashen trunks had stood naked in the autumn winds for nearly two months. The Arctic hare and ptarmigan had turned from brown to white, the bears had gone into caves for their winter sleep, and the grey days had grown very short indeed before the longed-for freeze-up finally arrived. At last, one morning at the end of the first week in November men woke to find the river frozen.

Naturally, the freeze-up was more dramatic if you were making your way down river in a desperate attempt to reach Dawson before you were caught in the ice! London's description of Smoke Bellew and his companions making this final effort gives a vivid picture of one of the most characteristic phenomena of the Arctic regions.

> The sky was clear, and in the light of the cold, leaping stars they caught occasional glimpses of the loom of mountains on either hand. At eleven o'clock, from below, came a dull grinding roar. Their speed began to diminish and cakes of ice to up-end and crash and smash about them. The river was jamming. One cake, forced upward, slid across their cake and carried one side of the boat away. It did not sink, for its own cake still up-bore it, but in a whirl they saw dark water show for an instant within a foot of them. Then all movement ceased. At the end of half an hour, the whole river picked itself up and began to move. This continued for an hour, when again it was brought to rest by a jam. Once again it started, running swiftly and savagely, with a great grinding. Then they saw lights ashore, and, when abreast, gravity and the Yukon surrendered, and the river ceased for six months.

It was on November 5 that Dawson woke to find the river frozen. It was on this same day, according to the books in the gold-records office, that Jack London filed claim for his gold strike on Henderson Creek. This cost him ten dollars for a mining licence and fifteen dollars for filing his first claim. That he had waited eighteen days after reaching the capital of the North-west Territory before filing strongly suggests that he didn't put much faith in the claim. Or he may have been waiting to win the twenty-five dollars in a faro game. Or he may have been too busy talking to Klondikers and seeing the sights in Dawson. The last seems the most unlikely explanation for his delay, for the resources offered by Dawson gossip and sights were soon exhausted. London still had another month to look around before going back to Split-up Island.

The year-old mining centre of Dawson, which sprawled over the triangle formed by the Klondike and Yukon rivers and the abrupt

Moosehide Mountain (the latter named for the scar on its side), was as raw and ugly as that scar on the hill behind it. Its principal buildings, none of them known for their pleasing architecture, stretched along Front Street parallel to the Yukon. Of these, the ones most often mentioned by London in his fiction were the Catholic hospital at the upper end of town, where the remarkable Father Judge helped many sick and wounded, the barracks of the North-west Mounted Police at the lower end, and the establishments of the two rival trading companies which formed the heart of the town. These companies were all-important, for they brought supplies into the region and owned the Yukon steamers.

"The Company" was the original Alaska Commercial Company (A. C. Company), which had long held a monopoly in the Yukon Valley. Its rival was the North American Trading and Transportation Company (N. A. T. & T.), newer and more popular. This latter enterprise, financed, like the A. C., in the United States, was headed in Dawson by John J. Healy, hunter, trapper, soldier, prospector, whiskey-trader, editor, guide, Indian scout, and sheriff. After establishing a trading post at Dyea, Healy had moved into the Yukon Valley, when Fortymile was still the focus of men's hopes and Dawson had not yet been dreamed of. With his cowlick and his goatee and his ramrod figure, the crusty, powerful Healy probably served as the original of London's Jacob Welse, father of the heroine and leading exponent of Anglo-Saxon individualism in *A Daughter of the Snows*. According to London, Welse was "an economic missionary, a commercial St. Paul," who "preached the doctrines of expediency and force." Devoted to the doctrine that "competition was the secret of creation," he fought the economic fight with no holds barred and still found time in his softer moments to read Browning and to love his daughter, who was truly a "man's woman" if there ever was one.

The commercial store in London's books, whether it be the A. C. Company or the N. A. T. & T., was a large building constructed of logs with brown moss stuffed between them, trimmed with rough, unstained boards. Along the length of the building ran a long counter with the gold scales perhaps more prominent than the piles of furs and the mining equipment. The shelves ordinarily used for canned goods were nearly bare, and there was little flour, no sugar, in sight. Huge red-hot wood-burning stoves made the room inhabitable; whiskbrooms hung near the door so that visitors could brush the snow from moccasins and parkas to keep the room decent. A dim light came through small-paned windows, real glass windows, a luxury in the Yukon.

Prices were high at the trading companies during the fall of 1897, but the really formidable inflation was found in the restaurants, such as Shavovitch's, which appeared often in London's fiction. Five dollars for a meal of beans, apples, bread, and coffee was a standard price. London later played up shortages of sugar and eggs in his fiction; probably he himself did little eating in restaurants in Dawson, for he and Thompson had brought provisions with them from Split-up Island just to avoid such a contingency.

The saloons were another thing. Naturally, many scenes in London's stories take place in saloons, for this was the customary place for Klondikers to foregather. Here they escaped the cold, they drank, they heard the latest news and took part in arguments, and they met the girls. London's stories mention the Eldorado, the Monte Carlo, the Elkhorn, the Moosehorn, the M & G, and the M & M. Probably the last was Pete McDonald's M & N Saloon and Dancehall, where the gambling was usually for heavy stakes and it cost a dollar a go to dance with the silk-clad girls. The dances were so short that McDonald was able to pack in as many as one hundred twenty-five dances in a single night's entertainment.

That London would spend a fair amount of time in the saloons is to be taken for granted. One of the few bits of direct evidence on this point is to be found in Edward E. P. Morgan's *God's Loaded Dice,* one of the many books of reminiscences by Klondikers. Of London he writes:

I first met London in a Dawson bar in the late fall of 1897. . . . London was surely prospecting, but it was at bars that he sought his material. I believe that he had staked a claim, and it is probable that his hatred of capitalism did not extend to acquiring wealth for himself, but I never saw him working one, never met him on the trail, and do not remember ever having seen him except in some Dawson bar. . . . I remember him as a muscular youth of little more than average stature, with a weather-beaten countenance in which a healthy colour showed, and a shock of yellow hair, customarily unkempt and in keeping with his usual slovenly appearance. It seemed to me that whenever I saw him at the bar he was always in conversation with some veteran sourdough or noted character in the life of Dawson. And how he did talk.

It is to be noted that Morgan dictated this account when he was an old man, and thus his evidence does not weigh very heavily. However, he acknowledges that London at the time "was only a youth who had not yet made a name for himself," showing clearly that he could distinguish between the famous London and the unknown one he had met on the Yukon. Other old-timers have often been unable to make this distinction. In talking in 1954 to sourdoughs then living at Dawson, I found a number who maintained that they could remember London but only one who convinced me that he actually had met him. One "acquaintance" admitted unguardedly that he reached Dawson after London had left; another swore that he had seen him write *The Call of the Wild* in a local cabin; and still another averred that London had been sent down river after a miners' meeting because he had failed to replace the firewood in a mountain shack, thus breaking one of the cardinal rules of Northland living. But John Korbo, who came in the spring of 1897, convinced me that he had in fact known London. He remembered that a friend had called him into a saloon to settle an argument with a pleasant chap named "London" and that they had talked on for many minutes without coming to a conclusion. This sounds entirely likely, entirely typical, and fits in very well with Morgan's testimony.

In the bars of Dawson City, London had plenty of opportunities of both seeing and hearing old-timers as they expressed the brag of the country. Nowhere else was the line as clearly drawn between sourdough and cheechako, a distinction explained in detail in *White Fang*. The wolf-pup was making his first contact with civilization, in Fort Yukon. "A small number of white men lived in Fort Yukon. These men had been long in the country. They called themselves Sour-doughs, and took great pride in so classifying themselves. For other men, new in the land, they felt nothing but disdain. The men who came ashore from the steamers were newcomers. They were known as *chechaquos,* and they always wilted at the application of the name. They made their bread with baking-powder. This was the invidious distinction between them and the Sour-doughs, who, forsooth, made their bread from sour-dough because they had no baking-powder." The sourdoughs were proud of their adaptability to famine and cold, contemptuous of the complaining cheechako. "Aw, you tenderfeet make me tired," explodes Dave Harney in *Scorn of Women*. "I never seen the beat of you critters. Better men than you have starved in this country, an' they didn't make no bones about it neither—they was all bones I calkilate. What do you think this is? A Sunday picnic? Jes' come in, eh? An' you're clean scairt. Look at me—oldtimer, sir, a sour-dough, an' proud of it! I come into this country before there was any blamed Company, fished for my breakfast, an' hunted my supper. An' when the fish didn't bite an' they wa'n't any game, jes' cinched my belt tighter an' hiked along, livin' on salmon-bellies and rabbit tracks an' eatin' my moccasins."

Dave Harney could have added that the sourdoughs were also famous for gambling away their fortunes in just such bars as London was frequenting. In *Burning Daylight* the hero, who had not hesitated to gamble fifty thousand dollars in a poker game in Circle City before the Klondike was discovered, was appalled at the waste he saw displayed in Dawson.

> He watched the lavish waste of the mushroom millionaires, and failed quite to understand it. According to his nature and outlook, it was all very well to toss an ante away in a night's frolic. That was what he had done the night of the poker-game in Circle City when he lost fifty thousand . . . as a mere ante. When it came to millions, it was different. Such a fortune was a stake, and was not to be sown on bar-room floors, literally sown, flung broadcast out of the moosehide sacks by drunken millionaires who had lost all sense of proportion. There was McMann, who ran up a single bar-room bill of thirty-eight thousand dollars; and Jimmie the Rough, who spent one hundred thousand a month for four months in riotous living, and then fell down drunk in the snow one March night and was frozen to death; and Swiftwater Bill, who, after spending three valuable claims in an extravagance of debauchery, borrowed three thousand dollars with which to leave the country . . . .

Besides drinking, talking, and gambling, there were singing and dancing to be found in the Monte Carlo and Eldorado, the Orpheum and the Tivoli. The saloon-*cum*-dance hall which plays the most prominent part in London's stories is the grandiloquently named Opera House, which was burned up the night before Thanksgiving in 1897, along with most of the rest of Dawson, in a fire that started when an M & N dance-hall girl threw a lamp at her rival. Whether

London was in the M & N when the lamp was thrown or in the Opera House when the customary Thanksgiving eve masked ball came to an end, he certainly was in town when the flames spread to most of Dawson's buildings. In his fiction he used the Opera House not as the scene of a holocaust but a place to hold community dances, parties which are featured in *A Daughter of the Snows* and "The Wife of A King." A passage from *A Daughter of the Snows* presents Opera House society in all its rough grandeur.

The crowded room was thick with tobacco smoke. A hundred men or so, garbed in furs and warm-coloured wools, lined the walls and looked on. But the mumble of their general conversation destroyed the spectacular feature of the scene and gave to it the geniality of common comradeship. For all its bizarre appearance, it was very like the living-room of the home when the members of the household came together after the work of the day. Kerosene lamps and tallow candles glimmered feebly in the murky atmosphere, while large stoves roared their red-hot and white-hot cheer.

On the floor a score of couples pulsed rhythmically to the swinging waltz-time music. Starched shirts and frock coats were not. The men wore their wolf-and beaver-skin caps, with the gay-tasselled ear-flaps flying free, while on their feet were the moose-skin moccasins and walrus-hide muclucs òf the north. Here and there was a woman in moccasins, though the majority danced in frail ball-room slippers of silk and satin. At one end of the hall a great open doorway gave glimpse of another large room where the crowd was even denser. From this room, in the lulls in the music, came the pop of corks and the clink of glasses, and as an undertone the steady click and clatter of chips and roulette balls.

This party ended in a fist-fight.

In *Scorn of Women* London uses the masked ball, this time held in Pioneer Hall, as a device for a confrontation between his two heroines, a dance-hall girl and the leader of Dawson society, insisting that they are sisters under the skin and both devoted to noble purposes. Almost without exception, the dance-hall girls in London's Klondike fiction are treated kindly, not to mention gallantly. Lucile in *A Daughter of the Snows* quotes Browning by the yard and hides a very sensitive heart; and Freda Moloof in *Scorn of Women* owns a grand piano, hires a maid, and plots to save a "good girl" from disaster. A leading character in *A Daughter of the Snows* expresses a completely romantic view of the girls: " 'Butterflies, bits of light and song and laughter, dancing, dancing down the last tail-reach of hell. Not only Lucile, but the rest of them. Look at May, there, with the brow of a Madonna and the tongue of a gutter-devil. And Myrtle—for all the world one of Gainsborough's old English beauties stepped down from the canvas to riot out the century in Dawson's dancehalls. And Laura, there, wouldn't she make a mother? Can't you see the child in the curve of her arm against her breast!' " This is a far cry from Addison Mizner's acid comments on Dawson "beauties" in his *The Many Mizners:* "Glass-eyed Annie sang beautifully; Myrtle Drummond had charm; diamond-toothed Gertie was tough, but attractive; over-flowing Flora, who looked like mud squeezing up from between your toes, had lovely eyes; but, most of the rest—my Gawd—what sights.... I remember once asking an invalid friend of mine, who had a cook named Jennie, aged seventy-five, with one tooth and cockeyes, 'How long do you stay in this lonely spot?' 'Until Jennie begins to look good to me,' he replied."

Jack London did not say in his fiction that many of these girls could be had for the hour or for the night at very fancy prices, nor does he mention the more common whores who lived in the cribs in Paradise Alley or in the swampland well back of the business district known as "Hell's Half Acre," or the lowest of the low who were relegated to Louse Town. From his books you would never suspect that prostitution existed. (He was writing in the early nineteen hundreds.)

Death was another matter—it stalked grim and final in many of London's stories. When one thinks of dwellings in Dawson, he does not remember the house owned by a dancer with its gilt French clock, bearskin rugs and sturdy furniture, "luxurious, comfortable, picturesque, emphasizing the contact of civilization and the wilderness,"[5] but the "sody-bottle window" cabin in which the protagonist of "The One Thousand Dozen" killed himself. "He re-entered the cabin and drew the latch in after him. The smoke from the cindered steak made his eyes smart. He stood on the bunk, passed the lashing over the ridge-pole, and measured the swing-off with his eye. It did not seem to satisfy, for he put the stool on the bunk and climbed upon the stool. He drove a noose in the end of the lashing and slipped his head through. The other end he made fast. Then he kicked the stool out from under."

There was also the attempted suicide of the dance-hall girl called "the Virgin," who was saved in the nick of time by Burning

Daylight. In "The League of the Old Men" there was the man frozen sitting upright on a sled in the main street where the men passed to and fro. "They thought the man was resting, but later, when they touched him, they found him stiff and cold, frozen to death in the midst of the busy street. To undouble him, that he might fit into a coffin, they had been forced to lug him to a fire and thaw him out a bit."

The task of disposing of the dead did not cease with thawing them out to get them into coffins. There was the long haul up the hill back of town to the graveyard. The hero and heroine climb that hill in *A Daughter of the Snows* and incidentally discover what a task it is to transport a Dawson corpse to its last resting place.

> At their feet, under the great vault of heaven, a speck in the midst of the white vastness, huddled the golden city— puny and sordid, feebly protesting against immensity, man's challenge to the infinite! Calls of men and cries of encouragement came sharply to them from close at hand, and they halted. There was an eager yelping, a scratching of feet, and a string of ice-rimed wolf-dogs, with hot-lolling tongues and dripping jaws, pulled up the slope and turned into the path ahead of them. On the sled, a long and narrow box of rough-sawed spruce told the nature of the freight. Two dog-drivers, a woman walking blindly, and a black-robed priest, made up the funeral cortege. A few paces farther on the dogs were again put against the steep, and with whine and shout and clatter the unheeding clay was hauled on and upward to its ice-hewn hillside chamber.

Of the hardest task of all, to dig a grave in the perma-frost, London tells in "The Unexpected." "The ground was frozen. It was impervious to blow of the pick. They first gathered wood, then scraped the snow away and on the frozen surface built a fire. When the fire had burned for an hour, several inches of dirt had thawed. This they shovelled out and then built a fresh fire. Their descent into the earth progressed at the rate of two or three inches an hour. It was hard and bitter work. The flurrying snow did not permit the fire to burn any too well, while the wind cut through their clothes and chilled their bodies." Eight hours of hard work found the graves completed. "They were shallow, not more than two feet deep, but they would serve the purpose."

Always in the consciousness of men in Dawson City was the cold, indifferent environment; the low hills of scrub fir and birch around them; the abrupt bluffs across the Yukon which hemmed them in; the clear sky when the thick fog which so often rose from the river was not pressing upon them; the breathless air, for weeks unmoving under the stable Arctic high; the vivid, unfeeling stars. Joaquin Miller, who also was spending the winter in a Dawson cabin, described the oppressive stillness as "this vast white silence, as if all earth lay still and stark dead in her white shroud waiting the judgment day." He complained that the sun was skulking behind the broken Klondike steeps, that he had not seen its cheery face for days and did not expect to see it again for weeks. "Let me not be caught here again," he moaned, "for caught I am like a wary old rat in a trap."[6]

In this inhuman natural theatre, the aurora borealis, melodramatic though it was, did not seem out of place. Time and again London etched the scene, its vocal accompaniment furnished by the howling of uneasy dogs. A typical example is found in *A Daughter of the Snows.*

It was a clear, cold night, not over-cold—not more than forty below—and the land was bathed in a soft, diffused flood of light which found its source not in the stars, nor yet in the moon, which was somewhere over on the other side of the world. From the southeast to the northwest a pale-greenish glow fringed the rim of the heavens, and it was from this the dim radiance was exhaled.

Suddenly, like the ray of a search-light, a band of white light ploughed overhead. Night turned to ghostly day on the instant, then blacker night descended. But to the south-east a noiseless commotion was apparent. The glowing greenish gauze was in a ferment, bubbling, uprearing, downfalling, and tentatively thrusting huge bodiless hands into the upper ether. Once more a cyclopean rocket twisted its fiery way across the sky, from horizon to zenith, and on, and on, in tremendous flight, to horizon again. But the span could not hold, and in its wake the black night brooded. And yet again, broader, stronger, deeper, lavishly spilling streamers to right and left, it flaunted the mid-most zenith with its gorgeous flare, and passed on and down to the further edge of the world. Heaven was bridged at last, and the bridge endured!

At this flaming triumph the silence of earth was broken, and ten thousand wolf-dogs, in long-drawn unisoned howls, sobbed their dismay and grief.

They were not all northern dogs in Dawson that winter, though huskies and malemutes were in the majority. It was a winter for dogs, this and the winter of early 1898, when Yukon transportation depended almost wholly upon them. Later horses took their place, and the dogs became a picturesque rarity. But in 1897 dogs of all sorts had been sent up from Canada and the States. Many of them were too small or too weak to be of much use, but some drivers found that the best of the large "outside" dogs suited the sudden needs of the area as well as the native huskies. Jack London had come to know one of these imports, a cross between a St. Bernard and a Scotch collie, owned by Louis Bond, near whose cabin he had camped when he first reached Dawson. Louis Bond was the son of Judge Bond of Santa Clara, California, who was to appear as Judge Miller in *The Call of the Wild,* while Louis Bond was to lend some of his traits to Stanley Prince in *The Son of the Wolf.* Louis' dog, still to be seen in old photographs, was the original of Buck, both in breed and in temperament.

When the fictional Buck reached Dawson after sledding over the Klondike trail during the same winter that London spent in the North, he found Dawson City a regular capital city of dogland.

Here were many men, and countless dogs, and Buck found them all at work. It seemed the ordained order of things that dogs should work. All day they swung up and down the main street in long teams, and in the night their jingling bells still went by. They hauled cabin logs and firewood, freighted up to the mines, and did all manner of work that horses did in the Santa Clara Valley. Here and there Buck met Southland dogs, but in the main they were the wild wolf husky breed. Every night, regularly, at nine, at twelve, at three, they lifted a nocturnal song, a weird and eerie chant, in which it was Buck's delight to join.

With the aurora borealis flaming coldly overhead, or the stars leaping in the frost dance, and the land numb and frozen under its pall of snow, this song of the huskies might have been the defiance of life, only it was pitched in minor key, with long-drawn wailing and half-sobs, and was more the pleading of life, the articulate travail of existence. It was an old song, old as the breed itself—one of the first songs of the younger world in a day when songs were sad. It was invested with the woe of unnumbered generations, this plaint by which Buck was so strangely stirred. When he moaned and sobbed, it was with the pain of living that was of old the pain of his wild fathers, and the fear and mystery of the cold and dark that was to them fear and mystery. And that he should be stirred by it marked the completeness with which he harked back through the ages of fire and roof to the raw beginnings of life in the howling ages.

It is not unlikely that, as Jack London idled through the weeks of early winter in Dawson City, he saw more than one prized dog put through the test of breaking out a heavily-laden sled from the frozen snow crust. Thus he would have the background detail for the magnificent scene in which Buck lives up to the confidence of his master, John Thornton, by starting a sled loaded with twenty fifty-pound sacks of flour. Thornton had accepted a wager from a Bonanza King that his dog, a hundred and fifty pounds of "grit and virility," could not possibly budge such a load. The sourdoughs and cheechakos at the Eldorado poured out into the snow (it was sixty degrees below zero) to watch the trial of strength. Every reader of *The Call of the Wild* remembers the passage:

> Buck threw himself forward, tightening the traces with a jarring lunge. His whole body was gathered compactly together in the tremendous effort, the muscles writhing and knotting like live things under the silky fur. His great chest was low to the ground, his head forward and down, while his feet were flying like mad, the claws scarring the hard-packed snow in parallel grooves. The sled swayed and trembled, half-started forward. One of his feet slipped, and one man groaned aloud. Then the sled lurched ahead in what appeared a rapid succession of jerks, though it never really came to a dead stop again . . . half an inch . . . two inches. . . . The jerks perceptibly diminished; as the sled gained momentum, he caught them up, till it was moving steadily along.

It is less likely that London saw any dog like White Fang, half-husky and half-wolf, exhibited in Dawson for fifty cents a head, penned in a cage as a "Fighting Wolf." White Fang, captive from the remote "Northland Wild," was beginning his journey from raw nature to civilization, where he eventually would be won over by the love of man. But Beauty Smith, the primordial bully who was exhibiting White Fang, was hardly calculated to hasten this process. In Dawson, he pitted White Fang against any animal that would fight him. The fights took place outside town in order to avoid interference from the Mounties, or "Yellow-Legs"; it is possible that London, with his interest in the primordial, saw more than one such fight while he was in the Klondike. White Fang conquered the best of the native dogs, fought successfully with a lynx (later London was to be attacked as a "nature fakir" by Teddy Roosevelt for pitting a lynx against a dog), but was nearly killed by a tenacious bulldog, from which he was rescued near death by an outraged bystander, who was to provide him with the warmth and generosity of a good human master.

Arguing in bars like the Moosehorn, gambling in dives like the Eldorado, dancing at masked balls in the ill-fated Opera House, watching men test their dogs on Front Street or fight them on the far side of the Yukon—these occupations might well have provided relief from the dull routine of cooking beans and bacon and sourdough bread, scraping out ice from the cabin or tent, chopping wood, mending torn clothes, and dragging heavy buckets of water up from ice holes in the river. There were two of these last which figured in London's fiction, one down near the barracks, where the Klondike joined the Yukon, the other at the north end of town near the hospital and the sawmill. During the late fall, men raised water through these holes; as the winter tightened its grip, they found the holes frozen and were forced to chop ice for their water supply, now toting it up the steep bank in sacks rather than in buckets.

Did London ever walk the dozen miles up the Klondike to the Bonanza diggings or continue even farther to the fabulous Eldorado placer claims or to those on the Hunker? Did he see anything of the burrowing operations that were going on the banks of these streams back of Dawson, talk to any of the miners who were piling up frozen tailings for the spring thaw? A description in *Burning Daylight* strongly suggests that he saw something of the mines.

Six thousand spent the winter of 1897 in Dawson, work on the creeks went on apace, while beyond the passes it was reported that one hundred thousand more were waiting for the spring. Late one brief afternoon, Daylight, on the benches between French Hill and Skookum Hill, caught a wider vision of things. Beneath him lay the richest part of Eldorado Creek, while up and down Bonanza he could see for miles. It was a scene of a vast devastation. The hills, to their tops, had been shorn of trees, and their naked sides showed signs of goring and perforating that even the mantle of snow could not hide. Beneath him, in every direction, were the cabins of men. But not many men were visible. A blanket of smoke filled the valleys and turned the gray day to melancholy twilight. Smoke arose from a thousand holes in the snow, where, deep down on bed-rock, in the frozen muck and gravel, men crept and scratched and dug, and ever built more fires to break the grip of the frost. Here and there, where new shafts were starting, these fires flamed redly. Figures of men crawled out of the holes, or disappeared into them, or, on raised platforms of hand-hewn timber, windlassed the thawed gravel to the surface, where it immediately froze. The wreckage of the spring washing appeared everywhere—piles of sluice-boxes, sections of elevated flumes, huge water-wheels—all the debris of an army of gold-mad men.

As Daylight looked on this scene, he thought some of the thoughts London expressed in his article "Economics in the Klondike," an essay devoted to the thesis that not all the gold in the Yukon equalled the outlay in cash of the individuals who pursued it. And the rape of nature compounded the deficit. Daylight "looked at the naked hills and realized the enormous wastage of wood that had taken place. From this bird's-eye view he realized the monstrous confusion of their excited workings. It was a gigantic inadequacy. Each worked for himself, and the result was chaos. In this richest of diggings it cost one dollar to mine two dollars, and for every dollar taken out by their feverish, unthinking methods another dollar was left hopelessly in the earth. Given another year, and most of the claims would be worked out, and the sum of the gold taken out would no more than equal what was left behind."

This was the mood of a later day, however. At the moment, London was more likely to have thrown his enthusiasm into one or more of the stampedes which periodically emptied Dawson of its inhabitants in a mad dash to still another creek. Almost every commentator on the Klondike rush remarks on these stampedes, recognized as largely futile but tremendously exciting. After all, with the many rich creeks near Dawson fully staked, it was not out of character to rush farther away in hopes there would be some reward for the ardours of reaching the Klondike and the discomforts of living there.

London includes three stampedes in his fiction, but two of them, the substance of the early story, "Thanksgiving on Slav Creek" and the chapter in *Smoke Bellew* entitled "The Stampede to Squaw Creek," prove on close examination to be the same event, retold to fit *Smoke Bellew* long after Dawson had become a ghost town. It is a typical stampede, starting in the middle of the night. The word has gone round of a rich find on a creek thirty miles up the Yukon, and each man is keeping the information to himself or merely confiding it to a partner. All of Dawson is awake, though, as the lights from windows suggest. Soon men are slipping out with light stampede-packs (sure signs of a secret abroad), scuttling for the river, where they slide down a thirty-foot ice chute and pile up at the bottom. Crossing the frozen river, a confusion of jam-packed ice cakes, proves to be such a difficult task that men light candles to find their way, candles which burn steadily in the windless air. Fireflies are now dancing all over the river. "It was a mile across the jams to the west bank of the Yukon, and candles flickered the full length of the twisting trail. Behind them, clear to the top of the bank they had descended, were more candles."

Across the river the stampeders turned south along the sled trail to Dyea. For the rest of the night they pushed on in the cold. Frequently the faster men floundered through the snow up to their waists in order to pass the more stolid hikers on the hard-packed trail. Morning came with its pink dawn to find half of Dawson up a frozen creek, not a worthwhile prospect in sight. The next day saw the stampeders back in their cabins and tents, joking about what suckers they had been. It was not all fun, however; gradually news of disaster along the trail seeped back to Dawson. "Nor did they learn till afterward the horrors of that night. Exhausted men sat down to rest by the way and failed to get up again. Seven were frozen to death, while scores of amputations of toes, feet and fingers were performed in the Dawson hospitals on the surviviors. For the stampede to Squaw Creek occurred on the coldest night of the year. Before morning the spirit thermometers at Dawson registered seventy degrees below zero." Exaggeration was inherent in the story. Probably no men froze, but they might have. Here was excitement, at least, in what one writer has called the world of "the young, strong, and stupid."[7] Such a stampede was fit punctuation for a winter in Dawson.

# Notes

1. Files of Mining Recorder, Dawson, Y.T. Grant No. 2080.
2. Jack London to Con Gepfert, May 5, 1900. Bancroft Library.
3. Quoted in Pierre Berton, *The Klondike Fever,* p. 172.
4. Ibid., p. 178.
5. *Scorn of Women,* p. 180.
6. Letter dated Dec. 17, 1897, quoted in Harr Wagner's *Joaquin Miller and His Other Self* (1929), p. 178.
7. Addison Mizner, *The Many Mizners,* p. 120.

# Chapter 6

# Selected Early Reviews of *The Call of the Wild*

# A "Nature" Story—*The Call of the Wild\** by Jack London

In these days of the development of "laureates of nature" and biographers of field and forest folk,—who are producing volume upon volume of what in years past would have been dull "natural history" books, appealing only to the few,—it is hard to find a new key in which to sound the praises of nature and animal life. This Jack London has done, albeit the resonance is of the same quality first given out by Charles G. D. Roberts in "The Kindred of the Wild." Here, too, is an astonishing similarity in the title. There is perhaps not that finesse to be noted in London's work that is apparent in every line written by Professor Roberts, but this is easily accounted for.

*The Call of the Wild,* which depicts the life-story of a dog taken from his home in a California valley to the wilds of Alaska, where he finally becomes the leader of a pack of Alaskan wolves, is a story of the robust variety which is never the work of any but a strong and original mind.

London has the subject and its detail well within his grasp. He writes from experience as to the latter, and with appreciation and insight of the former.

If you like dogs, you will like this book. If you wish to know more of the incident and life of the Alaskan trails, you will find here a fund of first-hand information, and withal a story of the first rank as to its conception and purport.

---

*An unsigned review from *Literary World* 34 (September, 1903): p. 229.

# The Call of the Wild*

## by J. Stewart Doubleday

The power of Jack London lies not alone in his clear-sighted depiction of life, but in his suggestion of the eternal principles that underlie it. The writer who can suggest these principles forcibly and well, though he may not be actually great, has something in him closely allied to greatness. Mr. London is one of the most original and impressive authors ·this country has known. His voice is large and vibrant, his manner straightforward and free, and we predict for him a success in Western narrative equalled only by that of Mr. Stewart Edward White.

*The Call of the Wild* is the story of a dog, reared in comfort in Southern California, but afterwards broken to the sled on the desolate Alaskan trail, where his experiences are related with a candor and ring of genuineness, exciting yet ofttimes heart rending in the extreme. The philosophy of the survival of the fittest runs through every page of Mr. London's book; the call of the wild evidently signifies the appeal (and in Buck's case, the triumph) of barbarian life over civilized life; in fact, this dog becomes, after a series of bloodcurdling incidents ending at the murder of a beloved master, the eventual leader of a pack of timber wolves, in whom, following a fang fight for individual supremacy, he recognizes the

---

*From *Reader* 2 (September, 1903): pp. 408-9.

"wild brother," and joins the savage horde. The book, very brief, is filled from cover to cover with thrilling scenes; the Northern Territory is brought home to us with convincing vividness; every sentence is pregnant with original life; probably no such sympathetic, yet wholly unsentimental, story of a dog has ever found print before; the achievement may, without exaggeration, be termed "wonderful."

Yet it is cruel reading—often relentless reading; we feel at times the blood lashing in our faces at what seems the continual maltreatment of a dumb animal; we can scarce endure the naked brutality of the thing; our sense of the creature's perplexity in suffering is almost absolutely unrelieved; we sicken of the analysis of the separate tortures of this dog's Arctic Inferno. Not seldom we incline to remonstrate, "Hang it, Jack London, what the deuce do you mean by 'drawing' on us so?" But we forgive the writer at last because he is true! He is not sentimental, tricky; he is at harmony with himself and nature. He gives an irresistible groan sometimes—like Gorky; but this is only because he does, after all, feel for humanity—yes, down to the bottom of his big California heart.

It must be patent to all, we think, that the man who can, through the simple story of a dog set us thought-wandering over illimitable ways, is a man of language to be respectfully classed and reckoned with. There is nothing local or narrow about Jack London. Sectionalism is smaller than he. His voice is the voice of a man in the presence of the multitude, and he utters the word that is as bread to him. He has not, to say truly, much humor; the theme of necessary toil and suffering overburdens and drowns the casual note of laughter—he is buoyant rather than bright. Sometimes we are wearied by his too ecstatic hymning of the primitive, the rude, the elemental in spirit and nature—we begin to desire a little more mildness and beauty, a possible mercy and femininity, a hope; but these we must look for in other writers than the stalwart youthful leader of the promising Far West. In his own field he is master; and more than this we ought not to exact of any man. The book is profusely and excellently illustrated.

# Anonymous Review*

When Jack London, four years ago, wrote the stories that were gathered in *The Son of the Wolf,* all the critics recognized in him a master of the life of the Arctic, as all, a decade before, had acclaimed Kipling the master of the older and more complex life in India. There was no question of London's intimate first-hand knowledge of the trail under the midnight sun and of the fierce lust for gold that arouses in the miner the passions of the cave man of the stone age. This knowledge was stamped on every line. With it was joined a marvelous story-telling faculty that gripped the reader's interest and never let go until the end was reached. With it, too, went a purely pagan joy in living and fighting, and overcoming the obstacles that nature in the Far North throws in the way of man. Stripped of all sentimentality, these stories lay hold upon one like the tales told by one who comes out from the very presence of dreadful death and in whose eyes yet linger the glow of superb courage. Other stories Jack London has told in the meanwhile, but he has never reached the height of those first tales until he produced *The Call of the Wild,* which the MacMillan Company of New York bring out now in fine style, with a number of illustrations by Philip R. Goodwin and Charles Livingston Bull. It is the story of a dog's life in the Far North, but this record of a splendid canine hero is really a marvelously graphic picture of the great gold rush to the

---

*From *The San Francisco Chronicle* (August 2, 1903), p. 32.

Klondike in 1897, and of the life of the packer and the miner in Alaska. Compared with this all other stories or sketches of this second great gold rush of the nineteenth century pale into insignificance. Fierce, brutal, splashed with blood, and alive with the crack of whip and blow of club, it is yet a story that sounds the deep note of tenderness between man and beast, and that loyalty and fidelity which never falters even in the jaws of death. And beyond all this is the strange haunting charm of "the call of the wild" to the savage strain in the big dog, arousing dormant instincts that have come down to him from his wolf ancestors. At times this is pushed perilously far, but in nothing has Jack London shown more clearly his artistic mastery than in making real to the reader the hereditary instincts that the savage life of the north brings out in the great dog, the hero of this story. Once only is a false note struck, and that is at the end, when he makes the dog return every year to mourn over the grave of the master whom he loved.

Buck, the hero, is a huge animal, a cross between a St. Bernard and a Scotch shepherd. He is stolen from his comfortable home in the Santa Clara valley and sold to a man, who takes him to Seattle. There he passes into the hands of a professional dealer in dogs, who makes him understand the power of a club wielded by a skillful hand. Then he is sold at a high price as a dog fit to draw a sledge over the frozen snow and ice from Skagway to Dawson. And now begins a really thrilling story of the training of this dog in the mastery of the trail, until he becomes not only the champion fighter of the Klondike, but the finest sledge dog in the Arctic. Very skillfully London develops the advantages which his good blood brings him. He is early taught what the author calls "the law of club and fang." He learns that this life and death struggle on the trail admits of no sentiment and no honors; that mercy enters not into it, nor kindness. He learns that dogs and men respect only the supremacy of brute force and cunning, and that justice is dealt out with unsparing hand. He quickly learns all that is to be taught of the lore of the trail, but his ambition rises to be master of the team on which he works. Before many weeks he has had his first great fight for supremacy with the old leader of the team. He conquers, and the old dog goes down to death under his savage fangs. He has several owners, mostly half-breeds, who carry the mail and official dispatches from tide water to Dawson. These men are drawn with only a few strokes, but each one stands out clear and recognizable, even to his mongrel French-English. Then, when Buck and the other dogs are worn to the bone with the fatigue of forced marches, they are sold by the Government to a tenderfoot party. From the handling of masters of the trail they pass to the cruelty of incompetents. Nothing in the book is better done than the short episode of the two men and one woman, who start for the land of gold with no training and no qualities of strength, patience and endurance that would make them able to cope with cold, fatigue and hardship. At White River the dogs drop in their traces and the brutal driver is beating Buck to death, when John Thornton, a prospector, interferes and saves the dog's life. The tenderfoot gang, in the face of warnings, press on and soon go down to death in the river through a hole in the rotten ice.

Then begins a new life for Buck. His master is slowly recovering from the effects of frozen feet and is waiting for his partners to return in the spring. Thornton learns to love the dog and he is repaid with a devotion that is sometimes startling. Twice the huge dog saves the life of the man who befriended him, and once he wins for him a large sum by putting forth his enormous strength. Finally Thornton and his partners strike rich ground in a remote section. There they stay many weeks. In his ample leisure Buck haunts the woods, and the visions of the old days when he roamed the forests as a wolf come back to him with renewed strength. But when he meets a wolf far in the woods and they fraternize, he cannot bring himself to abandon the man whom he loves. One day the instinct to hunt and kill comes over him when he espies a big bull moose. He follows the herd for hours, cuts out the bull, and, after two days, wears down its strength and kills it. On his return he finds that a band of Indians have attacked the mining camp and slain the prospectors. With a roar of rage and grief Buck suddenly leaps upon them, tearing at the men's throats, and so fierce is his attack and so fearful the wounds that he inflicts that the whole band is routed. Then, having avenged in some sort his master's murder, he turns to the woods and joins the band of wolves. Thus he succumbs at last to "the call of the wild."

Many passages were marked in the reading of this book, but most are too long for quotation. Good examples of fine dramatic power are the description of the breaking in of Buck at Seattle, the fight for the mastery of the team with Spitz, the winning of Thornton's wager and the trailing of the old moose. Some of the finest descriptive passages, cast in prose but full of poetic charm, are those which deal with the dog's harking back to his primordial days when he ranged over the north with the cave men. Here is a specimen of these visions which the dog dreamed by the campfire:

The Sunland was very dim and distant, and such memories had no power over him. Far more potent were the memories of his heredity that gave things he had never seen before a seeming familiarity; the instincts (which were but the memories of his ancestors become habits), which had lapsed in later days, and still later, in him, quickened and become alive again. Sometimes, as he crouched there, blinking dreamily at the flames, it seemed that the flames were of another fire, and that as he crouched by this other fire he saw another and different man from the half-breed cook before him. This other man was shorter of leg and longer of arm, with muscles that were stringy and knotty, rather than rounded and swelling. The hair of this man was long and matted, and his head slanted back under it from the eyes. He uttered strange sounds, and seemed very much afraid of the darkness, into which he peered continually.

At other times this hairy man squatted by the fire with head between his legs and slept. On such occasions his elbows were on his knees, his hands clasped above his head, as though to shed rain by the hairy arms. And beyond that fire, in the circling darkness, Buck could see many gleaming coals, two by two, always two by two, which he knew to be the eyes of great beasts of prey. And he could hear the crashing of their bodies through the undergrowth, and the noises they made in the night. And dreaming there by the Yukon bank, with lazy eyes blinking at the fire, these sights and sounds of another world would make the hair to rise along his back and to stand on end across his shoulders and up his neck, till he whimpered low and suppressedly, or growled softly, and the half-breed cook shouted at him. "Hey, you, Buck, wake up!" Whereupon the other world would vanish and the real world come into his eyes, and he would get up and yawn and stretch as though he had been asleep.

There is space here for only one more extract, which is a powerful reiteration of the law of the survival of the fittest:

His face and body were scarred by the teeth of many dogs and he fought as fiercely as ever and more shrewdly. And Buck was merciless. He had learned well the law of club and fang, and he never forewent an advantage or drew back from a foe he had started on the way to death. He had lessoned from Spitz and from the chief fighting dogs of the police and mail, and knew there was no middle course. He must master or be mastered; while to show mercy was a weakness.

Mercy did not exist in the primordial life. It was misunderstood for fear, and such misunderstandings made for death. Kill or be killed, eat or be eaten, was the law, and this mandate, down out of the depths of time, he obeyed.

And equally true with this is the pride of the sledge dog in his efficiency. Buck illustrates this when he claims the leader's position after he had killed Spitz, and Dave, the old wheel dog, also illustrates it very pathetically in his terrible efforts to keep up with the team and in his despair when he can no longer pull in the traces. It would be idle to recommend this book to any one who wishes love or sentiment. It is a man's book, through and through, but any one fond of dogs or of life and adventure in the Far North will be glad to read the book, and to read it more than once. In nothing else that Jack London has written has he shown so clearly as in this his complete mastery of his material and that unconscious molding of style to thought which marks real from make-believe literature.

# Review of
# *The Call of the Wild**

## by Kate B. Stillé

A clear, strong picture of the battlefield of life with the colors laid on in a way that brings to the strong and thoughtful the consciousness to the spiritual and material conflict that rages between civilization and savagery. A dog, not a man, is the hero of the story which is less fiction than a serious problem, that reaches down into the heart of life, with an anguish that throbs and cries aloud on every page. Buck, the master-spirit, is a dog, well-born and well-bred; all that is interesting in the men comes out through their intercourse with this splendid dog. A cross between the St. Bernard and the Shepherd, gives the size, the endurance, the placidity, the intelligence, the gentleness and faithfulness that count in civilization and in the struggle of life.

*The Call of the Wild* is the heart laid bare in that forcible, thrilling way that makes one groan in desperate resistance to the savage that is not worlds away, nor in ancestors dead and buried centuries ago, but within us. The truths of life under the skilful handling of Jack London take possession and press themselves into the soul in such a way that we seem in the horrors of a nightmare powerless to resist, unnerved and helpless under "the law of club and fang." All phases of life are touched with the unerring skill of the true artist.

---

*From *Book News Monthly* 22 (September, 1903): pp. 7-10.

The brush brings out softly the sensuous captivating life in Southern California.

Civilization is both beautiful and capable, is at home on Judge Miller's place. Buck is "neither house-dog nor kennel-dog. The whole realm was his," but he was saved from being the pampered house-dog by hunting and outdoor sports, which the author cleverly shows is the type of the country gentleman who is ease-taking and at the same time has the careful oversight of the details which makes his estate great. Buck was kidnapped and sold into the Klondyke by the gardener's helper, whose character and needs are graphically told in that he was a gambler, had faith in it, "which made his damnation certain." He required money for his sin, and "the wages of the gardener's helper do not lap-over the needs of a wife and numerous progeny." The result of the passion and the necessity bring to us such suffering on the part of the dog, and such brutality from men that we comprehend as never before, that there is a devil in man and that the savage is not on the frontier, but at our door.

Buck knew not fear until he was beaten; he was of gentle blood and understood that he stood no chance against the man with the club, but his splendid lineage saved him from cowardice and stood the test of starvation and merciless toil. He was put to work to draw sledges, subjected to cruelty and toil, but when he learned "the law of club and fang" he won the leadership of the team. We see the passiveness drop and watch until the toil of the traces becomes the best expression of life. Then comes the transformation, necessitated by the ruthless struggle for existence. How swift and terrible the going to pieces of moral nature, which is a vain thing and a heavy handicap under strenuous circumstances. This is the primitive code for man and beast—not to rob openly, but cunningly, "out of respect for club and fang," not to steal for joy; "but because of the clamor of an empty stomach."

This going down of the true man, this awakening of the primeval man, is desperately real. Sight and sense grow keen, instincts long dead are alive, the savage nature is quickened, and the old tricks come back without effort. Buck came to his own again "when on the still cold nights he pointed his nose at a star and howled long and wolf-like, it was his ancestors, dead and dust, pointing nose at star and howling down through the centuries, and through him. And his cadences were their cadences, and the cadences, which voiced their woe, and what to them was the meaning of the stillness and the cold and dark."

Through starvation and abuse Buck grew responsive to the call of the wild, and this he obeyed when Thornton, his only friend, was killed by the Indians.

Through the "comprehensive relation of things" Jack London shows that the heights and depths of the universe are within the soul, and no one has put it with such force and feeling, though all have known it.

How splendidly civilization brings out the fine steely strength that endures and triumphs; and how squarely the conditions of life are met. The thriftless, complaining go down! The strong and brutal overcome.

The telling thing in the book is its deep underlying truth. The call of the wild is no fiction. The things pointed out are the nameless things we feel, and the author shows clearly, unobtrusively that it is "the old instincts which at stated periods drive men out from the sounding cities to forest and plain to kill things." That man and dog alike are mastered by the wolf-cry, striving after things alive, as it flees before them. Both sounding the deeps of his nature and of the parts of his nature that were deeper than he, "going back into the womb of Time."

*The Call of the Wild* penetrates to the very marrow and flows in the blood of the veins. Its manifestations are everywhere.

When the society girl "camps out for fun" and tyrannizes over and neglects her pets, ignores and treats the old with scant courtesy she as surely obeys "the law of the club and fang" as Buck, when he relentlessly pursued the "foe he had started on the way to death."

This is true of soldiers, of university men, who enter mining camps and take to ranching, of men who leave their wives and firesides to sleep on the bare ground, of the nation's Chief, whose delight is in pursuing and killing big game, and who devotes the Cabinet room to sport, filling it with boxing gloves, swords, and foils.

These may all be taken as the legitimate guides to the trend of the times, which muzzles and massacres the individual, that touches society with decay, and drags men back to the primeval forest where their hairy ancestors clung with long arms to the trees.

The unknown self stands out on the pages of this thrilling romance, and from the depths of his heart the author says, Behold, you are no better than the—

> "New caught peoples,
>       Half devil, half child."

To bring us to our waking life, more literature like *The Call of the Wild* is needed, and more men like Herbert Welsh, these the benefactors of humanity, teach us to lift men rather than club them. True leadership always is in humanity, and it is not enough to possess pity and mercy, but we must be possessed by them. These give real authority and go to the heart, moves and persuades it, though this is not the language of greed and blood, but that of the Divine will.

There is sublime and pathetic beauty in the way the brute comes out in this noble dog. Driven to his own by man's cruelty and yet triumphing over the brute, becoming the master and leader of the pack, outdoing them in cunning, defying the bravest hunter, like man, and yet unlike him, always surrounded with mystery, through the touch of the human. Alone every year the dog goes down to the spot where his master was killed, and with one long mournful howl, stands motionless as a statue, the wolfish nature dead before the unforgettable Love that drew him there.

In this little drama we are brought face to face with that which we refuse to confess to ourselves, and are chilled by the realism of *The Call of the Wild,* and bidden by it to listen to the Voice of the Divine, which also is a part of our being.

# Chapter 7

## Critical Essays

# Jack London*

## by Earle Labor

London said he wrote *The Call of the Wild* to redeem the species. "I started it as a companion to my other dog-story 'Bâtard,' which you may remember; but it got away from me, and instead of 4,000 words it ran 32,000 before I could call a halt" (*Book of Jack London,* I, 388). Joan London tells us that so far as her father was concerned, this masterpiece was "a purely fortuitous piece of work, a lucky shot in the dark that had unexpectedly found its mark," and that, when reviewers enthusiastically interpreted *The Call of the Wild* as a brilliant human allegory, he was astonished: " 'I plead guilty,' he admitted, 'but I was unconscious of it at the time. I did not mean to do it.' "[1] However, he was not entirely oblivious to the story's unusual merit; in a letter to his publisher George Brett, he wrote: "It is an animal story, utterly different in subject and treatment from the rest of the animal stories which have been so successful; and yet it seems popular enough for the 'Saturday Evening Post,' for they snapped it up right away."[2]

Though London may not have understood the full import of this statement, his story was in fact "utterly different" from the

---

* From *Jack London* by Earle Labor, pp. 71-78; copyright 1974 by Twayne Publishers, Inc. Reprinted with permission of Twayne Publishers, a division of G. K. Hall & Co.

humanized beasts in Kipling's "Mowgli" stories and from the sentimental projections of Margaret Marshall Saunders's *Beautiful Joe*
and Ernest Seton's *Biography of a Grizzly,* which were enormously
popular in London's day and which can still be found in the children's sections of public libraries. Charles G. D. Roberts, writing
about the appeal of such literature at the turn of the century,
explained that "the animal story, as we now have it, is a potent
emancipator. It frees us for a little while from the world of shop-
worn utilities, and from the mean tenement of self of which we do
well to grow weary. . . . It has ever the more significance, it has ever
the richer gift of refreshment and renewal, the more humane the
heart and spiritual the understanding which we bring to the
intimacy of it."[3] This explanation holds true for *The Call of the
Wild* as well as for the other wild animal stories: London's work
offers the "gift of refreshment and renewal," as well as a certain
escapism. The difference is its radical departure from the conventional animal story in style and substance—the manner in which it
is, to use the psychoanalytic term, "overdetermined" in its multi-
layered meaning.[4]

Maxwell Geismar gives a clue to the deeper layer of meaning
when he classifies the work as "a beautiful prose poem, or *nouvelle,*
of gold and death on the instinctual level" and as a "handsome
parable of the buried impulses."[5] We need only interpolate that
these "buried impulses" are essentially human, not canine, and that
the reader identifies more closely than he realizes with the
protagonist of that *nouvelle.* The plot is animated by one of the
most basic of archetypal motifs: the Myth of the Hero. The call to
adventure, departure, initiation, the perilous journey to the "world
navel" or mysterious life-center, transformation, and apotheosis—these are the phases of the Myth; and all are present in Buck's
progress from the civilized world through the natural and beyond to
the supernatural world.[6] His journey carries him not only through
space but also through time and, ultimately, into the still center of a
world that is timeless.

Richard Chase points out that in the type of long fiction most
properly designated as the *romance,* character becomes "somewhat
abstract and ideal," and plot is "highly colored": "Astonishing
events may occur, and these are likely to have a symbolic or

ideological, rather than a realistic, plausibility. Being less committed to the immediate rendition of reality than the novel, the romance will more freely veer toward mythic, allegorical, and symbolistic forms."[7] All of these remarks are directly applicable to *The Call of the Wild,* in which the richly symbolistic form ultimately becomes the content of the fiction. The seven chapters of the work fall into four major parts or movements. Each of these movements is distinguished by its own theme, rhythm, and tone; each is climaxed by an event of dramatic intensity; and each marks a stage in the hero's transformation from a phenomenal into an ideal figure.

Part I, consisting of three chapters, is, with its emphasis on physical violence and amoral survival, the most Naturalistic—and the most literal—of the book. Its rhythms are quick, fierce, muscular. Images of intense struggle, pain, and blood predominate. Chapter I, "Into the Primitive," describes the great dog's kidnapping from Judge Miller's pastoral ranch and his subsequent endurance of the first rites of his initiation—the beginning of the transformation that ultimately carries him deep into Nature's heart of darkness: "For two days and nights he neither ate nor drank, and during those two days and nights of torment, he accumulated a fund of wrath that boded ill for whoever first fell foul of him. His eyes turned blood-shot, and he was metamorphosed into a raging fiend. So changed was he that the Judge himself would not have recognized him; and the express messengers breathed with relief when they bundled him off the train at Seattle."[8]

The high priest of Buck's first initiatory rites is the symbolic figure in the red sweater, the man with the club who relentlessly pounds the hero into a disciplined submission to the code of violence and toil. "Well, Buck, my boy," the man calmly observes after the merciless beating, "we've had our little ruction, and the best thing we can do is to let it go at that. You've learned your place, and I know mine" (*15*).* Like all of London's heroes who survive the rigors of the White Silence, Buck has passed the first test: that of adaptability.

Chapter II, "The Law of Club and Fang," takes the hero to the Northland. On the Dyea beach he encounters the dogs and men who are to become his traveling companions in the long hard months

---

* Page references to *The Call of the Wild* are to the text included in this volume.

ahead. He also continues to absorb the lessons of survival. Curly, the most amiable of the newly arrived pack, is knocked down by a veteran husky, then ripped apart by the horde of canine spectators. The scene remains vividly etched in Buck's memory: "So that was the way. No fairplay. Once down, that was the end of you." (20). Later, as he is broken into his traces for the trail, he awakens to the great driving motivation of the veteran sled-dogs: the extraordinary love of toil. But more significant is the metamorphosis of his moral values. He learns, for example, that stealing, an unthinkable misdeed in his former state, can be the difference between survival and death:

> [His] first theft marked Buck as fit to survive in the hostile Northland environment. It marked his adaptability, his capacity to adjust himself to changing conditions, the lack of which would have meant swift and terrible death. It marked, further, the decay or going to pieces of his moral nature, a vain thing and a handicap in the ruthless struggle for existence. It was all well enough in the Southland, under the law of love and fellowship, to respect private property and personal feelings; but in the Northland, under the law of club and fang, whoso took such things into account was a fool, and in so far as he observed them he would fail to prosper. (25)

Chapter III, "The Dominant Primordial Beast," marks the conclusion of the first major phase of Buck's initiation; for it reveals that he is not merely qualified as a member of the pack but that he is worthy of leadership. In this chapter, there is a pronounced modulation of style to signal the glimmerings of Buck's mythic destiny; instead of sharply detailed physical description, we begin to encounter passages of tone-poetry:

> With the aurora borealis flaming coldly overhead, or the stars leaping in the frost dance, and the land numb and frozen under its pall of snow, this song of the huskies might have been the defiance of life, only it was pitched in minor key, with long-drawn wailings and half-sobs, and was more the pleading of life, the articulate travail of existence. . . . When he moaned and sobbed, it was with the pain of living that was of old the pain of his wild fathers, and the fear and mystery of the cold and dark that was to them fear and mystery. (34)

London's style becomes increasingly lyrical as the narrative rises from literal to symbolic level, and it reaches such intensity near the end of Chapter III that we now realize that Buck's is no common animal story:

> There is an ecstasy that marks the summit of life, and beyond which life cannot rise. And such is the paradox of living, this ecstasy comes when one is most alive, and it comes as a complete forgetfulness that one is alive. This ecstasy, this forgetfulness of living, comes to the artist, caught up and out of himself in a sheet of flame; it comes to the soldier, war-mad on a stricken field and refusing quarter; and it came to Buck, leading the pack, sounding the old wolf-cry, straining after the food that was alive and that fled swiftly before him through the moonlight. He was sounding the deeps of his nature, and of the parts of his nature that were deeper than he, going back into the womb of Time. He was mastered by the sheer surging of life, the tidal wave of being, the perfect joy of each separate muscle, joint, and sinew in that it was everything that was not death, that it was aglow and rampant, expressing itself in movement, flying exultantly under the stars and over the face of dead matter that did not move. (*36*)

This paragraph is a thematic epitome of the whole work, and it functions as a prologue to the weird moonlit scene in which Buck challenges Spitz for leadership of the team, a scene noted by Geismar as "a perfect instance of the 'son-horde' theory which Frazer traced in *The Golden Bough,* and of that primitive ritual to which Freud himself attributed both a sense of original sin and the fundamental ceremony of religious exorcism" (*Rebels and Ancestors,* pp.150-51).

Even though Buck has now "Won to Mastership" (Chapter IV), he is not ready for apotheosis; he is a leader and a hero—but he is not yet a god. His divinity must be confirmed, as prescribed by ritual, through death and rebirth. After the climactic pulsations of Chapter III, there is a slowing of beat in the second movement. Death occurs symbolically, almost literally, in Chapter V ("The Toil of Trace and Trail"). Clustering darkly, the dominant images are those of pain and fatigue as Buck and his teammates suffer under the ownership of the three *chechaquos:* Charles, his wife Mercedes, and her brother Hal—"a nice family party." Like the two Incapables of "In a Far Country," they display all the fatal symptoms of incompetence and unfitness: "Buck felt vaguely that there was no depending upon these two men and the woman. They did not know how to do anything, and as days went by it became apparent that they could not learn. They were slack in all things, without order or discipline"(*52*). Without a sense of economy or the will to work and endure hardships themselves, they overwork, starve, and beat their dogs—then they turn on one another: "Their irritability arose out of their misery, increased with it, doubled upon it, outdistanced it. The wonderful patience of the trail which comes to all men who toil hard and suffer sore, and remain sweet of speech and kindly, did not come to these two men and the woman. They had no inkling of such a patience. They were stiff and in pain; their muscles ached, their bones ached, their very hearts ached; and because of this they became sharp of speech, and hard words were first on their lips in the morning and last at night"(*53*). This ordeal is the second long and difficult phase of Buck's initiation. The "long journey" is described in increasingly morbid imagery as the "perambulating skeletons" and "wayfarers of death" approach closer to their fatal end in the thawing ice of Yukon River; the journey ends with Buck's symbolic crucifixion as he is beaten nearly to death by Hal shortly before the ghostly caravan moves on without him and disappears into the lethal river.

Buck's rebirth comes in Chapter VI, "For the Love of a Man," which also functions as the third and transitional movement of the narrative. Having been rescued by John Thornton, the benign helper who traditionally appears in the Myth to lead the hero toward his goal, Buck is now being readied for the final phase of his odyssey. Appropriately, the season is spring; and the mood is idyllic as he wins back his strength, "lying by the river bank through the long spring days, watching the running water, listening lazily to the songs of the birds and the hum of nature. . . . (*61*) And during this same convalescent period, the hints of his destiny grow more insistent: "He was older than the days he had seen and the breaths he had drawn. He linked the past with the present, and the eternity behind him throbbed through him in a mighty rhythm to which he swayed as the tides and seasons swayed. . . . Deep in the forest a call was sounding. . . . But as often as he gained the soft unbroken earth and the green shade, the love for John Thornton drew him back. . . ." (*69*) The passionate devotion to Thornton climaxes in the final scene of Chapter VI when Buck wins a thousand-dollar wager for his master by moving a half-ton sled a hundred yards; this legendary feat, which concludes the third movement of the narrative, foreshadows the hero's supernatural appointment in the fourth and final movement.

Chapter VII, "The Sounding of the Call," consummates Buck's transformation. In keeping with this change, London shifts both the setting and the tone. Thornton, taking the money earned by Buck in the wager, begins his last quest "into the East after a fabled lost mine, the history of which was as old as the history of the country . . . steeped in tragedy and shrouded in mystery." As the small party moves into the wilderness, the scene assumes a mythic atmosphere, and the caravan is enveloped in a strange aura of timelessness:

> The months came and went, and back and forth they twisted through the uncharted vastness, where no men were and yet where men had been if the Lost Cabin were true. They went across divides in summer blizzards, shivered under the midnight sun on naked mountains between the timber line and the eternal snows, dropped into summer valleys amid swarming gnats and flies, and in the shadows of glaciers picked strawberries and flowers as ripe and fair as any the Southland could boast. In the fall of the year they penetrated a weird lake country, sad and silent, where wild-fowl had been, but where then there was no life nor sign of life—only the blowing of chill winds, the forming of ice in sheltered places, and the melancholy rippling of waves on lonely beaches. (*74*)

The weirdness of the atmosphere is part of the "call to adventure" described by Joseph Campbell in *The Hero with a Thousand Faces,* which "signifies that destiny has summoned the hero and transferred his spiritual center of gravity from within the pale of society to a zone unknown. This fateful region of both treasure and danger may be variously represented: as a distant land, a forest . . . or profound dream state; but it is always a place of strangely fluid and polymorphous beings, unimaginable torments, superhuman deeds and impossible delight." (*58*) This "fateful region of both treasure and danger" is a far cry from Judge Miller's pastoral ranch and from the raw frontier of the Klondike gold rush: it is the landscape of myth. The party finally arrives at its destination, a mysterious and incredibly rich placer-valley where "Like giants they toiled, days flashing on the heels of days like dreams as they heaped the treasure up." (*75*)

His role fulfilled as guide into the unknown zone to the "World Navel," Thornton and his party are killed by the savage Yeehats;

and Buck is released from the bond of love to fulfill the last phase of his apotheosis as he is transformed into the immortal Ghost Dog of Northland legend; he incarnates the eternal mystery of creation and life: "[And when] the long winter nights come on and the wolves follow their meat into the lower valleys ... a great, gloriously coated wolf, like, and yet unlike, all other wolves ... may be seen running at the head of the pack through the pale moonlight or glimmering borealis, leaping gigantic above his fellows, his great throat abellow as he sings a song of the younger world, which is the song of the pack." (*86*)

Though *The Call of the Wild* was perhaps no luckier than any other great artistic achievement, it was "a shot in the dark" in an unintended sense—into the dark wilderness of the unconscious. And as with other great literary works, its ultimate meaning eludes us. But at least a significant part of that meaning relates to the area of human experience which cannot be translated into discursive terms and which must therefore be approached tentatively and obliquely. After granting this much, we may infer that the animating force of London's wild romance is the vital energy Jung called *libido* and that London's hero is a projection of the reader's own *self* which is eternally striving for psychic integration in the process called *individuation*. Such an inference accounts for the appropriateness of London's division of his narrative into seven chapters which fall naturally into four movements: quaternity symbolizing, in Jung's words, "the ideal of completeness" and "the totality of the personality"—seven, the archetypal number of perfect order and the consummation of a cycle.[9] But, of course, we do not need such a technical explanation to know that the call to which we respond as the great Ghost Dog flashes through the glimmering borealis singing his song of the younger world is the faint but clear echo of a music deep within ourselves.

# Notes

from Earle Labor's *Jack London*

1. Joan London, *Jack London and His Times*, p. 252. Cf. C. G. Jung's explanation of the "primordial vision" as "an experience ...which cannot be accepted by the conscious outlook" in *Modern Man in Search of a Soul*, p. 159.
2. Letter to George P. Brett, February 12, 1903 (Huntington file).

3. Charles G. D. Roberts, *The Kindred of the Wild* (Boston, 1902), p. 29.
4. See Simon O. Lesser, *Fiction and the Unconscious* (Boston, 1957), p. 113.
5. Maxwell Geismer, ed., "Introduction," *Jack London: Short Stories,* American Century Series (New York, 1960), pp. ix-x.
6. See Joseph Campbell, *The Hero with a Thousand Faces,* Meridian Ed. (New York, 1956), pp. 34-36.
7. Richard Chase, *The American Novel and Its Tradition,* Anchor Ed. (Garden City, N. Y., 1957), p. 13.
8. *The Call of the Wild* (New York, 1903), p. 26. [Page 14 of this casebook]
9. See J. E. Cirlot, *A Dictionary of Symbols,* trans. Jack Sage (New York, 1962), p. 223.

# The Ghost Dog, A Motif in *The Call of the Wild**

## by Lawrence Clayton

In *The Call of the Wild* Jack London pictures Buck in the last stage of his atavistic transformation interbreeding with the wolves and terrorizing the Indians of the area. London indicates that these Indians later come to believe the ferocious animal is a Ghost Dog with preternatural powers and cunning.

The artistically appropriate conclusion to the transformation of the "super" dog is closely related to a folk motif recorded in an area close to where London gathered the material for his Alaskan stories. Stith Thompson's *Motif-Index of Folk-Literature* lists a legend of ghost dogs (E 521.1) belonging to the Eskimos of the Bering Strait area. The source referred to by Thompson is Edward William Nelson's *The Eskimos About Bering Strait* in the *Eighteenth Annual Report of the Bureau of American Ethnology* for 1896-1897.[1] Though Nelson's collected version of the folk tale contains the motif,[2] the story deals primarily with the return from the dead of a village girl. The element significant in a discussion of *The Call of the Wild* is that she returns from the "village of the dog shades" where dead people "can see how the living dogs feel when beaten."[3] The assumption utilized by London is that Buck is punishing the Indians in this life, a reversal of the situation in the folk tale. The

* Reprinted from *Jack London Newsletter* 5 (September-December, 1972): p. 158, with permission of Hensley C. Woodbridge, ed.

plot is so noticeably different from that of the novel that London obviously did not seek to use the old story, even if he had heard it in a form similar to that recorded by Nelson. The Indian belief in the existence of a "shade" or ghostly afterworld is, however, confirmed by the tale. How widespread the tale was in London's time is unknown, but the motif of the ghost dog, an idea apparently otherwise rare in recent American literature, is contained in both stories. It seems plausible that London became acquainted with the idea of a ghost dog during that Alaskan winter when he was stranded and utilized the folk belief to provide the conclusion for his story.

# Notes

1. pp. 19-518.
2. pp. 488-90.
3. p. 488.

# The Romantic Necessity in Literary Naturalism: Jack London*

## by Jay Gurian

Jack London's work is puzzling only when viewed from the alleged opposition of naturalism and romanticism. From such a view Alfred Kazin remarks of London and Upton Sinclair, "the curious thing about these leading Socialist 'fictioneers' is that they were the most romantic novelists of their time."[1] But there is no fundamental mutual exclusiveness between modern romanticism and the modern view of a causative naturalist universe. In another paragraph Kazin unwittingly takes the curiousness out of the thing when he says that London's "heroes stormed the heights of their own minds, and shouted that they were storming the world."[2] Modern romanticism may be defined as the storming by private vision and power to comprehend and affect the universe; and London is, very simply, a romantic in his exultation of private visions which he takes to be visions of the modern world.

But as every nineteenth-century man came to fear, and as every twentieth-century man has come to know, there are two worlds against which to storm: the supernatural and the natural. Perhaps

* Reprinted from *American Literature*, 38 (March 1966): pp. 112-14, by permission of Duke University Press.

in keeping with the modern temper these had better be called "forces." Faust fought the devil, but could not win against the supernatural force; Santiago, in Hemingway's *The Old Man and the Sea,* fought old age, the marlin's strength and will, and finally the marauder sharks, but could not win against these natural forces. Yet both these men are "heroes" of a private struggle against the forces that enclose them.

In the same way, Jack London's men fight, as heroes, against surrounding forces. But here we find a curious ambiguity. For London depicts protagonists fighting to win in a causative naturalist universe; but he also depicts antagonists fighting to overcome the causative universe and to affirm beliefs not possible within the dialectics of that universe. For example, in *The Sea-Wolf* London presents two heroes: the titan Wolf Larsen and the "sissy" Humphrey Van Weyden. As narrator, Van Weyden introduces Wolf Larsen for his "strength," the kind "we are wont to associate with things primitive, with wild animals, and the creatures we imagine our tree-dwelling prototypes to have been—a strength savage, ferocious, alive in itself, the essence of life . . . the elemental stuff itself out of which the many forms of life have been molded."[3] But this indomitable man, who literally snaps men's arms and legs with little effort, who emerges from a forecastle brawl—of which he is the intended victim—with no bruises, has a great weakness: he is worried. And what is he worried about? He is worried about his own philosophy. When Van Weyden asks the atheist and Darwinian Larsen: "What do you believe, then?" he replies:

"I believe that life is a mess . . . . It is like yeast, a ferment, a thing that moves and may move for a minute, an hour, a year, or a hundred years, but that in the end will cease to move. The big eat the little that they may continue to move, the strong eat the weak that they may retain their strength. The lucky eat the most and move the longest, that is all."[4]

But his underlying uncertainty is indicated by the fact that he reads in the great classics—Shakespeare, Tennyson, Poe, De Quincey, Darwin, Tyndall, Bulfinch. And even more, there is evidence that Jack London himself is worried about Larsen's philosophy. For, though the first half of *The Sea-Wolf* is Larsen's story—the story of the strong man dominating the ship's little universe—it increasingly becomes the narrator's story as well.

Humphrey Van Weyden is a man of civilization. He calls himself a "temperamental idealist" trying to put into speech "a something felt, a something like the strains of music heard in sleep, a something that convinced yet transcended utterance."[5] In a few short weeks "Hump," as he is called, rises from bumbling cabin boy to effective first mate. He feels that his "hope and faith in human life still survived Wolf Larsen's destructive criticism," but he acknowledges that Larsen had been "a cause of change . . . had opened up for me the world of the real . . . from which I had always shrunk."[6] Hump learns to defend himself against the threat of a knifing, but also learns to answer Wolf's cruelty with strong-minded assertions of principle.

Thus, two contrasting hero-types emerge: Larsen, accepting the naturalist universe, fighting only to be its master; and Hump, rejecting that universe, retaining his idealism and learning to fight against what he has rejected.

This ambiguity of heroes will be seen most strikingly in the character of Martin Eden. But earlier in his writing career, Jack London was able to avoid the ambiguity by the fortunate stroke of creating a non-human hero. In *The Call of the Wild*, Buck, the massive, powerful domestic animal, is gradually converted by the necessity to survive (The Law of Club and Fang) into the "dominant primordial beast." In Buck's universe, as in Wolf Larsen's, it is survive or die: "He must master or be mastered; while to show mercy was a weakness. . . . Kill or be killed, eat or be eaten, was the law; and this mandate, down out of the depths of Time, he obeyed."[7] Gifted by nature with intelligence, physical strength and will, Buck conquers his enemy, Spitz, in a fight to the death, leads his pack of dogs in sled-harness, protects the man who saves him from the inhumanity of his former owners, avenges this man's death by killing his killers, then, compulsively, answers "the call of the wild" by becoming the dominant primordial beast among wild wolves. There is no ambiguity in Buck, the conquering hero in the naturalist universe. He does not read philosophers and poets; he does not suddenly develop a fatal cancer, as Wolf Larsen did. In a word, since he is only an animal, he can be only natural. *The Call of the Wild* is a perfect parable of a biologically and environmentally determined universe. There are no holes in the argument. Buck's highest achievement is to kill, till finally he achieves the killing of man, "the noblest game of all."[8]

But at the same time *The Call of the Wild* suggests the truth that a *wholly* naturalist human hero—operating in a wholly naturalist universe—is an impossibility. For then there could be no hero—no private vision—in a scheme that by definition precluded private variation. Such a scheme would remove from human beings their faculty for abstraction and for choice, that very faculty which raises them above the animal world.

# Notes

1. Alfred Kazin, *On Native Grounds* (New York, 1942), p. 110.
2. *Ibid.*, p. 115.
3. Jack London, *The Sea-Wolf* (New York, 1945), pp. 18-19.
4. *Ibid.*, p. 50.
5. *Ibid.*, pp. 83, 50.
6. *Ibid.*, p. 156.
7. Jack London, *The Call of the Wild* (New York, 1914), p. 153. (Page 63 of this casebook)
8. *Ibid.*, p. 154. (Page 84 of this casebook.)

# Jack London's Naturalism: The Example of *The Call of the Wild**

## by Earl J. Wilcox

Both Jack London's intentions and his accomplishments in *The Call of the Wild* account for the artistic success of the book. For the story which London intended to write—about a dog who merely reverts to the wild—developed into a full, 32,000 word novel. And the simplicity intended in the implicit atavism in the dog's reversion also became a more complex discussion that London apparently bargained for. But a fortuitous combination of events led London to produce the most popular and the best piece of fiction he ever wrote. Thus while he gauged his audience accurately in writing a popular account of Darwinian literature, at the same time the novel gave him an opportunity to explore the philosophical ideas which had been fermenting in his mind but which he had not found opportunity to express in full in his fiction.

Joan London reports her father as saying that he did not recognize "the human allegory in the dog's life-and-death struggle to adapt himself to a hostile environment."[1] And even after he had reread his story several times, he allegedly said, "I plead guilty, but I was unconscious of it at the time. I did not mean to do it."[2] London's disclaimer has been eagerly accepted by critics who point to the

---

*Reprinted from *Jack London Newsletter,* 20 (December, 1969): 91-101, with permission of Hensley C. Woodbridge, ed.

discrepancies in both his plot and his philosophy. Indeed Miss London accepts her father's reported statement as fact, as does, apparently, Roy W. Carlson, and others who can find little to praise in even London's finest work.[3] But London *was* aware of his intentions in the novel, at least in some of the "allegorical" aspects. For sometime later, in defending himself against charges of President Theodore Roosevelt and John Burroughs, who had accused him of being a "nature-faker," London states his artistic purpose in *The Call of the Wild* and *White Fang:*

> I have been guilty of writing two animal stories—two books about dogs. The writing of these two stories, on my part, was in truth a protest against the "humanizing" of animals, of which it seemed to me several "animal writers" had been profoundly guilty. Time and again, and many times, in my narratives, I wrote, speaking of my dog heroes: "He did not think these things; he merely did them," etc. And I did this repeatedly to the clogging of my narrative and in violation of my artistic canons; and I did it in order to hammer into the average human understanding that these dog-heroes of mine were not directed by abstract reasoning, but by instinct, sensation, and emotion, and by simple reasoning. Also, I endeavored to make my stories in line with the facts of evolution; I hewed them to the mark set by scientific research, and awoke, one day, to find myself bundled neck and crop into the camp of the nature-faker.[4]

Throughout the discussion in the essay, London relies on his rather thorough knowledge of Darwinian thought to defend his assertions. If London were not drawing inferences about man in his "dog-heroes," his entire literary career, particularly in relationship to the naturalistic movement, is called into question. For to leave the implications of his struggle-for-survival thesis in the realm of "lower" animals is to relegate the stories to mere animal adventures. Indeed, there would seem to be no London achievement worth quibbling about. But, in fact, in both the first stories and the first novel—in which human beings are clearly the protagonists—these precise themes and motifs are basic philosophy. The extent to which London makes the Darwinian or Spencerian allegory directly applicable to human existence is surely left for the reader to decide. For while there is confusion in London's understanding between the explicit relationships of the evolutionary and atavistic concepts developed by Darwin and the views advanced by Spencer, London seems little concerned about delineating either with a nice distinction. Nevertheless, precise qualification which focuses on naturalistic implications of the novel accounts for the meaning of the work.

The plot of *The Call of the Wild* is so familiar, because of its widespread popularity, that to review it would appear unnecessary, particularly in view of the haste with which London wrote it. Since he is ostensibly concerned with dogs in the naturalism here, however, a brief statement of the plot may be helpful. In simplest terms, Buck, a magnificent dog, lives on Judge Miller's ranch in California. He is kidnapped and taken to Alaska where through numerous hardships and encounters with the "wild" he recognizes his affinity to it and reverts to his primordial state.

It is clear that Buck is not precisely one of the pure breed for whom London held greatest respect, because Buck is a cross between a St. Bernard and a Scotch shepherd.[5] Still, Buck's preeminence, as London later explains, results from the lucky combination of his parents, a familiar philosophical idea emanating from London's views on natural selection. While the Judge is away at a meeting of the Raisin Growers' Association, Buck is stolen by Manuel, a ranch laborer, and sold for fifty dollars to a man who wants to use Buck in the Northern country.

In the suggestive initial chapter, "Into the Primitive," Buck first learns the difference between the "cold" world to which he is being taken and the "warm" world from which he comes. He has not been accustomed to harsh treatment, but being an exceptionally wise dog, he quickly adjusts. In fact, his adjustment and his adaptability become his salvation. Buck's first reaction to rough treatment is in a spirit of rebelliousness. But, London tells his reader before he has gone a dozen pages into the narrative, Buck recognizes a new "law" when he sees it:

> He saw, once for all, that he stood no chance against a man with a club. He had learned the lesson, and in all his after life he never forgot it. That club was a revelation. It was his introduction to the reign of primitive law, and he met the introduction halfway. The facts of life took on a fiercer aspect; and while he faced that aspect uncowed, he faced it with all the latent cunning of his nature aroused.[6]

And each dog who is brought receives the same treatment:

> As the days went by, other dogs came, in crates and at the end of
> ropes, some docilely, and some raging and roaring as he had come;
> and, one and all, he watched them pass under the dominion of the
> man in the red sweater. Again and again, as he looked at each brutal
> performance, the lesson was driven home to Buck: a man with a club
> was a law-giver, a master to be obeyed, though not necessarily
> conciliated. Of this last Buck was never guilty, though he did see
> beaten dogs that fawned upon the man, and wagged their tails, and
> licked his hand. Also he saw one dog, that would neither conciliate
> nor obey, finally killed in the struggle for mastery.[7]

How easily London has transferred his concept of law from the early
stories to this intriguing adventure of man's best friend is readily
observable through the eyes of Buck, for Buck directs the reader's
sympathies to the "good" and the "bad" as they pass through his
life. The story is, of course, not an objective account of the struggle,
not in any way an "experiment" in Zola's frame of reference.
Nevertheless, it is a forceful and powerful adventure through which
London explores the latent possibilities of his Darwinian and Spencerian views.

Buck is finally sold to two Frenchmen who take him into the
Klondike. There Buck learns a corollary law of the club, the law of
fang. It is by these laws that Buck's "primitive" ancestors lived.
And Buck's own translation is succinctly noted: "He had been
suddenly jerked from the heart of civilization and flung into the
heart of things primordial."[8] Contrasted with the soft world from
which Buck has come, in the primordial "all was confusion and
action. . . . There was imperative need to be constantly alert; for
these dogs and men were not town dogs and men. They were
savages, all of them, who knew no law but the law of club and
fang."[9]

Buck's first experience with the law of fang is in observing
another dog, Curly, make friendly overtures to a husky. Curly is
quickly struck, and as soon as she is down, ". . .(the pack) closed in
upon her, snarling and yelping, and she was buried, screaming with
agony, beneath the bristling mass of bodies."[10] And Buck's mind
quickly reaches its first significant conclusion:

> So that was the way. No fair play. Once down, that was the end of
> you. Well, he would see to it that he never went down. Spitz ran out

his tongue and laughed again, and from that moment Buck hated him
with a bitter and deathless hatred.[11]

From this moment Buck's most dangerous enemy is Spitz, a dog who
has arrived with Buck for the new adventures. The allegory in their
action is too obvious, the melodramatic tone is unmistakably clear:
even as Scruff MacKenzie (an early London protagonist in a short
story) fought for his life, Buck early discovers both the "rules" of
"game" and the "laws" which govern the environment into which he
has come.

London's implicit suggestion that the law of club and fang is
supreme in the wild is weakened somewhat by his insistence that
Buck learns unusually fast. And part of Buck's education grows out
of his rebelliousness as much as his need for survival. For Buck
apparently needs only one lesson to know whom to approach, when
to act, and how to act. Always, London says, "he was learning fast,"
and, later Buck is described as "apt scholar." Nevertheless, his
schooling becomes important, for his mobility in adjusting to the
environment precipitates the early sensations he has about his
"call," the urgency to return to the primordial world from which he
has evolved. Using a familiar naturalistic image, the "trap,"[12]
London describes the prescience which surrounds Buck as he
dreams of being caught and devoured by the pack. Even when he
experiences his first snowfall and wakes to find himself buried,

> . . . a great surge of fear swept through him—the fear of the wild
> thing for the trap. It was a token that he was harking back through
> his own life to the lives of his forebears, for he was a civilized dog, an
> unduly civilized dog and of his own experience knew no trap and so
> could not of himself fear it.[13]

Watching and learning, Buck discovers that self-preservation
means more than defensive action. Offensive maneuvers are also a
part of the "law," particularly in regard to the procurement of food.
Like Theodore Dreiser's Carrie, who "adjusts" to Chicago to live,
Buck steals food to live. But London cannot resist propagandizing,
and he comments in non-Dreiserian terms.

> This first theft marked Buck as fit to survive in the hostile Northland
> environment. It marked his adaptability, his capacity to adjust him-
> self to changing conditions, the lack of which would have meant swift
> and terrible death. It marked, further, the decay or going to pieces of

his moral nature, a vain thing and a handicap in the ruthless struggle for existence. It was all well enough in the Southland, under the law of love and fellowship, to respect private property and personal feelings; but in the Northland, under the law of club and fang, whoso took such things into account was a fool, and in so far as he observed them he would fail to prosper.[14]

C. C. Walcutt has noted the similarity between this passage and the one in which London describes the adaptability of Vance Corliss, one of London's earlier protagonists.[15] For once Buck learns to adjust, "his development (or retrogression) was rapid."[16] Experience is his teacher, even as it had been Sister Carrie's or Stephen Crane's Maggie. But his morality is not questioned by the reader because Buck is a dog—or because London chooses to ignore the moral implications of Buck's thievery. For Buck's "new" way of life is new to him only momentarily. As London closes out his discourse on the law of club and fang, he comments on Buck's strange awareness of memories of a previous life in which his ancestors had lived precisely as he is now having to live in his struggle for survival.[17] As the culture of generations of civilizations fell from Scruff Mackenzie, the same process occurs through Buck's atavism.

> The domesticated generations fell from him. In vague ways he remembered back to the youth of the breed, to the time the wild dogs ranged in packs through the primeval forest, and killed their meat as they ran it down. It was no task for him to learn to fight with cut and slash and the quick wolf snap. In this manner had fought forgotten ancestors.[18]

Buck's evolutionary process is a combination of natural selection and of other Darwinian "accidents" through which he has evolved. The probability of his existence, a product of no clearly definable pattern, had characterized, for example, the view of Fortune La Perle (in an earlier London short story), who also knew life as chance. About Buck, too, London again asserts:

> Thus, as token of what a puppet thing life is the ancient song surged through him and he came into his own again; and he came because men had found a yellow metal in the North, and because Manuel was a gardener's helper whose wages did not lap over the needs of his wife and divers small copies of himself.[19]

It is London the pessimist who speaks for Buck in this cryptic manner.

The highest achievement of the novel is clearly Chapter III, "The Dominant Primordial Beast." Following themes, images, and tonal qualities upon which Frank Norris had dwelt in his descriptions of McTeague and Trina, and with which Stephen Crane described his central figures in *Maggie*, London is emphatic and convincing: "The dominant primordial beast was strong in Buck, and under the fierce conditions of trail life it grew and grew."[20] By now Buck has had many hours of schooling which have prepared him for the supreme test. The lead dog, whose job it is to keep the others in line, even if killing is necessary, is Spitz. From the first, Spitz and Buck[21] have been deadly enemies. When Spitz tries to steal Buck's bed, Buck reacts, and "The beast in him roared."[22] Even when Francois or Perrault, the masters, try to separate the dogs, Buck is eager to continue the fracas. Once in the grip of the new morality, "fairplay was a forgotten code," and Buck springs on Spitz.[23] While these minor clashes characterize the long trips which Buck and his friends are making, Buck discovers also that he is soft from years in civilization. Buck's feet tell the tale: "(They) were not so compact and hard as the feet of the huskies. His had softened during the many generations since the day his last wild ancestor was tamed by a cave dweller or river man."[24]

The inevitable, bloody showdown between Buck and Spitz is soon to come. And "Buck wanted it. He wanted it because it was his nature. . . ."[25] For Buck had endured thus far because he was different from the Southland dogs: "He alone endured and prospered, matching the husky in strength, savagery, and cunning."[26]

London leads his reader along at a rapid pace as he points toward the supreme effort of Buck's life, his fight with Spitz. In the precision of moving toward the battle, London again shows the explicit parallel between the lives of the dogs whom he is describing and the lives of humanity whom he also has in mind. In perhaps the most poetic passage London ever wrote, he says:

> With the aurora borealis flaming coldly overhead, or the stars leaping in the frost dance, and the land numb and frozen under its pall of snow, this song of the huskies might have been the defiance of life, only it was pitched in minor key, with long-drawn wailings and half-sobs, and was more the pleading of life, the articulate travail of

existence. It was an old song, old as the breed itself—one of the first songs of the younger world in a day when songs were sad. It was invested with the woe of unnumbered generations, this plaint by which Buck was so strangely stirred. When he moaned and sobbed, it was with the pain of living that was of old, the pain of his wild fathers, and the fear and mystery of the cold and dark that was to them fear and mystery. And that he should be stirred by it marked the completeness with which he harked back through the ages of fire and hoof to the raw beginnings of life in the howling ages.[27]

Finally, Buck is given the pre-eminent position as leader of the pack because the others respect his strength and his skill. Even Spitz resists open fighting, though grumbling has set in among some of the pack before the final stretch of a long journey between Dawson and Salt Water.

The call which has been haunting Buck returns one evening as he and the others relax after a day in the traces. A snowshoe rabbit is treed, and the pack is off after it. While leading the pack in the chase, Buck remembers his primordial past:

All that stirring of old instincts which at stated periods drives men out from the sounding cities to forest and plain to kill things by chemically propelled leaden pellets, the blood lust, the joy to kill—all this was Buck's, only it was infinitely more intimate. He was ranging at the head of the pack, running the wild thing down, the living meat, to kill with his own teeth and wash his muzzle to the eyes in warm blood.[28]

And in the description of this thrill of the chase, the joy, the ecstasy of living, London evinces a significant materialistic attitude that links him profoundly with the naturalists. Buck becomes, perhaps, the epitome of London's own materialistic impulses, in his exulting in the joy of living, the joy of life for its own sake. For Buck is also "mastered by the verb 'to live'" in precisely the same manner of Jan, the Unrepentant, and Sturgis Owens, and Scruff Macken-zie—all human protagonists in London's first short stories. Later, London depicted Wolf Larsen, a man, in similar terms; here it is Buck, the dog, who finds the life-urge, the sense of impulse, the will to live, dominating all else.

There is an ecstasy that marks the summit of life, and beyond which life cannot rise. And such is the paradox of living, this ecstasy comes when one is most alive, and it comes as a complete forgetfulness that one is alive. This ecstasy, this forgetfulness of living, comes to the artist, caught up and out of himself in a sheet of flame; it comes to the soldier, war-mad on a stricken field and refusing quarter; and it came to Buck, leading the pack, sounding the old wolf-cry, straining after the food that was alive and that fled swiftly before him through the moonlight. He was sounding the deeps of his nature, and of the parts of his nature that were deeper than he, going back into the womb of Time. He was mastered by the sheer surging of life, the tidal wave of being, the perfect joy of each separate muscle, joint, and sinew and that it was everything that was not death, that it was aglow and rampant, expressing itself in movement, flying exultingly under the stars and over the face of dead matter that did not move.[29]

This formula is characterized by impulse emerging from self-forgetfulness, and the individual who partakes does so without reason. In the comment, it is obvious that man and animal become one in this materialistic view.

Following immediately in the narrative is the passage which tells of Spitz's intention to prevent Buck's remaining the leader. The fight to death ensues. When Spitz attacks, Buck knows the meaning instantly:

In a flash Buck knew it. The time had come. It was to the death. As they circled about, snarling, ears laid back, keenly watching for the advantage, the scene came to Buck with a sense of familiarity. He seemed to remember it all,—the white woods, and earth, and moonlight, and the thrill of battle. . . . To Buck it was nothing new or strange, this scene of old time. It was as though it had always been, the wonted way of things.[30]

The resulting battle is a bloody, ugly affair. It is won by Buck because he has imagination. The quality of mind which produces Buck's victory is indeed a strange and perplexing psychological feat for a mere animal, but as odd as it appears, it does not leave room for mercy. That was "a thing reserved for gentler climes."[31] Buck reigns supreme, "the successful champion, the dominant primordial beast who had made his kill and found it good."[32] London is not explicit in arguing for survival as the motivation for Buck's fight, though it is certainly implicit in all that Buck does from the first encounter with Spitz. The capture of the rabbit is likewise not necessary for survival, but it is artistically relevant since it precipitates Spitz's desire to attack Buck.

After this chapter, which itself is episodic, the remainder of the novel seems almost anti-climactic, though in reality it is not. For London still manages in the scenes following to carry out his central thesis, Buck's return to a former, primitive state. So Buck becomes the leader of the pack, and the team successfully makes its trips between Dawson and other cities. In the leisure between trips, while lying by the fire, Buck's mind wanders back to Judge Miller's home, and London makes the dream of the call nearer:

> The Sunland was very dim and distant, and such memories had no power over him. Far more potent were the memories of his heredity that gave things he had never seen before a seeming familiarity; the instincts (which were but the memories of his ancestors become habit) which had lapsed in later days, and still later, in him, quickened and became alive again.[33]

And in Buck's dreams of the ancestral world of the primitive, described in a manner very similar to the setting in London's earlier "The First Poet" and the later book, *Before Adam*, Buck sees another man:

> This other man was shorter of leg and longer of arm, with muscles that were stringy and knotty rather than rounded and swelling. The hair of this man was long and matted, and his head slanted back under it from the eyes. He uttered strange sounds, and seemed very much afraid of the darkness, into which he peered continually, clutching in his hand, which hung midway between knee and foot, a stick with a heavy stone made fast to the end. He was all but naked, a ragged and fire-scorched skin hanging part way down his back, but on his body there was much hair. In some places, across the chest and shoulders and down the outside of the arms and thighs, it was matted into almost a thick fur. He did not stand erect, but with trunk inclined forward from the hips, on legs that bent at the knees. About his body there was a peculiar springiness, or resiliency, almost catlike, and quick alertness as of one who lived in perpetual fear of things seen and unseen.[34]

With each passing day Buck and his mates are given sleds too heavy to pull, until finally their masters overwork them, and the entire pack crawls, half-dead into Dawson. There Buck is sold to a group of tenderfeet who try also to pack too much on a sled for the tired dogs to pull. In this dull little episode, Buck learns that not all people have a knowledge of even the rudiments of survival, for "Hal," "Charles," and "Mercedes" first quarrel, then fight, and finally resort to beating the dogs into moving the heavy sleds. John Thornton, an informed and interested trapper, warns the tenderfeet to stop beating the dogs and to go no further on the frozen river. After seeing their particularly harsh treatment of Buck, he rescues Buck from the group, and the naive trappers dash on, only to fall through the ice and drown.

In the penultimate chapter, the one most often remembered but far less characteristic of the book's themes, London sentimentalizes his story to make effective the contrast of the last chapter where Buck answers the call of the wild. Thornton revives memories of the soft days before Buck came north. Still the episode only quickens Buck's dilemma. Buck cannot decide between the call of Thornton's love and the lure of the wild. In the structural *tour de force* of the novel, London parallels Buck's journey back to the wild with the literal journey the sled teams take to the wild country of Alaska:

> He was older than the days he had seen and the breaths he had drawn. He linked the past with the present, and the eternity behind him throbbed through him in a mighty rhythm to which he swayed as the tides and seasons swayed. He sat by John Thornton's fire, a broad-breasted dog, white-fanged, and long furred; but behind him were the shades of all manner of dogs, half-wolves, and wild wolves. . . .
>
> So peremptorily did these shades beckon him, that each day mankind and the claims of mankind slipped farther from him. Deep in the forest a call was sounding, and as often as he heard this call, mysteriously thrilling and luring, he felt compelled to turn his back upon the fire and the beaten earth around it, and to plunge into the forest. . . .[35]

London says that "Buck earned sixteen hundred dollars in five minutes for John Thornton," in summarizing the events that characterize Buck's "love of man." But the love and the fame of his feats in civilization cannot forever restrain Buck. The more he is on the trail with the man he loves, the more also the vision; and in all his visions, the "trap" is prominent. Except for his love for Thornton, Buck's return to his "first" love becomes complete. In daydreams, while his masters work their claims, Buck wanders through the wilds until at last he cannot resist the call: "And he knew it, in the old familiar way, as a sound heard before."[36] In answering the call, Buck finds a friend in the wolf he has heard. But the two ways of life persist in his mind, even with increased perplexity as he returns to be with Thornton briefly. At last Buck's killing a bull moose assures him that it is with the wild he belongs:

There is a patience of the wild—dogged, tireless, persistent as life itself—that holds motionless for endless hours the spider in its web, the snake in its coils, the panther in its ambuscade; this patience belongs peculiarly to life when it hunts its living food; and it belonged to Buck as he clung to the flank of the herd. . . .[37]

Trying to break completely with civilization, Buck discovers that it is not easy to leave the man he loves, but returning to find his master dead, Buck knows that "the last tie was broken. Man and the claims of man no longer bound him."[38] Thornton's death, Buck discovers, is at the hands of a tribe of Yeehats. In his revenge, Buck achieves his highest aim, his action pointing to the implicit allegory of the novel: "He had killed man, the noblest game of all, and he had killed in the face of the law of club and fang."[39] Symbolically, the law of survival has become explicit; the law of club and fang both pays and extracts its fee in the merging of the killing of the Indianman by the dog-man.

Once in the wild permanently, Buck soon successfully defends his life against a pack of wolves; then he knows that he was right to answer the call.

London's Darwinian epic is neatly concluded:

And here may well end the story of Buck. The years were not many when the Yeehats noted a change in the breed of timber wolves; for some were seen with splashes of brown on head and muzzle, with a rift of white centering down the chest.[40]

It is the Ghost dog, as elusive in its forays into the Indians' camp as the Evil Spirit into which the dog eventually evolves in the Indian mythology. London apostrophizes the call, noting that Buck still exists in the folklore of the Yeehats, the primitive forerunner of man. And Buck and his "pack" still permeate the world:

But he is not always alone. When the long winter nights come on and the wolves follow their meat into the lower valleys, he may be seen running at the head of the pack through the pale moonlight, or glimmering borealis, leaping gigantic above his fellows, his great throat a-bellow as he sings a song of the younger world, which is the song of the pack.[41]

The naturalism that characterizes this novel is not consistently developed. But neither is the naturalism always of a rigid, definable pattern in, for example, Norris's romantic ending of McTeague, or Dreiser's, or Crane's notable lack of reform (to choose random motifs historically associated with naturalism). In *The Call of the Wild* one does not learn how atavism is biologically or scientifically plausible, nor does one learn how the implicit determinism at work behind Buck's existence comes about. In London's mind, it is merely an assertion, an accepted, "Irrefragable fact," not a scientifically controlled experiment. The book gives no help to either the sociologist or the biologist who turns here expecting to find Taine's, Darwin's, or Spencer's theories put into practice in fiction. Indeed the ideas of Spencer and Darwin are certainly confused in the philosophy which does come through. For Spencer felt that whatever evolutionary processes should work out in creating a complex society, the individual would never notice the changes. In Buck, however, the dominant operating pressure is clearly an evolutionary process, though not rationally defended by London, which the individual not only senses but ultimately knows. While Jung's and Freud's psychology later supported London's legend of the purlieu of a dog world, Darwinism was generally not intent on showing that in the descent of man the intuitive memories of a former state were a prerequisite to man's having been there. Nevertheless, while some technical difficulties preclude one's making rigid and categorical assertions about London's understanding and use of naturalistic theory, he was clearly writing for a popular audience that had no doubt about either his intentions or his accomplishments.

# Notes

1. Joan London, *Jack London and His Times* (New York, 1932), p. 252.
2. Ibid.
3. Roy W. Carlson, "Jack London's Heroes: A Study of Evolutionary Thought" (unpublished Ph.D. dissertation, Department of American Studies, University of New Mexico, 1961), p. 101.

4. Jack London, "The Other Animals" in *Revolution and Other Essays* (New York, 1912), p. 238.
5. Carlson argues that the mixture in Buck's ancestry shows London's failure to see the human allegory in the novel (Carlson, p. 109). But one notices that London's heroic figures are seldom "pure," as for example Martin Eden.
6. Jack London, *The Call of the Wild* (New York, 1963), p. 9. [15. Bracketed page numbers refer to the *Call of the Wild* text included in this casebook.]
7. Ibid., p. 9-10. [15-16]
8. Ibid., p. 13. [19]
9. Ibid. [19]
10. Ibid., p. 14. [19]
11. Ibid. [20]
12. Norris had used it in *McTeague*; Dreiser in *Sister Carrie*.
13. London, *The Call of the Wild,* pp. 17-18. [22]
14. Ibid., p. 21. [25] A year later, London wrote a fine short story, "Diable, A Dog," in which the outlines of Buck's learning the law of club and fang are followed almost exactly. The law of survival, biological and anthropological evolution, and the beast in man motifs are also explored. In a companion piece in the same vein, particularly the survival thesis, see "Too Much Gold," produced in 1904.
15. C. C. Walcutt, *American Literary Naturalism: A Divided Stream* (Minneapolis, 1956), p. 104.
16. London, *The Call of the Wild,* p. 21. [25]
17. Ibid., p. 21. [26] Three years later London devoted an entire novel, *Before Adam,* to a study of the memories of a "civilized" boy of his primordial ancestors.
18. Ibid., pp. 22-23. [26]
19. Ibid. [26]
20. Ibid., p. 24. [27]
21. One remembers the man-dog parallels in *McTeague*. Marcus Schouler and McTeague's battles, parodied in the novel by the dogs who keep growling at each other, bear a striking resemblance to Buck and Spitz's encounters.
22. London, *The Call of the Wild,* p. 29. [28]
23. Ibid., p. 32 [28]
24. Ibid., p. 29. [31]

25. Ibid., p. 31. [32]
26. Ibid. [32]
27. Ibid., pp. 33-34. [34]
28. Ibid., pp. 35-36. [36]
29. Ibid., p. 36. [36]
30. Ibid., p. 37. [37]
31. Ibid., p. 39. [38]
32. Ibid. [38]
33. Ibid., p. 45. [43]
34. Ibid., pp. 45-46. [43]
35. Ibid., p. 72. [63-64]
36. Ibid., p. 88. [76]
37. Ibid., p. 94. [80]
38. Ibid., p. 100. [84]
39. Ibid., p. 99. [84]
40. Ibid., p. 101. [85]
41. Ibid., p. 102. [86]

# The Wolf in London's Mirror*

## by Ann Upton

If one were painting or sculpting Jack London as the old Greek gods were pictured with their animals, London's companion would, of course, be the wolf. He signed his letters "Wolf"; he called his never-occupied, great stone castle "Wolf House"; he once had a great, grey wolf as a pet; a wolf's head adorned his book marks; wolves frequently appear as characters in his novels and short stories and the word "wolf" itself often appears in the titles of many. How does one explain London's attraction to this animal? What was there in his own personality that responded instinctively to the wolf-image?

There is, first, the archetypal image of the wolf as both preserver and destroyer, embodying the two conflicting wishes of mankind, the life wish and the death wish. In the story of creation according to Norse mythology, the sun and the moon are pursued by a pack of wolves which try to devour them and thus end everything. The wolf is also a creature of Odin, feasting on the slain and haunting the warrior paradise, with one great, grey wolf watching the abode of the gods like Fate, knowing his time will come. Yet, as a creature dedicated to Odin, the giver of victory, the wolf is also a propitious sign. In Greek mythology, where everything was conceived in the likeness of man or beast, the wolf is the destructive principle; but by

*From *Jack London Newsletter,* 6 (September-December, 1973), pp. 111-18, with permission of Hensley C. Woodbridge, ed.

carrying away the old and unfit, he made way for new life and thus shared in the creative function.[1] In Celtic myth, the wolf-dog (destroyer) is associated with the stag-dog (preserver), and here the association is clearly that of life-and-death-upon-one-tether.[2] From our pastoral ancestors, we inherit the concept of the wolf as destroyer of the life-sustaining sheep. A "wolf in sheep's clothing" is also an image that dramatizes the difference between the appearance and the reality; it is a representation of the destroyer masked as the sustainer, and suggests the dual nature of all forces. Among the early agricultural tribes, according to Frazer in *The Golden Bough* (Vol. 1, p. 270), the wolf was one of the embodiments of the corn-spirit which must be caught and killed in the last sheaf of corn so that the corn would come up next year. As the corn-spirit, the wolf was the sustainer of life so long as he was imprisoned in the corn; but escaped from control, he could be the destroyer by taking the spirit away from the corn and so preventing the food crop from growing the next year.

In the legend of Romulus and Remus, in the story of Mowgli in Kipling's *Jungle Book,* and in some old Irish legends, the wolf becomes the preserver by suckling babies, imparting with milk, perhaps, supernatural powers. Since London was never sure of the identity of his father, the adolescent fantasy of discovering one's "real" parents to be more admirable or desirable than the parents he lives with may have caused him to imagine them as animals and himself as the son of a wolf. In fact, in one of his first published stories, "Son of the Wolf," London has the Indians call all white men the sons of the wolf. The notion that a man can take on the form of a wolf has persisted from the time of older Roman writings (Petronious, in *The Satyricon,* relates one of the stories told at the banquet of Trimalchio of a man who turns into a wolf); through the loup-garou hysteria in 16th century France when wolf-men, believed to have eaten children, were burned at the stake; to the *Dr. Jekyll and Mr. Hyde* of Robert Louis Stevenson. Whether London, familiar with these stories, selected the wolf image from them or whether he found the image in that collective unconscious Jung claims we share is immaterial. It is his strong, consistent identification with the symbol that is intriguing.

Two contemporaneous influences that could have suggested the wolf image to London were the growing competitiveness of business and the gold rush of the Klondike. Idiomatic expressions using "wolf" fit in well with the competitive atmosphere of business in London's time. The "wolf at the door" and "to throw to the wolves" suggest that nineteenth century capitalism in its drive for profits was like a hungry wolf pack in search of food, a constant threat to the weak. A "lone wolf" carries the idea of independence, self-sufficiency—an idea in harmony with London's image of himself; but it also suggests a lack of social concern, a concept that London did not find so appealing and sought to remedy by his affiliation with the Socialist movement. "To wolf one's food" is to eat voraciously, to gobble up whatever in sight tempts one's appetite. In terms of the growing corporations, the application of the expression is clear; in terms of London personally, the expressions had a sinister meaning which is discussed below.

As for the Klondike, that dream of wealth and adventure that drew so many men of London's age, one met there the wolf of myth and legend: the destroyer who was also cosmic energy, a heat force, the primal warmth amid all that desolate cold. Man could identify with this image and through the identification, renew his strength, courage, adaptability, *elan vital*.

Jack London, as a product of his time, could not have escaped the influence of these suggestions, nor the dichotomy of feeling generated by them. His innate perceptiveness, though, went farther, causing him to associate his own opposing sympathies with the two faces of the wolf. One London face—the adventurous, virile, combative, "natural" man face, typified by the blond, Anglo-Saxon Nietzschean superman—corresponded to the lone wolf, sufficient against the forces of nature in his universe, taking what he wanted, secure in his superiority. The other face—the friendship-seeking, justice-loving, intellectual product of education and civilization that sought expression in Socialism—was like the wolf when he ran in packs, answering the longing for brotherhood and mutual aid. In the wolf-symbol, then, were the two sides of London's nature united.

Through the use of this symbol, London was able to explore the depths of his own nature. A wild counterpart of the dog, the wolf has no structural differences from his domesticated brother. The only distinction between them is founded on their habits; wolves will even mate with larger domestic dogs. Thus it is easy for the wolf-dog to slip from civilization back to the primeval state as Buck does

in *Call of the Wild;* or he may turn from the wild state to civilization as White Fang does. Civilized man, even though he sees the
primitive man in himself inadequately glossed over with civilization,
can only play these interchangeable roles in dreams of fantasies.
Yet by identifying with an animal which looks the same in both wild
and domesticated states, he can vicariously journey from domestication into the primitive and back again. The journeys of London's two
most famous dog-heroes are an attempt at vicarious atavism, and
mirror image of London's two faces.

Buck, in *Call of the Wild,* is the natural man, reverting to the
primitive; the story concerns his experiences while learning to adapt
to life's demands. The book ends when Buck is accepted into the
wolf pack; he has successfully made the journey back to the roots of
his nature. Buck's journey follows closely the journey of the hero as
described by Joseph Campbell in *Hero with a Thousand Faces.*
There is a call of adventure:

> Irresistible impulses seized [Buck]. . . . He would be lying in camp,
> dozing lazily in the heat of day, when suddenly his head would lift
> and his ears cock up, intent and listening . . . seeking for the
> mysterious something that called—called waking or sleeping, at all
> times, for him to come.[3]

And the hero ventures forth from the common world into a region
of supernatural wonder, the dark night of the soul, Dante's "dark
wood":

> He sprang through the sleeping camp and in swift silence dashed
> through the woods. As he drew closer to the cry he went more slowly,
> with caution in every movement, till he came to an open place among
> the trees. . . . *(Call of the Wild, p. 76)**

Fabulous forces are there encountered and a decisive victory won:

> . . . looking out [he] saw, erect on haunches, with nose pointed to the sky,
> a long, lean timber wolf. *(Call of the Wild, p. 76)*

There is, however, no victory in this encounter, for Buck does not
go deep enough into the dark night or the dark forest:

> He knew he was at last answering the call, running by the side of his
> wood brother toward the place from where the call surely

---

*Page references to *The Call of the Wild* are to the text included in this casebook.

came...(but) Buck remembered John Thornton. He sat down ...(then) turned about and started slowly on the back track. *(Call of the Wild, p. 77)*

After Thornton's death, though, Buck answers the call again and this time he fights the whole wolf pack, winning the hero's decisive victory. Buck does not return as the hero should; he remains in the wild and we leave him running with the pack in the dark of the northern winter. If the light is consciousness, Buck is left in the depth of the unconscious. And here a strange parallel with London's life develops.

Jung has said that the archetype has a distinctly numinous character; it drives with remorseless logic to its goal and draws the subject under its spell.[4] The subject is at first unwilling, then no longer able to free himself. It is as though London drew from his unconscious the wolf-dog figure to answer by proxy his call to adventure, then the wolf-dog began to draw him. London said that, unlike his other writing which was laborious, *Call of the Wild* seemed to write itself, the story unfolding like an effortless slipping into unconsciousness. The experience should have brought a depth and fullness of meaning to both London and his archetypal hero, as Campbell says it brings to the hero who is enriched by his adventure and returns with power to bestow boons. But what happens to Buck? His adventure is aborted. London reaches the depths through his proxy, but he can't or won't find his way back, hence he cannot complete the second half of the hero's life, the assimilating of the unconscious potential gained in the symbolic journey. Buck stays in the younger world, reborn to primitive instincts, but dead to the conscious world.

London, like Buck, is a product of the South and civilization, and as he fights to survive, he learns as Buck does that when he sounds the "deeps of his nature...parts of his nature...(are) deeper than he, going back to the womb of Time" *(Call of the Wild, p. 36)*. London, like Buck, leaves California and travels north to the Arctic Circle, finding successive depths of his nature as he travels north. Unlike Buck, however, he cannot stay in the wild. Jung says that "consciousness struggles in a regular panic against being swallowed up in the primitivity and unconsciousness of sheer instinctuality.... The closer one comes to the instinct world, the more violent is the urge to shy away from it. . . . Psychologically, however, the archetype as an image of instinct is a spiritual goal toward which the whole nature of man strives" (*Basic Writings*, p. 82). London, of course, had not yet read Jung (since *Call of the Wild* was published in 1903 and the first translations of Jung's writings appeared in the United States in 1916), but what he does with Buck and White Fang bears out the truth of Jung's observation. Wishing to leave a part of himself in the wild, or being urged by his nature both to stay and to go, London creates a surrogate to return to the conscious world—White Fang. White Fang makes his first voluntary move toward civilization when he goes back to Grey Beaver after spending a cold and lonely night at the deserted Indian campsite. He has sat in the center of the space Grey Beaver's tent has occupied, pointed his nose at the moon, and uttered his first long wolf-howl, a howl containing all "his apprehensions of sufferings and dangers to come."[5] With the coming of daylight, he decides to set out on "The Trail of the Gods." When he finally curls up by Grey Beaver's fire, and is fed, he is content, "secure in the knowledge that the morrow would find him, not wandering forlorn through bleak forest-stretches, but...with the gods to whom he had given himself" (*White Fang*, p. 194). Physical comforts, companionship, and object to worship—all have a part in his choosing civilization at this time.

Later, though, with Weedon Scott, White Fang's choice is tantamount to obligation, and seems to be more of a turning toward death than a return to consciousness. It is true that he travels to the south and warmth, but the old wild ecstacy is missing. In one of the early chapters of the book, killing the ptarmigan,

> [White Fang] was too busy and happy to know that he was happy.... He was thrilling and exulting.... The pitch to which he was aroused was tremendous. All the fighting blood of his breed was up in him and surging through him. This was living, though he did not know it.
> (*White Fang*, p. 158)

And even when White Fang is being tormented by Beauty Smith, "The mere sight of Beauty Smith was sufficient to send him into transports of fury" (*White Fang*, p. 229). The word "transports" here suggests rapture—a pinnacle of living. It is reminiscent of the passage in *The Sea Wolf* when Humphrey Van Weyden wonders why Wolf Larsen does not kill the sailor, Leach, who hates him so. Larsen explains:

It gives a thrill to life. . . . Why should I deny myself the joy of exciting Leach's soul to fever pitch? For that matter, I do him a kindness. . . . He is living more royally than any man for'ard . . . he is living deep and high. I doubt that he has ever lived so swiftly and keenly before, and I honestly envy him sometimes when I see him raging at the summit of passion and sensibility.[6]

It is hate that arouses this passion, but it is a life-passion.

Significantly, London titles the chapter in *White Fang,* in which comes the real turning point for White Fang, "The Clinging Death." The Clinging Death is a bull dog with whom White Fang fights. The dog does not fight like any animal White Fang has ever known. He waddles in good naturedly, never seems to become aroused, gets a grip on White Fang's throat and holds on, slowly squeezing the life out of him. The bull dog, as impersonal as a force of nature, motivated neither by the thrill of battle nor the desire for life, subdues White Fang. After this, White Fang's hold on life seems loosened, for Weedon Scott rescues him, becomes his new god and demands of him, through love, the final obligation of any god—death. White Fang follows Weedon Scott south and the reader leaves White Fang lying "with half-shut, patient eyes, drowsing in the sun."

Compare that with the last glimpse of Buck:

When the long winter nights come on and the wolves follow their meat into the lower valleys, he may be seen running at the head of the pack through the pale moonlight or glimmering borealis, leaping gigantic above his fellows, his great throat a-bellow as he sings a song of the younger world, which is the song of the pack. *(86)*

There is poetry and vigor in the expression of the earlier book, while by the end of *White Fang,* even the style seems to drowse. Clearly, White Fang's journey is toward a more subdued life (if not death) while Buck's is toward a more intense one. Yet London himself thought *White Fang* the better book. It may be that he was trying to prove something to himself, or to justify his own return.

Then does London return from the Klondike follow the pattern of White Fang's journey? London comes out sick, needing in order to sustain life, the fresh foods of the South and civilization. He may also have come out for his love-god, Mabel Appelgarth; or he may only have been completing the journey of the hero. His return, however, is not the triumphant hero's return: he fails to bring back the boon he sought—the elixir that restores the world. For London, the "stinging things of the spirit" are gone. When he tries to recapture them in Socialism, in women, in fame or security, he fails; only in his stories of the far North does he approach the early ecstacy of life. Later, in the autobiographical *Martin Eden,* London makes his dark journey of withdrawal from the external to the internal world; when he retreats to the peace within, he regresses to what Jung calls the infantile unconscious. And to make the analogy even stronger, Martin Eden (London's surrogate), apathetic, finding life an intolerable burden, slips into the sea and drowns himself. In Jungian symbolism the sea stands for the womb, so that in effect Jack London, through his character Martin Eden, finishes his heroes quest by deciding life is not worth living and returning to the womb. In terms of London's own life it is eerily prophetic.

Prophetic also is the emphasis in *White Fang* on the law of survival: "Eat or be eaten." As Maxwell Geismar in *Rebels and Ancestors* says of *White Fang:* "All love, affection, sense of trust [is reduced] to an oral context, stronger, more continuous and basic than the sexual drive itself. The law of life became only and purely the law of meat." When White Fang's father, old One Eye, is stalking the lynx, he watches as the lynx lies crouched, waiting for a porcupine to open himself up. Wolf, lynx, and porcupine are all "intent on life; and such was the curiousness of the game, the way of life for one lay in eating the other and the way of life for the other lay in not being eaten" *(White Fang, p. 145).* In fact, London repeats the law "eat or be eaten" so often that he apparently convinces himself; for when he is forty, overweight, and sick with uremia, he continues to eat two raw ducks a day. It is reminiscent of the man in London's story "Love of Life" who stuffs his mattress with food because he has once been so hungry. But it is also a way of using the wolf's voracious appetite to eat oneself to death.

London certainly felt a deep instinctual identification with the wolf-dog figures in *Call of the Wild* and *White Fang.* Van Wyck Brooks called it London's "literary lycanthropy." Sidney Alexander[7] claims Jack London wasn't sure whether he was a man or a wolf. Although this assertion does seem a trifle exaggerated, it does indicate how deeply every London reader feels this identification and how remarkable was London's insight into his own character to choose and develop this image.

# Notes

1. H. R. Ellis Davidson, *Gods and Myths of Northern Europe* (Middlesex, England: Penguin Books, Ltd., 1964).
2. Anne Ross, *Pagan Celtic Britain* (London: Routledge and Kegan Paul, 1967), p. 341.
3. Jack London, *The Call of the Wild and White Fang* (New York: Bantam Pathfinder Editions, 1963), p. 89. [Page 76 of this casebook]
4. Carl Jung, *The Basic Writings of C. G. Jung,* ed. Violet Staub de Laszle (New York: Modern Library, 1959), p. 75.
5. *Call of the Wild and White Fang.* Hereafter references to either *Call of the Wild* or *White Fang* are to the edition cited in footnote three.
6. Jack London, *The Sea Wolf and Selected Stories* (New York: The New American Library, Inc., 1964), p. 121.
7. Sidney Alexander, "Jack London's Literary Lycanthropy," *Reporter,* 16 (1957), 46-48.

# Jack London's *Mondo Cane: The Call of the Wild* and *White Fang**

## by Earle Labor

### I

At a meeting of the Michigan College English Association a few
years ago, Sam Baskett—then MCEA President—told a story that
serves neatly as an "objective correlative" for Jack London's current
reputation among the literati. The anecdote, as I recall it, went
something like this. One evening during his pre-doctoral salad days
Sam was chatting with several other graduate students, sharing
those dreams of scholarly glory so often aroused by too many hours
in the library, too much coffee, and too little sleep. One member of
the group explained that he was writing a definitive prolegomenon to
*Finnegans Wake*; another had deciphered the true nature of Henry
James's "obscure hurt"; and a third had managed to explicate all
thirteen ways of looking at a blackbird. After each had assured the
group of his certain success, it was Sam's turn to confide that he was
devoting his energies to the revival of a major if neglected American
literary naturalist—Jack London. His announcement was received

*From *Jack London Newsletter* 1 (September-December, 1967), pp. 2-13, with
permission of Hensley C. Woodbridge, ed.

with an awkward silence. Finally, the Joycean brightly volunteered: "Oh yes, he was the fellow who wrote the stories about the dogs!"

Professor Baskett's story reveals two things. First—and obviously—among contemporary graduate students, Joyce, James, and Stevens are "in"; London is "out." Moreover, those of us who are indiscreet enough to manifest a critical enthusiasm for London's works are likely to be labeled as "low camp." But more important, if less apparent, the story indicates that London's dogs have a curious way of sticking in our memories—even in the memories of sophisticated young critics who have put aside the simple literary pleasures of childhood.

Among the world's common readers there is little indication that this kind of pleasure has diminished. *The Call of the Wild* has been translated into more than thirty languages; Macmillan has sold over two million hardcover copies; and the current volume of *Books in Print* lists thirteen separate editions of the novel, not all of which are by any means juvenilia. Sales and printing of *White Fang*, though slightly less in number, are also impressive. Despite the critics' relegation of London's works to the dead-letter office, his dog stories evidently remain very much alive on the popular market; and despite the disparagement and short notice he receives in most of our literary histories, *The Call of the Wild* is, oddly enough, usually mentioned as "a masterpiece" of its type. Even so, the reasons for its enduring appeal have not been elaborated; nor has it (or *White Fang*) received more than cursory attention from the literary analysts.

One explanation for this kind of critical neglect lies in the very skill with which London made his stories so easy to read. As Simon O. Lesser has pointed out in his *Fiction and the Unconscious* (Boston, 1957), we tend to disparage that which is effortless, and the "tendency to assume that by and large the value of reading matter is proportionate to the amount of difficulty it offers . . . manifests itself frequently in literary criticism and scholarship" (p. 5). It would seem that the current vogue of such writers as James, Joyce, and Stevens is due in part to the complexities of their styles as well as to the intrinsic literary merit which their works undoubtedly possess. In other words, their works offer an intellectual challenge to the critical puzzle-solver which may or may not be related directly to more basic aesthetic considerations: the aspiring young critic can make his reputation by ingenious explication and stylistic analysis of such works without concern for less precise if more fundamental problems of "the philosophy of literature as art." But Jack London is difficult for the critics because he is so easy for his readers. In contrast to the meticulous attention insisted upon by Henry James, the willing suspension of disbelief required by Wallace Stevens, and the leap of faith demanded by James Joyce, London asks no more of his reader than a modicum of literacy and sincere desire to be entertained by a good story (I am referring here to London's fiction—not to his sociological treatises). As he explained in his pamphlet "Eight Great Factors of Literary Success,"

> [Herbert Spencer's *Philosophy of Style*] taught me the subtle and manifold operations necessary to transmute thought, beauty, sensation and emotion into black symbols on white paper; which symbols, through the reader's eye, were taken into his brain, and by his brain transmuted into thought, beauty, sensations and emotions that fairly corresponded with mine. Among other things, this taught me to *know* the brain of my reader, in order to select the symbols that would compel his brain to realize my thought, or vision, or emotion. Also, I learned that the right symbols were the ones that would require the expenditure of the minimum of my reader's brain energy, leaving the maximum of his brain energy to realize and enjoy the content of my mind, as conveyed to his mind.[1]

London's great popularity attests to the thoroughness with which he knew the brain of the common reader; he could not have cared less about the brain of the literary critic, whom he regarded as "a deedless, actionless thinker."[2]

This is no excuse, however, for condescension on the part of the critic, whose role—regardless of the creative writer's contempt—must be to procure a viable meaning for the readers of his time and place.[3] The modern critic has been inexcusably remiss in attempting to procure such meaning from London's fiction. Mr. Lesser is of course right in saying that "No one person can hope to see, much less to say, all the true and important things which ought to be said about any single masterpiece of narrative art. . . . All one can hope to do is to identify some of the more important factors—some of the urgent needs which cause us to read, some of the basic characteristics of fiction which enable it to satisfy those needs." Lesser's statement sets the guidelines for this essay on London's *Call of the Wild* and *White Fang.* What I hope to do, essentially, is to identify "some of the more important factors" that have given these two novels their lasting appeal. I hope also to explain why *The Call* has greater appeal than *White Fang* and to justify my classification of the first as a "great" book and the second as merely a "very good" one.

One point should be made clear at the outset. These narratives are stories about dogs in a superficial sense only. They are, more accurately, beast fables. Stated simply, our interest in them—unconsciously if not consciously—centers in what they reveal not about animals as animals but about the human situation. By using canine rather than human protagonists, London was able to say a good deal more about this situation than he might have been otherwise allowed by the editors of such publications as the *Saturday Evening Post* and *Cosmopolitan,* who had to be careful not to offend the moral sensibilities of their Victorian readers. Just as Poe had masked the naked realities of sex under the cloak of Gothicism two generations earlier, so London could present such realities without undue offense as long as he dramatized them at a subhuman level and avoided calling a spade a spade. A case in point is his vivid presentation of "the lovemaking of the Wild, the sex-tragedy of the natural world" in the early pages of *White Fang* when old One Eye and the ambitious young wolf fight to the death while "the she-wolf, the cause of it all," sits and watches with sadistic pleasure. Another, more to the point, is Buck's ethical retrogression in *The Call of the Wild:* we can accept his learning to steal and rob without scruple and to kill without pity because he is "just a dog," whereas such behavior on the part of a human protagonist would necessarily affect us with revulsion. In fiction as in dreams we are protected by a "censor" which disguises, and shields us from, what Freud called the "moral chaos of the id." Writing during an era in which gentility was regarded as a considerably higher good than frankness, London wisely sublimated these grosser realities by means of the art of fable.

## II

A proper understanding of *The Call of the Wild* and *White Fang* should perhaps begin with examination of "Bâtard," an earlier dog story published in the June, 1902, issue of *Cosmopolitan* under the discreet title "Diable—A Dog." Although its relationship to the two later works is inverse, this story shares with them both the fabulistic element and—especially with *White Fang*—the naturalistic theme of hereditary and environmental determinism. In a sense the three works might be regarded as two sides and the edge of a single coin: London's version, as it were, of *Mondo Cane*. Superficially, we could say that the common theme of all three is that "It's a dog's world." Beyond this glib generalization, however, they are very different stories. "Bâtard" is an anatomy of hatred, and its canine protagonist—"Hell's Spawn," as he is called by some—is the antithesis of everything that man's best friend is supposed to be. Yet it is clear that such devils are not merely born; they are also made:

> Bâtard did not know his father—hence his name—but, as John Hamlin [the storekeeper of the Sixty Mile Post] knew, his father was a great gray timber wolf. But the mother of Bâtard, as he dimly remembered her, was a snarling, bickering, obscene husky, full-fronted and heavy-chested, with a malign eye, a cat-like grip on life, and a genius for trickery and evil. There was neither faith nor trust in her. Her treachery alone could be relied upon, and her wild-wood amours attested her general depravity. Much of evil and much of strength were there in these, Bâtard's progenitors, and, bone and flesh of their bone and flesh, he had inherited it all. And then came Black Lèclerè, to lay his heavy hand on the bit of pulsating puppy life, to press and prod and mould till it became a big bristling beast, acute in knavery, overspilling with hate, sinister, malignant, diabolical. With a proper master Bâtard might have made an ordinary fairly efficient sled-dog. He never got the chance: Lèclerè but confirmed him in his congenital iniquity.[4]

It is his sadistic treatment at the hand of his human antagonist, the dissolute voyageur, which finally transforms Bâtard into the incarnation of evil. Half-starved, tortured, beaten, and cursed, the dog grows progressively more vicious and cunning—yet he refuses to leave his master, biding with a preternatural sufferance his time for revenge. Nor can Black Lèclerè resist his compulsion to cultivate this hatred; even after Bâtard has attacked him in his sleep, slitting his throat, he refuses to accept the advice of old-timers who urge him to let them shoot the dog. The strange, passionate bond between them is very like the kind of love-hate relationship that D. H. Lawrence has delineated with disturbing effectiveness in his fiction; and, like Lawrence, London employs the lower animal as a symbol of man's unconscious brute impulses. Lèclerè, whose blackness—a libidinous lack of moral restraint—is merely human, is ultimately no match for the superhuman malevolence that he has fostered; and he is hoisted on his own petard. Near the end of the story, unjustly convicted of murdering a gold miner, he is forced to mount a large box after his hands have been tied and a noose has been slipped over his head. He gets a last-minute reprieve, but the miners leave him alone—still tied and standing precariously on the box—to meditate upon his sinful ways while they go downriver to pick up the real murderer. This is the chance Bâtard has been so patiently waiting for. . . .

> Fifteen minutes later, Slackwater Charley and Webster Shaw, returning, caught a glimpse of a ghostly pendulum swinging back and forth in the dim light. As they hurriedly drew in closer, they made out the man's inert body, and a live thing that clung to it, and shook and worried, and gave to it the swaying motion. (p. *101*)*

There is a ghastly poetic justice in London's conclusion, and the moral lesson is implicit but fundamental: the man who deliberately plays with hellfire will surely be burnt.

*The Call of the Wild* was written to redeem the species. Originally planned as a short story, comparable but antithetical to "Bâtard," it grew into an incomparable novel. London wrote to his close friend Anna Strunsky on March 13, 1903, "I started it as a companion to my other dog-story 'Bâtard,' which you may remember; but it got away from me, and instead of 4,000 words it ran 32,000 before I could call a halt."[5] Joan London reports that, so far as her father was concerned, this masterpiece was "a purely fortuitous piece of work, a lucky shot in the dark that had unexpectedly found its mark," and that when reviewers enthusiastically interpreted *The Call of the Wild* as a brilliant human allegory, London was astonished: " 'I plead guilty,' he admitted, 'but I was unconscious of it at the time. I did not mean to do it.' "[6] Not an uncommon phenomenon among artists, particularly those gifted with what Carl Jung has called "primordial vision," here was an instance in which the author wrote better than he knew. Yet to

*Page references to *The Call of the Wild* and "Bâtard" are to the texts included in this casebook.

consider this book as only a "lucky shot in the dark" is to overlook the significance of the thirty Klondike stories and the novel that London had already published before *The Call of the Wild*. The novel (*A Daughter of the Snows*, 1902) had been a failure, but it was an instructive failure; and many of the stories were first-rate work—work that repeatedly manifests the artistic qualities which coalesce in his masterpiece. Regarded from this perspective, *The Call of the Wild* is no luckier a shot than *Huckleberry Finn, The Great Gatsby,* or *The Sound and The Fury*. Moreover, London was not entirely oblivious to the book's unusual merit; on February 12, 1903, he described it to his publisher George Brett: "It is an animal story, utterly different in subject and treatment from the rest of the animal stories which have been so successful; and yet it seems popular enough for the 'Saturday Evening Post,' for they snapped it up right away."[7] Though London may not have understood the full implications of his statement, *The Call* was, in fact, "utterly different" from the humanized beasts in Kipling's "Mowgli" stories and from the sentimentalized animals in Anna Sewell's *Black Beauty,* Margaret Marshall Saunders' *Beautiful Joe* and Ernest Seton's *Biography of a Grizzly,* all of which were enormously popular in London's day and can still be found in the children's sections of our libraries. Writing about the appeal of such stories for adult readers at the turn of the century, Charles G. D. Roberts explained in *The Kindred of the Wild* (Boston, 1902):

> The animal story, as we now have it, is a potent emancipator. It frees us for a little while from the world of shop-worn utilities, and from the mean tenement of self of which we do well to grow weary. It helps us to return to nature, without requiring that we at the same time return to barbarism. It leads us back to the old kinship of earth, without asking us to relinquish by way of toll any part of the wisdom of the ages, any fine essential of the "large result of time." The clear and candid life to which it reinitiates us, far behind though it lies in the long upward march of being, holds for us this quality. It has ever the more significance, it has ever the richer gift of refreshment and renewal, the more humane the heart and spiritual the understanding which we bring to the intimacy of it. (P. 29)

Roberts' explanation is germane to *The Call of the Wild* as well as to the other animal stories. London's book offers the "gift of refreshment and renewal," and it shares with these other works a certain quality of escapism. The essential difference, however, is its radical departure from the conventional animal story in style and substance—the manner in which it is "overdetermined" in its multi-layered meaning. The story of the great dog Buck's transformation from ranch pet to Ghost Dog of the Wilderness *is* entertaining escape literature, but to read the novel on this level is equivalent to reading *Moby-Dick* as a lively if somewhat long-winded fisherman's yarn. Mere escape novels do not become world classics, unless our definition of "escape" is subtler than the ordinary one.

Pearl Buck has said that, although great literature does offer escape, it is an escape "deeper into the world and not away from it." *The Call of the Wild* is an "escape" book in this sense. Maxwell Geismar provides an important clue to this deeper meaning when he classifies the work as "a beautiful prose poem, or *nouvelle,* of gold and death on the instinctual level," a "handsome parable of the buried impulses."[8] We need only interpolate that these "buried impulses" are essentially human, not canine, and that the reader identifies with Buck more profoundly than he realizes. Strictly speaking, *The Call* is not a novel but a poem informed by the rhythms of epic and myth. The basic pattern of its action derives from a motif of immemorial antiquity: the Myth of the Hero. The call to adventure, departure, initiation, the perilous journey to the "world navel" or mysterious life-source, transformation, and apotheosis: these are the essential phases of the Myth, and all are present in Buck's progress from the civilized through the natural to the supernatural world.[9] His journey carries him not only through space but also through time and, ultimately, into the still center of a world that is timeless.

Appropriately, London's style accommodates itself to this progress. Aside from the rather clumsy verse epigraph at the beginning of the story, nothing could be more prosaic than the opening sentence: "Buck did not read the newspapers, or he would have known that trouble was brewing, not alone for himself, but for every tidewater dog, strong of muscle and with warm, long hair, from Puget Sound to San Diego." After having been forcibly dis-abused of his civilized code first by the man in the red sweater, a nicely symbolic figure, and then by his fellow sled-dogs led by Spitz, Buck is now prepared to hear the first faint call of the primeval; and with this change in his character occurs a corresponding stylistic modulation in Chapter 3, "The Dominant Primordial Beast":

> With the aurora borealis flaming coldly overhead, or the stars leaping in the frost dance, and the land numb and frozen under its pall of snow, this song of the huskies might have been the defiance of life, only it was pitched in minor key, with long-drawn wailings and half-sobs, and was more the pleading of life, the articulate travail of existence. It was an old song, old as the breed itself—one of the first songs of the younger world in a day when songs were sad. It was invested with the woe of unnumbered generations, this plaint by which Buck was so strangely stirred. When he moaned and sobbed, it was with the pain of the living that was of old the pain of his wild fathers, and the fear and the mystery of the cold and dark that was to them fear and mystery. And that he should be stirred by it marked the completeness with which he harked back through the ages of fire and roof to the raw beginnings of life in the howling ages. (P. *34*)

Moving from prose to poetry and from the material world to the world of myth, London achieves one of his finest passages here, and another near the end of this chapter; both reveal that Buck's is no common animal story.

> There is an ecstasy that marks the summit of life, and beyond which life cannot rise. And such is the paradox of living, this ecstasy comes when one is most alive. This ecstasy, this forgetfulness of living, comes to the artist, caught up and out of himself in a sheet of flame; it comes to the soldier, war-mad on a stricken field and refusing quarter; and it came to Buck, leading the pack, sounding the old wolf-cry, straining after the food that was alive and that fled swiftly before him through the moonlight. He was sounding the deeps of his nature, and the parts of his nature that were deeper than he, going back into the womb of Time. He was mastered by the sheer surging of life, the tidal wave of being, the perfect joy of each separate muscle, joint, and sinew in that it was everything that was not death, that it was aglow and rampant, expressing itself in movement, flying exultantly under the stars and over the face of dead matter that did not move. (P. *36*)

This paragraph, a thematic epitome of the whole book, immediately prefaces the weirdly moving scene in which Buck and Spitz engage in fatal battle for leadership of the team, a scene noted by Professor Geismar as "a perfect instance of the 'son-horde' theory which Frazer traced in *The Golden Bough*, and of that primitive ritual to which Freud himself attributed both a sense of original sin and the fundamental ceremony of religious exorcism."[10]

Even though he has "won to mastership," Buck is still not ready for apotheosis; he is a leader and a hero—but he is not yet divine. His divinity must be confirmed through death and rebirth. Death occurs symbolically—almost literally—in Chapter 5, "The Toil of Trace and Trail," after the hero has suffered through his terrible ordeal under "the newcomers" Hal, Charles, and Mercedes, who are fittingly removed from the scene after they have fulfilled their role in the ritual. Rebirth comes with spring under the protective love of John Thornton, the benign companion who traditionally appears in the Myth to lead the hero toward his goal. Adumbrations of this goal appear in Chapter 6 as Buck grows stronger: "He was older than the days he had seen and the breaths he had drawn. He linked the past with the present, and the eternity behind him throbbed through him in a mighty rhythm to which he swayed as the tides and seasons swayed." (Pp. *63-64*)

It is in the seventh and final chapter that the hero achieves apotheosis. Here London modulates both setting and style poetically to enhance Buck's transformation. With the sixteen hundred dollars the dog has won miraculously by pulling a sled loaded with a half-ton of flour, Thornton pays off his debts and buys supplies "to journey into the East after a fabled lost mine, the history of which was as old as the history of the country." From the opening paragraph of this chapter it is evident that the place toward which the group is moving is extraordinary: "Many men had sought it; few had found it; and more than a few there were who had never returned from the quest. This lost mine was steeped in tragedy and shrouded in mystery. No one knew of the first man. The oldest tradition stopped before it got back to him." The land into which Thornton's party ventures coincides with that described in *The Hero with a Thousand Faces:*

> [The "call of adventure"] signifies that destiny has summoned the hero and transferred his spiritual center of gravity from within the pale of society to a zone unknown. This fateful region of both treasure and danger may be variously represented: as a distant land, a forest, a kingdom underground, beneath the waves, or above the sky, a secret island, lofty mountaintop, or profound dream state; but it is always a place of strangely fluid and polymorphous beings, unimaginable torments, superhuman deeds and impossible delight. (p. 58)

All semblance of familiar temporal and spatial reality vanishes as the group moves into this curious *ur-welt* which Geismar likens to "some opium-haunted paradise of De Quincey or an Arctic Xanadu" (p. 152):

> To Buck it was boundless delight, this hunting, fishing, and indefinite wandering through strange places. . . .
> The months came and went, and back and forth they twisted through the uncharted vastness. . . . They went across divides in summer blizzards, shivered under the midnight sun on naked mountains between the timber line and the eternal snows, dropped into summer valleys amid swarming gnats and flies, and in the shadows of glaciers picked strawberries and flowers as ripe and fair as any the Southland could boast. In the fall of the year they penetrated a weird lake country, sad and silent, where wild fowl had been, but where then there was no life nor sign of life—only the blowing of chill winds, the forming of ice in sheltered places, and the melancholy rippling of waves on lonely beaches.
> Spring came on once more, and at the end of all their wandering they found. . .a shallow placer in a broad valley where the gold showed like yellow butter across the bottom of the washing-pan. They sought no farther. Each day they worked earned them thousands of dollars in clean dust and nuggets, and they worked every day. The gold was sacked in moosehide bags, fifty pounds to the bag, and piled like so much firewood outside the sprucebough lodge. (p. *74*)

This "fateful region of both treasure and danger" is a far cry from Judge Miller's ranch and even from the raw frontier of the Klondike gold rush: enveloped in the atmosphere of the dream world, it is the timeless landscape of myth. And when London writes that, "Like giants they toiled, days flashing on the heels of days like dreams as they heaped the treasure up," he touches the chords of a farther and deeper music than that of the ordinary, phenomenal world. It is a strange music that, in the words of Carl Jung, "derives its existence from the hinterland of man's mind—that suggests the abyss of time separating us from pre-human ages, or evokes a super-human world of contrasting light and darkness. It is a primordial experience which surpasses man's understanding. . . . "[11] Since such experience cannot be rationally grasped, continues Jung, it "requires mythological imagery to give it form. In itself it offers no words or images, for it is a vision seen 'as in a glass, darkly.' It is merely a deep presentiment that strives to find expression" (p. 164). In other words, the world into which Buck moves at the end of the story is a world of the "collective unconscious," the primordial world which modern man has blocked off with the inhibiting barriers of reason and social convention but a nonetheless real world to which he would return, in dreams, to find his soul. Released by the death of John Thornton from the last bond that ties him to the conventional world, Buck achieves full apotheosis and the ultimate freedom for which all men unconsciously yearn. He is no longer a dog—not even a superdog—but a projection of the reader's essential mythic *self,* a dynamic symbol of libido, *elan vital,* the life force. And it is to this call—the faint but clear echo of an inner music—that we respond as the great Ghost Dog flashes "through the pale moonlight or glimmering borealis," singing his "song of the younger world."

### III

In 1904, following the immediate success of *The Call of the Wild,* London wrote to George Brett that he had decided to compose a "complete antithesis [and] companion piece": "I'm going to reverse the process. Instead of devolution or decivilization of a dog, I'm going to give the evolution, the civilization of a dog—development of domesticity, faithfulness, love, morality, and all the amenities and virtues."[12] Two years later the companion piece was published under the title of *White Fang.* Instead of being a companion and antithesis, however, *White Fang* is a completely different kind of book from *The Call of the Wild.* Structured upon ideas rather than upon myth, it is a more intellectualized and artificial (if less artful) work than *The Call.* A powerful but not a great book, it is nevertheless important to our understanding of the naturalistic philosophy propounded by London. Nature is depicted here as a vast intransigent force; men, as "puny adventurers...pitting themselves against the might of a world as remote and alien and pulseless as the abysses of space" (p. 99). This is not the Wild to which Buck reverts; it is "the savage, frozen-hearted Northland Wild," informed by the principle of death—not life:

> Life is an offence to it, for life is movement; and the Wild aims always to destroy movement. It freezes the water to prevent it running to the sea; it drives the sap out of the trees till they are frozen to their mighty hearts; and most ferociously and terribly of all does the Wild harry and crush into submission man—man, who is the most restless

to life, ever in revolt against the dictum that all movement must in the end come to the cessation of movement. (P. 99)

Set against this principle and providing the central tension of the novel is a cluster of contrasting values: Life, Love, Civilization, and the Southland. It is toward this latter pole that White Fang moves during his rites of passage. If *The Call of the Wild* may be classified as a denitiation story, *White Fang* is a proper initiation story: the hero follows the conventional pattern of separation, ordeal, transformation, return, and full integration into society (both integration and apotheosis may be inferred from the title of "The Blessed Wolf!" conferred upon him by Judge Scott's family at the end of the novel). Applying his theory of environmental determinism, London demonstrates that, given the proper care and climate, the most savage beast may be transformed into a gentle housedog: "Not alone was [White Fang] in the geographical Southland, for he was in the Southland of life. Human kindness was like a sun shining upon him, and he flourished like a flower planted in good soil" (p. 268). From this perspective, *White Fang* is a companion piece and antithesis—not to *The Call of the Wild*—but to "Bâtard." To emphasize his message, the author inserts a *ficelle* or reflector: the escaped convict Jim Hall, who is a human counterpart to Bâtard. Hall has been "ill-made in the making," and the harsh treatment he has received from society—"from the time he was a little pulpy boy in a San Francisco slum—soft clay in the hands of society and ready to be formed into something"—has turned him into "so terrible a beast that he can best be characterized as carnivorous" (pp. 274-75). And the dramatic confrontation between these two diametrically opposed products of environment, the humanized beast and the brutalized man, occurs when the convict enters Judge Scott's house to "wreak vengeance" on the man who has "railroaded" him. Jim Hall is a mad dog and must be destroyed for the safety of respectable citizens, but London has made it clear, as he did in "Bâtard," that the responsibility for such creatures rests squarely upon the society that molded them. The "lesson" of *White Fang* is stated explicitly by the author himself in the following quotation from Charmian London's *The Book of Jack London*:

I am an evolutionist, therefore a broad optimist, hence my love for the human (in the slime though he be) comes from my knowing him as he is and seeing the divine possibilities ahead of him. That's the whole motive of my 'White Fang.' Every atom of organic life is plastic. The finest specimens now in existence were once all pulpy infants capable of being molded this way or that. Let the pressure be one way and we have atavism—the reversion to the wild; the other the domestication, civilization. I have always been impressed with the awful plasticity of life and I feel that I can never lay enough stress upon the marvelous power and influence of environment. (II, 49-50)

*White Fang* is an impressive dramatic representation of this theme; and because London succeeded so well in his dramatization, the novel will continue to be read widely. But it is nevertheless a lesser artistic work than *The Call of the Wild* because it is written in what Eliseo Vivas has called the "transitive" mode: its function is to point toward the "cognitive" and the "moral." *The Call of the Wild,* on the other hand, is purely aesthetic and intransitive—engaging the reader in a rapt attention for no other purpose than the unique experience of art.[13] Rather than pointing outward to society and environment, *The Call of the Wild* points to something awesome and marvelous within man's own heart of darkness, the eternal mystery of the "artistic transaction" and, ultimately, of life itself. The book is, for this reason, an unforgettable classic while *White Fang* is merely a very memorable "story about a dog."

# Notes

1. Broadside, 1916; copy on file at the Utah State University Library, Logan.
2. Letter to Philo M. Buck, Jr., July 19, 1913; in *Creator and Critic,* ed. King Hendricks (Logan, Utah, 1961), p. 43.
3. See Oscar Cargil, *Toward a Pluralistic Criticism* (Carbondale, Ill., 1965), pp. xiii-xiv, 15-16; and "Criticism with a Core," *The CEA Critic,* XXX (Oct. 1967), 1, 4-5, 6.
4. *Great Short Works of Jack London,* ed. Earle Labor, Harper Perennial Classic (New York, 1965), pp. 2-3. [Pages 89-90 of this casebook. References for this story and for *The Call of the Wild*, given hereafter in parentheses following the quotes, are to this casebook.] Page references for...*White Fang*...are to [the Labor] edition.

5. Quoted in Charmian London, *The Book of Jack London,* 2 vols. (New York, 1921), 1, 388.
6. *Jack London and His Times* (New York, 1939), p. 252.
7. Copy of letter on file at the Utah State University Library.
8. *Jack London: Short Stories,* American Century Series (New York, 1960), pp. ix-x.
9. See Joseph Campbell, *The Hero with a Thousand Faces,* Meridian Ed. (New York, 1956), pp. 40–171 *passim.*
10. *Rebels and Ancestors* (Boston, 1953), pp. 150–151.
11. C. G. Jung, *Modern Man in Search of a Soul,* Harvest Ed. (New York, first publ. 1933), pp. 156–157.
12. *Letters from Jack London,* ed. King Hendricks and Irving Shephard (New York, 1956), p. 166.
13. *The Artistic Transaction* (Ohio State University Press, 1963), pp. 10, 30–31.

# Naturalism in the Works of Jack London*

## by Mary Kay Dodson

In the naturalistic sense, man is considered an animal. Heredi-tary, environmental, and biological forces determine what he is; he has little or no control over what he is and what he does. In 1900 London wrote that "the different families of man must yield to law, which has no knowledge of good or ill, right or wrong." As London grew older, his materialistic view of life grew stronger. Fifteen years later he wrote: "I am a hopeless materialist. I see the soul as nothing else than the sum of the activities of the organism plus personal habits, memories, and experiences, plus inherited habits, memories, experiences of the organism." He also wrote that "man is not a free agent, and free will as the power of ethical choice is a fallacy exploded by science long ago." London was also a believer in Darwin's ideas about the struggle for existence. Since this survival depends on superior forces or guile, London formulated the idea that man's will (as vital impulse or force) was the one positive fact upon which an individual could base his actions. In glorifying strength, he glorified the will (as vital force) which seems always to exist in a character who has superior cunning or power.[1] London's writings reflect his naturalistic philosophy. The primary symbol he uses for the purpose of showing the relationship between strength and the struggle for survival expressed in terms of Darwin's scientific determinism is the beast. His beasts are depicted both explicitly and implicitly. Buck, the protagonist in *The Call of the Wild,* is the most

*From *Jack London Newsletter* 4 (September-December, 1971), pp. 130-39, with permission of Hensley C. Woodbridge, ed.

forceful example of the former, whereas Wolf Larsen, in *The Sea-Wolf*, is the best example of the latter.

The characters[2] in London's works fight against their surrounding forces. According to Jay Gurian he "depicts protagonists fighting to win in a causative naturalist universe; but he also depicts antagonists fighting to overcome the causative universe and to affirm beliefs not possible within the dialects of that universe."[3] The characters must fight out their destiny, but they "must be explained in terms of purely material causation, and they must be so completely explained in these terms that impressions of free will and ethical responsibility do not intrude to disrupt the relentless operation of this material causation."[4]

Men in London's works are not only described in terms of animals; they are sometimes equated with them as in "Diable—a Dog." This story concerns the rivalry between Diable, a dog, and his master, Black Lèclerè. Note the following description of them from the opening paragraph: "The first time they met, Diable was a puppy, lean and hungry and with bitter eyes; and they met with snap and snarl and wicked looks, for Lèclerè's upper lip had a wolfish way of lifting and showing the cruel white teeth." (89).[5] As Diable attacked Lèclerè in his sleep later in the story, he "awoke to the pang of the fangs in his throat, and perfect animal that he was, he awoke clear-headed and with full comprehension." (92) As the fight broke into full force, Lèclerè could easily have used his knife or rifle. "But the beast in him was up and raging. He would do the thing with his hands—and his teeth." (93) The scene was that of "two beasts, locked in combat, snapping and snarling, raging madly about, panting, sobbing, cursing, straining, wild with passion, blind with lust, in a fury of murder, ripping, tearing and clawing in elemental brutishness." (94) Here there is no mistaking the fact that Black Lèclerè is as much of an animal as Diable himself.

Diable was a product of his environment and heredity. His father was a timber wolf and his mother "was a snarling, bickering husky, full-fronted and heavy-chested, with a malign eye, a catlike grip on life, and a genius for trickery and evil. There was neither faith nor trust in her." (89) Diable inherited these characteristics of his progenitors. As a puppy these traits were not particularly evident until Black Lèclerè became his master. He had only "to press and prod and mold it [the dog] till it became a big, bristling beast, acute

in knavery, overspilling with hate, sinister, malignant, diabolical."
(90) In other circumstances and with a different mother, Diable
might not have turned into a vicious beast; but Lèclerè "confirmed
him in his congenital iniquity." (90) Diable inherited his tenacious
grip on life, his stealth, and his cunning from his mother, and his
fierceness and valor from his father. Thus, both Diable's heredity
and environment are reflected in him to the extent that they make
him the beast that he is.

One of London's greatest successes in his writing about the vast
northern wilderness is *The Call of the Wild.* The universe
determined scientifically by heredity and environment is wrought
very masterfully in the novel. Many naturalistic elements already
discussed appear in *The Call of the Wild.* The use of Buck is
London's most explicit portrayal of the "beast." Buck's transformation from a domesticated, gentle dog into the dominant primordial
beast is inevitable because of the naturalistic universe; his heredity
and environment force him to kill or to be killed. The amiable Buck
was kidnapped from Judge Miller's California ranch by Manuel, a
ranch-hand, and sold. Then he was transported to the Yukon to be
used in a dog team which was run by Perrault, a French Canadian.
Buck learned quickly that he would have to adapt in order to
survive. He was cruelly treated in the beginning of the book; after
Perrault sold him, he was almost killed by his new master. John
Thornton, his final owner, saved him from this cruel master.

In *The Call of the Wild,* the portrayal of men as beasts is shown
as well as the portrayal of dog as beast. When Buck is caged after he
has been stolen, he is tormented by his captors. He has been put in a
baggage car and has had nothing to eat or drink for two days. As can
be expected, Buck is very angry. "In his anger he had met the first
advances of the express messengers with growls, and they had
retaliated by teasing him. When he flung himself against the bars,
quivering and frothing, they laughed at him and taunted him. They
growled and barked like detestable dogs. . . ." (*13*)

Buck's first introduction to primitive law—the law of the club and
fang—came at the hands of Perrault who beat him into submission
with a club. Buck learned quickly that he must avoid the club; he
was an intelligent dog who fought not only by instinct, but also by
his head. He "possessed a quality that made for greatness—imagination." (*38*) His imagination helped him not only to
survive, but also to adapt.

Buck's father was a huge St. Bernard and his mother a Scotch shepherd dog. During the four years he lived at Judge Miller's, he became accustomed to the genteel life. "But he had saved himself by not becoming a mere pampered house dog. Hunting and kindred outdoor delights had kept down the fat and hardened muscles; and to him, as to the cold-tubbing races, the love of water had been a tonic and a health preserver." (*10*) Because Buck was in good physical condition, one aspect of his adaption to the Yukon territory was made easier; he was capable of doing the work for which he had been stolen.

The powerful influence of Buck's heredity is carefully presented. He was not homesick because his memories of California were very dim and distant, and therefore not very powerful. "Far more potent were the memories of his heredity that gave things he had never seen before a seeming familiarity; the instincts (which were but the memories of his ancestors become habits) which had lapsed in later days, and still later, in him, quickened and became alive again." (*43*) Even though Buck's father too had been a companion of Judge Miller's, Buck quickly recognized his hereditary instincts. He responded to them because he was placed in an environment in which these hereditary factors were essential to survival. Had he remained in his comfortable surroundings at the ranch, he never would have felt this influence of his heredity.

Buck realized that his new environment was his natural habitat especially when he made friends with the wolf. The two of them

> . . . came down into a level country where were great stretches of forest and streams, and through these great stretches they ran steadily, hour after hour, the sun rising higher and the day growing warmer. Buck was wildly glad. He knew he was at last answering the call, running by the side of his wood brother toward the place from which the call surely came. Old memories were coming upon him fast, and he was stirring to them as of old he stirred to the realities of which they were the shadows. He had done this thing before, some-where in that other and dimly remembered world, and he was doing it again, now, running free in the open, the unpacked earth underfoot, the wide sky overhead. (*77*)

Buck, in responding to the call of the wild, was responding to the call of his ancestors—his heredity. As his hereditary forces came into the fore, he began to depend less and less upon the only decent human being he had encountered since leaving Judge Miller's. He learned to kill, but not just for the sake of killing; he killed to feed himself. "The blood longing became stronger than before. He was a killer, a thing that preyed, living on the things that lived, unaided, alone, by virtue of his own strength and prowess, surviving triumphantly in a hostile environment when only the strong survived. Because of all this he became possessed of a great pride in himself, which communicated itself like a contagion to his physical being." (*78*) His appearance was almost that of a gigantic wolf. The physical characteristics of his father and mother were blended in him:

> From his St. Bernard father he had inherited size and weight, but it was his shepherd mother who had given shape to that size and weight. His muzzle was the long wolf muzzle, save that it was larger than the muzzle of any wolf; and his head, somewhat broader, was the wolf head on a massive scale. His cunning was wolf cunning, and wild cunning; his intelligence, shepherd intelligence and St. Bernard intelligence; and all this, plus an experience gained in the fiercest of schools, made him as formidable a creature as any that roamed the wild. (*78*)

Thus Buck explicitly embodies the theory of naturalism. He is a product of biological, environmental, and hereditary forces.

Jack London did not confine himself to writing about experiences in the North. Much of his writing deals with life at sea; in these writings, he also brings naturalism to the fore. In a consideration of Wolf Larsen in *The Sea-Wolf* and others, London's characterizations of these people as demoniacs should be kept in mind. Samuel Shivers carefully defines the term *demoniac* in reference to London's characters as "a being of tremendous energy and determination who at the same time is possessed of an intensely evil quality . . . such a person is not intangible or ghostly, but very real and is driven by devilish impulses against which he does not struggle, as if he had no moral conscience or God-given sense of direction."[6] He goes on to say that the demoniacs are conceived along bestial lines in order that the actions of the characters proceed from a biological basis. When this is not completely possible, London emphasizes the primacy of the will over the body, and thus the concept of the demoniac is a debased *"Wille zur Macht"* combined with a Darwinian "survival of the fittest" concept. Therefore the use of the demoniac, as exemplified in many respects by the bestial imagery, is an important aspect of the naturalism presented by Jack London.

The chief elements of the London demoniac are:

1. He or it is a personification of instincts or passions;
2. The energy and drive are enormous, making the character almost unconquerable in one respect or another;
3. The animal, beastly qualities are emphasized, especially those equipping one to survive in the heartless world of natural competition;
4. There is no conscience or moral reflection;
5. There is an *idee fixe* in most cases;
6. The demoniac has a fine body, keen mind, and a strong and unrelenting will.[7]

Diable, the dog, can certainly be classified as a demoniac. However, the discussion concerning the demoniac as a facet of naturalism must center on Wolf Larsen. *The Sea-Wolf* concerns Wolf Larsen, the captain of the sealing craft, *The Ghost*, who picks up Humphrey Van Weyden in the San Francisco Bay. Larsen enslaves Hump in that he refuses to put him ashore. He gives two reasons for this: "(1) The hard experience of being shanghaied and put to rough usage will make a man out of the bookish 'mollycoddle.' (2) It is to Larsen's personal advantage that Van Weyden serve under him."[8] Wolf fulfills all of Shiver's essential elements of a demoniac.

It is no accident that Larsen is named Wolf. Time after time throughout the novel, Larsen's resemblance to a beast is explicitly stated. His strength was that which "we are wont to associate with things primitive . . . a strength savage, ferocious, alive in itself . . . in short, that which writhes the body of the snake when the head is cut off." (20) "The jaw, the chin, the brow rising to a goodly height and swelling heavily above the eyes—these, while strong in themselves, unusually strong, seemed to speak an immense vigor or virility of spirit that lay behind and beyond and out of sight." (24) In spite of his massive strength, he once sprang "to the deck with the weight and softness of a tiger." (63) Later Hump infuriated Larsen:

> . . . until the whole man of him was snarling. The dark sun-bronze of his face went black with wrath, his eyes were ablaze. There was no clearness or sanity in them, nothing but the terrific rage of a madman.

It was the wolf in him that I [Hump] saw, and a mad wolf at that. (71)

As Larsen was at the point of attacking Johnson, Larsen was three yards away from him and sitting down. "Nine feet! And yet he left the chair, just as he sat in it, squarely, springing from the sitting posture like a wild animal, a tiger, and like a tiger covered the intervening space." (93–94)

London is also explicit concerning conscience or moral reflection, or rather, lack of it, in Larsen. Moral suasion was unknown on the ship; it was ruled by brute force. Ironically Larsen is interested in reading and thinking, and as a result, develops a sort of comradeship with Hump with whom he can hold discussions. In one of their conversations, Hump mentions the *ethics*; Larsen says that it is the first time he ever heard the word. He then chides Hump for believing in such things as right and wrong. Larsen feels only that might is right and weakness is wrong.

Larsen has obviously read and studied some philosophy, but he rejects and selects portions according to his needs and desires. For instance, he relates that Spencer says a man must act first for his own benefit, then for the benefit of his children, and finally for the benefit of his race. But Larsen says: "I wouldn't stand for that. Couldn't see the necessity for it, nor the common sense. I cut out the race and the children. I would sacrifice nothing for them." (68)

At one point in the novel, after Hump finished making the bed, he looked at Larsen in fascination:

He was certainly a handsome man—beautiful in the masculine sense. And again, with never-failing wonder, I remarked the total lack of viciousness, or wickedness, or sinfulness in his face. It was the face, I am convinced, of a man who did no wrong. And by this I do not wish to be misunderstood. What I mean is that it was the face of a man who either did nothing contrary to the dictates of his conscience or who had no conscience. I am inclined to the latter way of accounting for it. He was a magnificent atavism, a man so purely primitive that he was of the type that came into the world before the development of the moral nature. He was not immoral, but merely unmoral. (81)

Larsen feels that Hump has the capabilities of doing great things in the world; in order to do this though, he would have to rid himself of conscience and moral instinct.

Larsen's *idee fixe* is success in seal hunting. He tolerates the hunters because they are necessary. "He frankly states that the position he takes is based on no moral grounds, that all the hunters could kill and eat one another so far as he is concerned were it not that he needs them alive for the hunting." (86) Larsen completely rejects the idea of conscience; for him it is desire which decides. He gives the following example:

> Here is a man who wants to, say, get drunk. Also, he doesn't want to get drunk. What does he do? How does he do it? He is a puppet. He is the creature of his desires, and of the two desires he obeys the strongest one, that is all. His soul hasn't anything to do with it. How can he be tempted to get drunk and refuse to get drunk? If the desire to remain sober prevails, it is because it is the strongest desire. Temptation plays no part, unless . . . he is tempted to remain sober. (194)

Nothing Hump says can sway Larsen from his ideas.

Larsen sees one objective in life—to kill and not be killed; his physical strength is devoted to this end. In this respect he is very similar to Buck. Hump did not argue with him because, as he says: "I had seen the mechanism of the primitive fighting beast, and I was as strongly impressed as if I had seen the engines of a great battleship or Atlantic liner." (117) Hump then asks Larsen what he believes. His philosophy of life is summed up in his reply:

> I believe that life is a mess. It is like yeast, a ferment, a thing that moves and may move for a minute, an hour, a year, or a hundred years, but that in the end will cease to move. The big eat the little that they may continue to move, the strong eat the weak that they may retain their strength. The lucky eat the most and move the longest, that is all. (45)

Larsen sacrificed Kelley's life to save a broken boat. Hump tells him that it wasn't worth it, but Larsen replies that "Kelley didn't amount to much. Good night." (137) Killing has no effect on Larsen; if someone gets in the way of his goal he simply kills him. He finds it difficult to understand why Hump cannot kill him. His remarks on this occasion reflect the effect of environment upon a person. "You are the slave to the opinions which have credence among the people you have known and read about. Their code has been drummed into your head from the time you lisped, and in spite of your philosophy and of what I have taught you, it won't let you kill an unarmed, unresisting man." (237)

Earlier Hump recognized the effect of Mugridge's environment on his actions. In him, Hump saw a malignant devil which impelled him to hate the world. "Life had been unfair to him. It had played a scurvy trick when it fashioned him into the thing he was, and it had played him scurvy tricks ever since. What chance had he to be anything else than he was?" (101) Mugridge clearly perceives the difference between himself and Hump, and he also understands the effect of heredity and environment, as is shown in his reply: "I'm already myde, an' myde our of leavin's and scraps. It's all right for you, 'Ump. You was born a gentleman." (101)

A character similar to Larsen is Captain Decker in "Poppy Cargo." The situation is similar; Decker has picked up some survivors in a lifeboat and keeps them shanghaied. His goal, rather than being seal hunting as it is with Larsen, is transporting opium. He will do anything to achieve his goal as does Larsen. Decker, too, is an obsessed man—a demoniac. One of the most vivid contrasts to men like Larsen and Decker appears in *The Sea-Wolf.* In the sailor Johnson, Hump found the complete refutation of Larsen's materialism. Johnson "was swayed by idea, by principle, and truth, and sincerity. He was right, he knew he was right, and he was unafraid. He would die for the right if needs be, he would be true to himself, sincere with his soul. And in this was portrayed the victory of the spirit over the flesh, the incomitability and moral grandeur of the soul that knows no restriction and rises above time and space and matter with a surety and invincibleness born of nothing else than eternity and immortality." (91)

Wolf Larsen is the protagonist in a naturalist universe and Humphrey Van Weyden, the antagonist against a naturalist universe. In the beginning of *Martin Eden*, Eden is a type of blood beast who might become either a Wolf Larsen or a Humphrey Van Weyden. The book concerns the young sailor, *Martin Eden,* who struggles to educate himself for the sake of winning the girl he is enamoured of. His struggle of becoming a writer no doubt reflects London's own struggle. Eden saves the life of a wealthy Arthur Morse, who invites him for dinner. There he meets Arthur's sister Ruth, with whom he falls in love. Eden begins to wish for the type of life represented by the Morse family; he begins his rise by devouring sociology, philosophy, and literature. He sets certain goals for himself and accomplishes them. He seems to be answering the call of the unwild much as Buck answered the call of the wild. But here the similarity ends. Buck is happy, whereas Eden becomes increasingly despondent and eventually commits suicide. He begins to see the middle class as represented by the Morse family as hypocritical. "It is this hypocrisy, this shrinking in the face of total commitment to the jungle law, that he comes to hate in Ruth. Ironically this reaction causes him to freeze her out of his life when he has finally succeeded in the bourgeois world by becoming a commercially successful author and thus 'acceptable' to Ruth's family, and to her."[9]

At the beginning of the book, Eden is described in terms of strength and "in the eyes there was an expression such as wild animals betray when they fear the trap." (2) Ruth immediately feels a strong attraction toward him when they meet. "A wave of intense virility seemed to surge out from him and impinge upon her. . . . It seemed to her that if she could lay her two hands upon that neck that all its strength and vigor would flow out to her." (10) He realizes the difference between them and his recollection of the girls he had known in the past serves to point out to him his primitive nature: "a grotesque and terrible nightmare brood—frowsy, shuffling creatures from the pavements of Whitechapel, ginbloated haps of the stews, and all the vast hell's following of harpies, vile-mouthed and filthy, that under the guise of monstrous female form prey upon sailors, the scrapings of the ports, the scum and slime of the human pit." (5)

After Eden achieves success as a writer, he gives up his naturalist philosophy, turning to altruism which in turn leads him to his feeling of emptiness and eventually to suicide. Philip S. Foner feels that Brissenden is the only one who recognizes Eden's talent and tries "to persuade him to join the socialist movement, predicting disillusionment for Martin if he does succeed as a writer and has nothing to hold him to life. But Martin Eden refuses to heed his advice. "As for myself," he says, "I am an individualist. I believe the race is to the swift, the battle to the strong. Such is the lesson I have learned from biology, or at least I think, I have learned. As I said, I am an individualist, and individualism is the hereditary and eternal foe of socialism."[10] Brissenden's prophecy is fulfilled, but not before he dies; Eden realizes that he has not gained anything and thus he drowns himself.

Jay Gurian feels that Eden is a romantic hero and that the romantic hero is necessary to literary naturalism:

> In sum, *Martin Eden* is London's fullest working out of the naturalist philosophy because Martin enacts the truth-and-consequences dialectic of the causative natural force which denies abstract morality and deity. Martin's is the private vision of the naturalist universe—his own romance of naturalism. Without a Martin to storm the universe, conquer its obstacles, and look around from its summit to find nothing, London would have been writing merely a biological, sociological, and faintly psychological essay.[11]

Thus, in the primary works discussed—*Martin Eden, The Call of the Wild, The Sea-Wolf, White Fang,* and "Diable—a Dog"—the element of naturalism prevails. Men and animals are seen both within and outside of their natural habitat. They are seen, in many cases, adapting to their environment and surviving. Hereditary, environmental, and biological forces to a large extent determine the man or animal in these representative works by Jack London.

# Notes

1. Charles Child Walcutt, "Naturalism and the Superman in the Novels of Jack London," *Papers of the Michigan Academy of Science, Arts, and Letters,* XXIV (1938), 91-92.
2. The word *character,* as it appears in this paper, refers to both men and animals.
3. Jay Gurian, "The Romantic Necessity in Literary Naturalism: Jack London," *American Literature,* XXXVIII (March 1966), 112.
4. Walcutt, p. 89.
5. Quotations from London's works are taken from the following editions: *Martin Eden* (New York: Holt, Rhinehart, and Co., 1956); *The She-Wolf* (New York: New American Library of World Literature, Inc., 1964); *White Fang* (New York: Airmont Publishing Co., 1956); "Diable—a Dog". . . , *Great Short Works of Jack London* (New York: Harper & Row, Publishers, Inc., 1965). [Page references to *The Call of the Wild* are to the text included in this casebook.]
6. *Samuel A. Shivers,* "The Demoniacs in Jack London," *The American Book Collector,* XII (September 1961), 11.
7. Ibid., p. 14.
8. Ibid., p. 11.
9. Gurian, p. 116.
10. Philip S. Foner, *Jack London, American Rebel* (New York, 1964), p. 102.
11. Gurian, p. 120.

# "Call of the Wild": Parental Metaphor*

## by Andrew Flink

As much as *The Call of the Wild* has been scrutinized, dissected, discussed, and categorized by observers over the years, it somehow retains a vitality and vigor unequalled in all London's other efforts. By his own admission the allegory inherent in the work is completely "accidental," "(but) I was unconscious of it at the time. I did not mean to do it"[1] was his answer to those who mentioned this allegory. It is however, significant and perhaps more so because of the element of accident and a closer look at "Call of the Wild" gives the feeling that the novel holds a more personal significance in relation to Jack London himself.

It has been pretty well established that Jack had been deeply hurt by William Chaney's rejection of fatherhood. By circumstances, however, Jack was able to transfer to John London the paternal affection he had to withhold from Chaney thus allowing some outlet for his feelings. As observed by E. B. Erbentraut in his paper titled "'A Thousand Deaths'—Hyperbolic Anger" Jack vented some of his feelings for Chaney in the short story "A Thousand Deaths." Erbentraut states:

> When the protagonist-narrator of the story invents the disintegrative force that blasts his father into a 'little pile of elementary solids,' what are we to think?

He goes on to say that:

* From *Jack London Newsletter*, 7 (May-August, 1974): 58-61, with permission of Hensley Woodbridge, ed.

The pile of elementary solids seems a problem which goes beyond blaming (and probably does not blame any particular person)—purified, settled. For the moment, emotions may be placed in proper perspective.[2]

But where did London's feelings go from there? The only recourse open to him in this regard was John London many years later. In *Sailor on Horseback* Irving Stone referred to John London as young Jack's idol[3] and comments also on the love and trust between Jack and his step-father and how they were together often.[4] Joan London tells of a deep affection for John (London).[5] To what extent their relationship grew is probably anyone's guess but one thing would seem certain: there was a genuine mutual affection between them. In the following examples from *The Call of the Wild* I'll show what I feel to be strong allegorical indications of this mutual affection. In the chapters "Toil of Trace and Trail," "For the Love of a Man" and "Sounding of the Call," John Thornton may have assumed the role in relation to Buck that John London occupied in Jack London's own life. Note here the similarity of the names *John London* and *John Thornton*.

London provides this description of John Thornton.

> John Thornton asked little of man or nature. He was unafraid of the wild. With a handful of salt and a rifle he could plunge into the wilderness and fare wherever he pleased and as long as he pleased. Being in no haste, Indian fashion, he kept on traveling. . . . (73)*

By comparison, this description of John Thornton is much like his description of John London provided years earlier in Jack London's letter to Houghton-Mifflin dated January 31, 1900, wherein London states that his father had a background as a backwoodsman and wandering trapper.[6]

In Joan London's biography of her father she states that John London had tremendous faith in Jack's ability to succeed and was certain Jack "would not fail."[7] In this vein, the chapter "For the Love of a Man" finds Buck winning a bet for John Thornton by pulling a thousand pound sled as based on an old legend of the north.

---

*This reference is to *The Call of the Wild* text included in this casebook.

He (John Thornton) had great faith in Buck's strength and had often
thought him capable of starting such a load. . . . [8]

Jack London upheld the faith his step-father had in him and more
and by being on hand at the right time, John London became a sort
of relief valve for the frustration left in the wake of Chaney's
rejection. In the chapter "Toil of Trace and Trail" the character of
Hal seems significant when he administers a beating to Buck but is
stopped by the intervention of John Thornton. Several paragraphs
later as Thornton is comforting Buck, Hal and his party literally
"drop out of sight" through the ice. Is Hal in this instance an
allegorical Chaney and the beating symbolic of Chaney's emphatic
rejection of fatherhood? If so, then John London in the person of
Thornton becomes the antithesis of Chaney (Hal) by taking over
with kindness and help. With the rejection damage already done,
Chaney disappears. He (figuratively speaking) "drops out of sight"
just as Hal dropped through the ice. In effect, Chaney's rejection
could have instilled the fear of losing parental love Jack had found
in John London. Note the following:

His (Buck's) transient masters since he had come into the northland
had bred in him a fear that no master could be permanent. He was
afraid that Thornton would pass out of his life as Perrault and
François and the Scotch half-breed had passed out. Even in the night,
in his dreams he was haunted by this fear.[9]

If the intensely portrayed anger expressed in "A Thousand
Deaths" is allegorical to his feelings for William Chaney, then Jack
London, years later, in *The Call of the Wild* must have expressed
his feelings for John London with the following:

But love that was feverish and burning, that was adoration, that was
madness, it had taken John Thornton to arouse.[10]

Further in this line, and on the basis of the foregoing that John
Thornton was the symbol of parental love, note the following:
Buck left John Thornton's camp on the longest outing he's taken
when he stalked the moose deep into the forest and here learns the
real art of survival. Returning to camp he finds Thornton dead. Not
only was the only remaining link between the wild and civilization
gone, but with Thornton went the only love and affection Buck had
known since the Santa Clara valley.

PARALLEL:

London goes to the Klondike, his longest adventure away from home, and returns to Oakland to find John London dead. Here, as with Buck, gone was the only paternal love and affection Jack London knew. His reaction is recounted on page 108 of Richard O'Connor's book *Jack London*.[11] Here, O'Connor states in effect that Jack did mourn for his step-father to the limit of his feeling remembering all the kindnesses including the giving of his name.

Buck's reaction to John Thornton's death serves to complete this interesting parallel:

> All day Buck brooded by the pool or roamed restlessly above the camp. Death, as a cessation of movement, as a passing out and away from the lives of the living, he knew, and he knew John Thornton was dead. It left a great void in him somewhat akin to hunger, but a void which ached and ached, and which food could not fill.[12]

Jack London's heavy sense of loss with the death of John London must have compared closely with Buck's feeling for the loss of John Thornton. From that segment of the story on to the conclusion is to be found some of London's most eloquent writing portrayed vividly with descriptions of haunting eloquence. You can almost feel Buck's grief hang in the chill of the fall air[13] and so it must have been with London when he returned from the Klondike (also in the fall of the year) and found John London had died.

If John London had not entered Jack London's life it would be interesting to consider how *The Call of the Wild* might have been written and what turns it may have taken. It seems that London's feelings in "A Thousand Deaths," as intensely and at the same time as negatively drawn as they are, would seem to be inversely proportional to his positive feelings for John London in *The Call of the Wild* and that once again as Erbentraut stated:

"Emotions are purified—settled. For the moment emotions may be placed in proper perspective."

* * * * *

At this point I wish to extend my thanks to those who advised and helped me in the preparation and the working out of this paper. Thanks also to the staff of the Huntington Library for their invaluable assistance and for the use of their reference material.

A.F.

# Notes

1. Joan London, *Jack London and His Times,* Seattle, University of Washington Press, 1969, p. 252.
2. Edwin B. Erbentraut, "A Thousand Deaths—Hyperbolic Anger," *Jack London Newsletter,* 4:128 (Sept.-Dec. 1971).
3. Irving Stone, *Sailor on Horseback,* New York, p. 17.
4. Ibid., p. 21.
5. Joan London, *op. cit.,* p. 135.
6. King Hendricks and Irving Shepard, *Letters from Jack London,* New York, Odyssey Press, 196, p. 86.
7. Joan London, *op. cit.,* p. 129.
8. Jack London, *Call of the Wild,* New York, Macmillan, 1904, p. 181. [68. Bracketed page numbers refer to the *Call of the Wild* text included in this volume.]
9. Ibid., p. 166. [63]
10. Ibid., p. 163. [62]
11. Richard O'Connor, *Jack London: a biography,* Boston, Little, Brown, 1964, p. 108.
12. London, *Call of the Wild,* p. 222. [83-84]
13. Ibid., p. 213. [73]

# A Syllabus for the 20th Century: Jack London's "The Call of the Wild"*

## by Jonathan H. Spinner

*The Call of the Wild* has usually been placed in the limbo of the "boys book," a designation that conjures up a cheap, though exciting, "action-packed adventure story." To be sure, it is a story filled with action and adventure. However, there is something deeper in this novella, something beyond the usual frontier "Shoot-em-up." For London describes an education, spiritually as well as physically, of a being suffering through the dilemma of existence of the modern world. What is presented by London is a syllabus for the twentieth century, a syllabus that states that the way to solve the dilemma of existence in a harsh world is to accept and glory in the cleansing fire of violence.

A syllabus usually states what the lesson to be learned consists of, what the problem to be solved is. The lesson that Buck must learn is how to cope with his loss of identity, his feeling of alienation, and his loss of faith in a world he neither created nor knew existed. In other words, Buck's problem is how to survive in a hostile world; not surprisingly, it is the same problem faced by modern man.

I may seem to be overextending the concept of a "dilemma of existence" for a dog, even one as larger-than-life as Buck. But London makes it clear that Buck certainly does suffer from a loss of identity and a feeling of alienation when he is first "dognapped" and thrown into a crate prior to being sent to the Klondike, for Buck

---

*From *Jack London Newsletter*, 7 (May-August, 1974): 73-78, with permission of Hensley C. Woodbridge, ed.

could not understand what it all meant. What did they want with him, these strange men? Why were they keeping him pent up in this narrow crate? He did not know why, but he felt oppressed by the vague sense of impending calamity.

These reactions are compounded by a loss of faith in both man and dog, first stated when he is finally freed on the Dyea Beach, as his first day there is

> like a nightmare. Every hour was filled with shock and surprise. He had been suddenly jerked from the heart of civilization and flung into the heart of things primordial. . . . Here was neither peace, nor rest, nor a moment's safety. All was confusion and action, and every moment life and limb were in peril. There was imperative need to be constantly alert; for these dogs and men were not town dogs and men. They were savages, all of them, who knew no law but the law of club and fang.

These chaotic feelings are the central focus of the first two chapters of the novella. Gradually, Buck is able to cope with such inner confusion as he learns of his new outer world. He quickly discovers certain natural laws in this universe far away from his Southland home. Buck sees "once for all, that he stood no chance against a man with a club." As far as how a dog in the Klondike is expected to fight, he learns that there was "no fair play. Once down, that was the end of you." And Buck learns another natural law of the North, that of the true relationship between man and dog, when he discovers that what Francois has fastened upon him was "an arrangement of straps and buckles. It was a harness, such as he had seen the grooms put on the horses at home."

These, Buck learns, are the Northland dog's three great laws: fear of man; no quarter among themselves; and the true constant in the equation, hard work. What permits Buck to absorb these lessons without being destroyed as other dogs are destroyed is the "latent cunning of his nature aroused," his "adaptability." Having once gained the knowledge of these three laws, Buck quickly learns all the other necessary tricks of survival in a hostile world. As he learns them with great speed, London states, the greater the

> decay or going to pieces of his moral nature, a vain thing and a handicap in the ruthless struggle for existence. It was all well enough in the Southland, under the law of love and fellowship, to respect private property and personal feelings; but in the Northland, under

the law of club and fang, whoso took such things into account was a fool, and in so far as he observed them he would fail to prosper.

It is this "decay" that is at the heart of Buck's learning process, and is the core of London's lesson. In a harsh and brutal world, it is imperative that Buck give up civilized ways for "instincts long dead." In order for Buck to solve the dilemma of his existence, a dilemma created by modern Fates, uncaring as their ancient sisters, it is necessary for Buck to shed his "domesticated generations" and become a "dominant primordial beast." Like modern men, Buck is thrown out of paradise somewhere much further than east of Eden, by forces unknown to him, beyond his control, and rooted in the industrial world, forces somehow tied into men finding "a yellow metal in the North, and because Manuel was a gardener's helper whose wages did not lap over the needs of his wife and divers small copies of himself."

By the third chapter, Buck has learned, in an unconscious way, all the tricks of survival. But London, being a wise teacher, does not end the story here, with a quick and successful fight against Spitz, and Buck's assumption of the mantle of lead sled dog. London does not wish to present a story of how a dog learns to survive in the wilderness. That is the nature of the usual adventure story. Rather, London wants to create a moral tale, a fable, and it is necessary that Buck become conscious of the changes in himself, even as the reader is informed. Further, London also wants to go beyond the lessons Buck has already gained; his true aim is the exploration and exploitation of his own Northland gold—the instinctual nature of blood and violence, the call of the wild.

London must, however, set the stage in the reader's heart by showing how treacherous and frightened Spitz is, by having him attack Buck in dangerous situations. It is not enough to win the adventure-story-buff's head by giving the story a pseudo-Darwinistic "survival of the fittest" patina, since the "fair play" credo is the accepted one in this genre. Thus, when the maddened huskies attack the camp, it is Spitz who slashes at Buck during the fighting. After being pursued by the rabid Dolly, it is Spitz who attacks Buck as he is trying to catch his breath. By setting up this situation, London is able to exploit it by having Buck then act in like spirit and attack

Spitz at inopportune times, while saying that for Buck, "fair play was a forgotten code."

One other element is added by London to this equation, an element that acts as a catalyst for the final showdown between Buck and Spitz, even as it promises to be one of the active ingredients in the rest of the story. It is the vital element of wildness, first expressed by Buck when he joins the wolf huskies in their "nocturnal song." For Buck

> this song of the huskies might have been the defiance of life, only it was pitched in minor key, with long-drawn wailings and half-sobs, and was more the pleading of life, the articulate travail of existence. It was an old song, old as the breed itself—one of the first songs of the younger world in a day when songs were sad. It was invested with the woe of unnumbered generations, this plaint by which Buck was so strangely stirred. When he moaned and sobbed, it was with the pain of living that was of old the pain of his wild fathers, and the fear and mystery of the cold and dark that was to them fear and mystery. And that he should be stirred by it marked the completeness with which he harked back through the ages of fire and roof to the raw beginnings of life in the howling ages.

Thus, when Dub scares out a snowshoe rabbit, the stage has been set not only for Buck to become the "dominant, primordial beast" by killing Spitz, but has been prepared as well for the succeeding acts leading to Buck's complete acceptance of the "call of the wild."

By ascending to the head of pack, Buck has merely crossed over from being a good Southland dog to being a good Northland dog. Only half of London's syllabus has been expounded and absorbed by Buck and the reader. It is time for Buck to begin to break two of the three natural laws he had learned so far as a Northland trace dog, as he learns new rules about violence as a way out of the modern dilemma of the "monotonous life" in which he worked with "machinelike regularity."

Like the situation surrounding Spitz' death, London sets up this further change in Buck's outer way of life by giving him tantalyzing glimpses of this paradise of instinctual violence that lies within Buck's reach. By having Buck dream of happier possibilities, London has shown the reader Buck's future potential. And by having Buck dream of the "far more potent . . . memories of his heredity," London is able to contrast these "memories of his ancestors" against "the Sunland" of Judge Miller's ranch, for which Buck is "not homesick," and thus use the weight of the pre-historic past to defeat the more recent, upstart civilized garden of eden in the "sun-kissed Santa Clara valley." Of course, since London is attempting to educate his human audience more than he is the dog Buck, it is not surprising that the first of Buck's dreams features a man "shorter of leg and longer of arm" sitting by a fire surrounded by "the eyes of great beasts of prey."

Having hooked the reader by a vision of his own possible ancestral paradise, London now proceeds to have Buck violate two of the three natural laws he has learned about the Northland, with the reader, if not applauding, at least understanding Buck's reasons for his actions. Buck is first shown what hard work does to every dog who survives the continual fights with the other sled-dogs, when Dave, one of the hardest working and most compulsive of the dogs, becomes ill yet refuses to stop pulling in his place in the sled-harness. A choice is given to Buck between the "natural" way of the wild, dying an honorable death in combat, and the "unnatural" way of the world of man by dying a death filled with "convulsive efforts" in the sled-harness. Thus, a dog like Buck, filled with pride and dignity, must choose to break the Northland law of hard work.

London clarifies Buck's choice when the team is sold to Hal, Charles, and Mercedes. Already beaten by the thirty-day drive from Dawson to Skagway, Buck and the rest of the team are sold to Southland people totally unequipped to handle a sled in the Klondike. Buck quickly realizes their lack of expertise as he "watched them apprehensively as they proceeded to take down the tent and load the sled. There was a great deal of effort about their manner, but no businesslike method." Buck's apprehension is proven to be more than a suspicion in the succeeding weeks, as the greenhorns' lack of expertise, combined with their cruelty, destroys the sled-team's already exhausted abilities. However, something else besides physical strength is destroyed as well; Buck learns that hard work done for people who neither understand nor appreciate it leaves one, as modern man has already learned, "jaded and tired . . . [and] bitter. His heart was not in the work."

So much for one of the laws of the Northland, hard work. Yet another law is to be broken on this trip with the greenhorn

Southerners, the law of the man with the club. This condition of the Klondike was the first that Buck was exposed to, and the most fearsome of the three. To overcome it then, is to free Buck from man. Buck does not defeat it by killing Hal, who torments Buck and the rest of the team; rather, like oppressed beings in the modern world, the dogs become "insensible to the bite of the lash or the bruise of the club. The pain of the beating was dull and distant." And compared to these beatings administered by a man, so much like death, is the natural world that is filled with the "bursting, rending, throbbing of awakening life."

At this point, John Thornton is brought into the story. Buck has reached the nadir of his existence in the Northland, a situation of life beyond the dilemma of existence, brought on by physical exhaustion and human cruelty beyond that first experience had by him on the Dyea Beach. If two laws of Klondike life are swept aside by Buck, it is because of the actions taken by beings outside Buck's control that force him to choose life over the death-giving aspects of these laws. John Thornton is necessary partially to release Buck from death, spiritually as well as physically.

The physical death facing Buck is clear enough, for as Hal beats him Buck feels that

> the blows did not hurt much. And as they continued to fall upon him, the spark of life within flickered and went down. It was nearly out. He felt strangely numb. As though from a great distance, he was aware that he was being beaten. The last sensation of pain left him. He no longer felt anything, though very faintly he could hear the impact of the club upon his body. But it was no longer his body, it seemed so far away.

As John Thornton springs to Buck's defense with a "cry that was inarticulate and more like the cry of an animal," he forces Buck into a new position, a position at once free of the Northland laws of hard work and respect for the man with a club while still tied to mankind and his civilization through the love for one man. And Thornton understands, perhaps unconsciously, what kind of animal he has helped, as he refers to Buck as " 'You poor devil.' " For Thornton, Buck will be an angel; to others, he will seem to be a devil, and a rather powerful one at that.

As Buck regains his strength under Thornton's ministrations, he senses two changes in himself. First, "love, genuine passionate love, was his for the first time"; secondly, "the strain of the primitive, which the Northland had aroused in him, remained alive and active." These changes are the last of the lessons of the Klondike, and they are the last of the choices Buck will have to make to determine his pattern of existence. That both love and violence are equally powerful lures is indicated by the actions Buck is willing to take in either case. For Thornton, Buck is willing to jump a chasm, to attack a man, to brave rapids, to pull a sled weighing a thousand pounds.

But there is the "stuff of his dreams." There is,

> deep in the forest a call . . . sounding, and as often as he heard this call, mysteriously thrilling and luring, he felt compelled to turn his back upon the fire and the beaten earth around it, and to plunge into the forest, on and on, he knew not where or why; nor did he wonder where or why, the call sounding imperiously, deep in the forest.

So there it is, the call of the heart against the call of the wild.

It is the Northland's, and London's, final lesson to Buck and to people of the twentieth century, that there is no choice involved. There is only one syllabus to be followed, only one passion that will cleanse the soul, and that is violence, not love. Love of this world is transient, because it depends on loving flesh-and-blood, which may wander away or in Thornton's case, be too weak to survive physically, and so disappear. Since neither London nor twentieth century man truly believes in God's love, only one passion can truly be called enduring, that of violence. Buck, like mankind in our time, chooses that which seems strongest, which will help him best survive in a cruel world.

Even with Thornton still alive, Buck is almost completely overwhelmed by the call of violence. Perhaps it is London's bit of irony that as Thornton is drawn to gold, to undreamed-of wealth, the perennial El Dorado of civilized man, Buck is drawn to his own El Dorado, the merciless ways of the wild. And as Thornton and his companions discover their sought-after mother-lode, so Buck discovers his own gold mine, his own treasure in the wild. Buck also discovers, through his dreams, what is at the root of his relationship to men other than Thornton, the basis for the relationship between all men and all dogs: man's fear of the unknown, of other beasts, of the wild itself. Buck realizes that man needs the dog to protect him from that which, every day and night, called to him and "filled him with a great unrest and strange desires."

When Buck discovers the wolf, he discovers a substitute for his love for John Thornton: the companionship of the wild pack. Buck knows that his choice is coming soon, and he guiltily "never left camp, never let Thornton out of his sight" for two days and nights, for he is "haunted by recollections of the wild brother." This substitute for his love for John Thornton, like the bond between teenagers in a gang, is strengthened by his "blood longing." London's lesson, like the lessons of the worst of the twentieth century, is that one must be a "killer, a thing that preyed, living on the things that lived," in order to survive "triumphantly in a hostile environment where only the strong survived."

Buck's long hunt of the bull moose is part of that blood longing, just as his detection of a "new stir in the land . . . different from the life which had been there throughout the summer." What he discovers on his return to camp is death, the death of John Thornton, not life. But there is something new in the land, as both the Yeehats who killed Thornton, and the wolves who come to devour Thornton's remains discover; it is Buck who is new, a Buck who is to become the incarnation of the Evil Spirit. For Buck, there is "a great void . . . somewhat akin to hunger, but a void, which ached and ached, and which food could not fill." There is also, however, the breaking of all ties with mankind and the loss of all fear of him. As Buck proves himself to the wolves and joins them to run "side by side with the wild brother," London's last lesson is driven home, his syllabus completed, and violence is shown to be the only way to overcome the dilemma of existence in the twentieth century.

London writes "and here may well end the story"; Buck leads the wolf pack, throws fear into the Yeehats, and generally becomes the embodiment of so much that twentieth century man has come to applaud, the cleansing force of violence. But Buck, having fulfilled his dreams of his ancestors' genetic call, remembers another vision, a vision not too distant in his own past, that of his love for a man, John Thornton. By the "yellow stream (that) flows from rotted moose-hide sacks and sinks into the ground," Buck "muses for a time, howling once, long and mournfully, ere he departs." Perhaps Buck's memorial visit is of greater sincerity than our present-day nostalgic remembrances of things past; but readers of today still may better understand Buck than did London's first readers of some seventy years ago. For Buck remembers and yearns for a moment, for that time in his life that was filled with love, like mankind when it speaks of belief in God nowadays, and how human beings in the past once believed fully, and God loved us completely. Like Buck, however, we soon return to our fellows and to our violence singing "a song of the younger world, which is the song of the pack."

# Bibliography

# Jack London: Primary Materials

*The Son of the Wolf, Tales of the Far North.* Boston: Houghton Mifflin, 1900.
*The God of His Fathers and Other Stories.* New York: McClure, Phillips, 1901.
*A Daughter of the Snows.* Philadelphia: Lippincott, 1902.
*The Cruise of the Dazzler.* New York: Century, 1902.
*Children of the Frost.* New York: Macmillan, 1902.
*The People of the Abyss.* New York: Macmillan, 1903.
*The Call of the Wild.* New York: Macmillan, 1903.
*The Kempton-Wace Letters* (with Anna Strunsky). New York: Macmillan, 1903.
*The Faith of Men and Other Stories.* New York: Macmillan, 1904.
*The Sea-Wolf.* New York: Macmillan, 1904.
*War of the Classes.* New York: Macmillan, 1905.
*The Game.* New York: Macmillan, 1905.
*Tales of the Fish Patrol.* New York: Macmillan, 1905.
*Scorn of Women* (play). New York: Macmillan, 1906.
*Moon-Face and Other Stories.* New York: Macmillan, 1906.
*White Fang.* New York: Macmillan, 1906.
*Before Adam.* New York: Macmillan, 1907.
*Love of Life and Other Stories.* New York: Macmillan, 1907.
*The Road.* New York: Macmillan, 1907.
*The Iron Heel.* New York: Macmillan, 1908.
*Martin Eden.* New York: Macmillan, 1909.
*Lost Face.* New York: Macmillan, 1910.
*Theft: A Play in Four Acts.* New York: Macmillan, 1910.
*Burning Daylight.* New York: Macmillan, 1910.
*Revolution and Other Essays.* New York: Macmillan, 1910.
*When God Laughs and Other Stories.* New York: Macmillan, 1911.
*Adventure.* New York: Macmillan, 1911.
*The Cruise of the Snark.* New York: Macmillan. 1911.
*South Sea Tales.* New York: Macmillan, 1911.
*The House of Pride and Other Tales of Hawaii.* New York: Macmillan, 1912.
*Smoke Bellew.* New York: Century, 1912.
*A Son of the Sun.* New York: Doubleday, Page, 1912.
*The Night-Born.* New York: Century, 1913.

*The Abysmal Brute.* New York: Century, 1913.
*John Barleycorn.* New York: Century, 1913.
*The Valley of the Moon.* New York: Macmillan, 1913.
*The Strength of the Strong.* New York: Macmillan, 1914.
*The Mutiny of the Elsinore.* New York: Macmillan, 1914.
*The Scarlet Plague.* New York: Macmillan, 1915.
*The Star Rover.* New York: Macmillan, 1915.
*The Little Lady of the Big House.* New York: Macmillan, 1916.
*The Acorn-Planter: A California Forest Play.* New York: Macmillan, 1916.
*The Turtles of Tasman.* New York: Macmillan, 1916.
*Jerry of the Islands.* New York: Macmillan, 1917.
*The Human Drift.* New York: Macmillan, 1917.
*Michael, Brother of Jerry.* New York: Macmillan, 1917.
*The Red One.* New York: Macmillan, 1918.
*On the Makaloa Mat.* New York: Macmillan, 1919.
*Hearts of Three.* New York: Macmillan, 1920.
*Dutch Courage and Other Stories.* New York: Macmillan, 1922.
*The Assassination Bureau, Ltd.* (finished by Robert L. Fish). New York: McGraw-Hill, 1963.
*Letters from Jack London.* Edited by King Hendricks and Irving Shephard. New York: Odyssey Press, 1965.
*Jack London Reports.* Edited by King Hendricks and Irving Shephard. New York: Doubleday, 1970.
*Daughters of the Rich.* Edited by James E. Sisson. Oakland, Calif.: Holmes Book Co., 1971.
*Gold.* (Three act play written with Herbert Heron). Edited by James Sisson. Oakland, Calif.: Holmes Book Co., 1972.

# Bibliography

Woodbridge, Hensley C., John London and George H. Tweney. *Jack London: A Bibliography.* Georgetown, Calif.: Talisman Press, 1966. Revised and Enlarged, Millwood, N.Y.: Kraus Reprint Corp., 1973. *The Jack London Newsletter* lists additions to this bibliography in each quarterly issue.

# Selected Criticism

Baskett, Sam. "Jack London's Heart of Darkness." *American Quarterly* 10 (1958): 66-77.

Baskett, Sam. "A Brace for London Criticism: An Essay Review." *Modern Fiction Studies* 22 (1976): 101-105.

Benoit, Raymond. "Jack London's *The Call of the Wild.*" *American Quarterly* 20 (1968): 246-48.

Berton, Pierre. *The Klondike Fever.* Toronto: McClelland and Stewart, 1958.

Brooks, Van Wyck. "Frank Norris and Jack London." In *The Confident Years, 1885-1915,* pp. 217-237. New York: Dutton, 1952.

Calder-Marshall, Arthur. "Introduction" to *The Bodley Head Jack London.* 4 vols. London: The Bodley Head, 1963-1966.

Carlson, Roy W. "Jack London's Heroes: A Study of Evolutionary Thought." Dissertation, University of New Mexico, 1961.

Clayton, Lawrence. "The Ghost Dog: A Motif in *The Call of the Wild.*" *Jack London Newsletter* 5 (1972): 158.

Collins, Billy G. "The Frontier in the Short Stories of Jack London." Dissertation, Kansas State University, 1970.

Dodson, Mary Kay. "Naturalism in the Works of Jack London." *Jack London Newsletter* 4 (1971): 130-39.

Feied, Frederick. *No Pie in the Sky: The Hobo as American Cultural Hero in the Works of Jack London, John Dos Passos and Jack Kerouac.* New York: Citadel, 1964.

Flink, Andrew. *"The Call of the Wild:* Parental Metaphor." *Jack London Newsletter* 7 (1974): 58-61.

Geismar, Maxwell. "Jack London: The Short Cut." In *Rebels and Ancestors: The American Novel, 1890-1915,* pp. 139-216. Boston: Houghton Mifflin, 1953.

Geismar, Maxwell, ed. "Introduction" to *Jack London: Short Stories,* pp. ix-xix. New York: Hill and Wang, 1960.

Giles, James R. "A Study of the Concept of Atavism in the Writings of Rudyard Kipling, Frank Norris, and Jack London." Dissertation, University of Texas, 1966.

Gurian, Jay. "The Romantic Necessity in Literary Naturalism: Jack London." *American Literature* 38 (1966): 112-20.

Jennings, Ann S. "Jack London's Code of the Northland." *Alaska Review* 1 (1964): 43-48.

Labor, Earle. *Jack London.* New York: Twayne, 1974.

Labor, Earle. "Jack London's *Mondo Cane: The Call of the Wild* and *White Fang.*" *Jack London Newsletter* 1 (1967): 2-13.

Lieberman, Elias. "A Glimpse at the Frozen North, Alaska—Jack London." In *The American Short Story,* pp. 150-157. Pinewood, New York: 1912.

London, Charmian. *The Book of Jack London.* 2 vols. New York: Century, 1921.

London, Joan. *Jack London and His Times.* New York: Doubleday, 1939. Second edition contains new "Introduction." Seattle: University of Washington Press, 1968.

Mills, Gordon H. "The Symbolic Wilderness: James Fenimore Cooper and Jack London." *Nineteenth Century Fiction* 13 (1959): 329-340.

Nichol, John. "The Role of 'Local Color' in Jack London's Alaska Wilderness Tales." *Western Review* 6 (1969): 51-56.

O'Connor, Richard. *High Jinks on the Klondike.* Indianapolis: Bobbs, Merrill, 1954.

Peterson, Clell T. "Jack London and the American Frontier." Dissertation, University of Minnesota, 1951.

Peterson, Clell T. "Jack London's Alaskan Stories." *American Book Collector* 8 (1959): 15-22.

Spinner, Jonathan. "A Syllabus for the 20th Century." *Jack London Newsletter* 7 (1974): 73-78.

Stone, Irving. *Sailor on Horseback: The Biography of Jack London.* Cambridge: Houghton Mifflin, The Riverside Press, 1938.

Upton, Ann. "The Wolf in Jack London's Mirror." *Jack London Newsletter* 6 (1973): 111-118.

Wagenknecht, Edward C. "Jack London and the Cult of Primitive Sensation." In *Cavalcade of the American Novel,* pp. 222-229. New York: Henry Holt, 1952.

Walcutt, Charles Child. "Jack London: Blond Beasts and Superman." In *American Literary Naturalism: A Divided Stream,* pp. 87-113. Minneapolis: University of Minnesota Press, 1956.

Walcutt, Charles Child. "Jack London." In *Seven Novelists in the American Naturalist Tradition,* edited by C. C. Walcutt, pp. 131-67. Minneapolis: University of Minnesota Press, 1974.

Walker, Dale, and James E. Sisson III, comps. *The Fiction of Jack London: A Chronological Bibliography.* El Paso: Texas Western Press, 1972.

Walker, Franklin. "Foreword" to *The Call of the Wild and Selected Stories,* pp. vii-xii. New York: New American Library, 1960.

Walker, Franklin. *Jack London and the Klondike: The Genesis of an American Writer.* San Marino, California: The Huntington Library, 1966.

Wilcox, Earl J. "Jack London and the Tradition of American Literary Naturalism." Dissertation, Vanderbilt University, 1966.

Wilcox, Earl J. "Jack London's Naturalism: The Example of *The Call of the Wild." Jack London Newsletter* 2 (1969): 91-101.

Woodward, Robert H. "Jack London's Code of Primitivism," *Folio* 18 (1953): 39-44.

# Index

# Index

Alaska Commercial Co., 132

Alexander, Sidney, 200

*Arena,* 111

*Atlantic,* 111

Baskett, Sam, 247

Benoit, Raymond, 247

Berton, Pierre, 247

Bond, Louis, 140

*Book News Monthly,* 157

Brett, George P., 114, 116, 119, 170, 208

Brooks, Van Wyck, 247

Buck, Pearl, 209

Bull, Charles Livingston, 152

Calder-Marshall, Arthur, 247

Cargil, Oscar, 215

Carlson, Roy W., 179, 247

Campbell, Joseph, 169, 196, 211

Chase, Richard, 164

Cirlot, J. E., 171

Clayton, Lawrence, 172

Collins, Billy B., 247

Conrad, Joseph, 117

Cosgrove, W. H., 114

Crane, Stephen, 184

Darwin, Charles, 179, 190

Davidson, H. R. Ellis, 201

Dodson, Mary Kay, 217

Doubleday, J. Stewart, 150

Dreiser, Theodore, 190

Erbentraut, E. B., 229-30

*Everybody's,* 114

*Examiner,* 114

Feied, Frederick, 247

Flink, Andrew, 229

Foner, Philip S., 228

Frazer, Sir James George, 194, 210

Geismar, Maxwell, 164, 167, 200, 210

Giles, James R., 248

Goodman, Jim, 125

Goodwin, Philip R., 152

Gurian, Jay, 174, 227

Haeckel, Ernest, 121

Houghton Mifflin Co., 109-12

Innis, Harold A., 127

Irving, Washington, 110

*Jack London and His Times,* 170

Jennings, Ann S., 248

Johns, Cloudesley, 113

Jung, Carl G., 197, 212

Kasper, Ralph, 121

*Kempton-Wace Letters,* 117

Kipling, Rudyard, 194, 208

Labor, Earle, 163, 202

*Leslie's,* 114

Lesser, Simon O., 171, 203

Lieberman, Elias, 248

*Literary World,* 149

London, Charmian, 214
London, Jack (Works Cited)
  *A Daughter of the Snows,* 136, 138, 139
  "Bâtard," 89-103, 205, 206, 214
  *Before Adam,* 120
  *Burning Daylight,* 126, 135, 142
  "Diable—A Dog," 218-19
  "Eight Great Factors of Literary Success," 204
  "Economics in the Klondike," 143
  "Great Interrogation," 118
  *God of His Fathers,* 118
  *Martin Eden,* 225
  "A Nose for the King," 119
  *Son of the Wolf,* 118
  "Priestly Prerogative," 118
  *Scorn of Women,* 119, 136
  *The Sea-Wolf,* 175, 198, 222-25
  *Smoke Bellew,* 143
  "The Unexpected," 138
  *White Fang,* 119, 134, 141, 198-99
  "The Wife of a King," 118

London, Joan, 248
Lowrie, C. F., 120

*McTeague,* 191
Mills, Gordon H., 248
Mizner, Addison, 137
Morgan, Edward E. P., 133

Nelson, Edward William, 172
Nichol, John, 248
Norris, Frank, 184, 190

O'Connor, Richard, 232, 248
*Overland Monthly,* 111

Peterson, Clell T., 248
*Reader,* 150
*Review of Reviews,* 111
Roberts, Charles G. D., 149, 164, 208
Ross, Anne, 201

*San Francisco Chronicle,* 152
*Saturday Evening Post,* 115, 116
Sisson, James E., III, 249
Shivers, Samuel, 221
Smoke Bellew, 131
Spinner, Jonathan H., 234
Stanford University, 109
Stevenson, Robert Louis, 194
Stillé, Kate B., 157
Strunsky, Anna, 107-9, 117

Thompson, Stith, 172
Tweney, George H., 246

Upton, Ann, 193

Wagenknecht, Edward, 248
Walcutt, Charles C., 183, 228, 249
Walker, Dale, 249
Walker, Franklin, 249
*Wave,* 111
White, Stewart Edward, 150
Wilcox, Earl J., 178, 249
Woodbridge, Hensley C., 246
Woodward, Robert H., 249

*Youth's Companion,* 111

Zola, Emile, 181